D0752743

A LOST AIRSHIP, A LOST EMPRESS, A LOST WORLD

Abner Perry had invented the Iron Mole which dug into the crust of the Earth to plunge into the hollow interior world, eternally lit by a central sun, and inhabited by cavemen and cave beasts. This was Pellucidar and, in it, Abner and his friend David Innes carved themselves an empire.

Abner's introduction of aeronautics into SAVAGE PELLUCIDAR was to plunge David and his primitive empress, Dian, into the dangers of a series of new adventures among the unexplored lands and untamed tribes. This is top-notch adventure—and also the last novel of Pellucidar that Edgar Rice Burroughs ever wrote.

EDGAR RICE BURROUGHS
1875-1950

One of Chicago's most famous sons was Edgar Rice Burroughs. Young Burroughs tried his hand at many businesses without success, until, at the age of thirty-five, he turned to writing. With the publication of *Tarzan of the Apes* and *A Princess of Mars,* his career was assured. The gratitude of a multitude of readers who found in his imagination exactly the kind of escape reading they loved assured him of a large fortune.

Edgar Rice Burroughs died at home in a town bearing the name of his brain child, Tarzana, California. But, to the countless millions who have enjoyed his works, he will live forever.

EDGAR RICE BURROUGHS

SAVAGE PELLUCIDAR

ace books

A Division of Charter Communications Inc.
1120 Avenue of the Americas
New York, N.Y. 10036

To my first grandson
JAMES MICHAEL PIERCE

A SPECIAL ANNOUNCEMENT TO ALL
ERB ENTHUSIASTS

Because of the widespread, continuing interest in the books of Edgar Rice Burroughs, we are listing below the names and addresses of various ERB fan club magazines. Additional information may be obtained from the editors of the magazines themselves.

—THE EDITORS

ERB-DOM
P. O. Box 550
Evergreen, Colorado 89439

THE BURROUGHS BIBLIOPHILES
6657 Locust Street
Kansas City, Missouri 64131

THE JASOOMIAN
P. O. Box 1305
Yuba City, California 95991

THE BURROUGHS NEWSBEAT
7710 Penn Avenue So., #206
Richfield, Minnesota 55423

ERBANIA
8001 Fernview Lane
Tampa, Florida 33615

PART I

THE RETURN TO PELLUCIDAR

I

DAVE INNES came back to Sari. He may have been gone a week, or he may have been gone for years. It was still noon. But Perry had completed his aeroplane. He was very proud of it. He could scarcely wait to show it to Dave Innes.

"Does it fly?" asked Innes.

"Of course it flies," snapped Perry. "What good would an aeroplane be which did not fly."

"None," replied Innes. "Have you flown it yet?"

"No, of course not. The day of the first flight is going to be epochal in the annals of Pellucidar. Do you think I'd fly it without you being here to see?"

"That's mighty nice of you, Abner; and I appreciate it. When are you going to fly it?"

"Right now, right now. Come and see it."

"Just what do you propose using an aeroplane for?" asked Innes.

"To drop bombs, of course. Just think of the havoc it will raise! Think of these poor people who have never seen an aeroplane before running out from their caves as it circles overhead. Think of the vast stride it will be in civilizing these people! Why, we should be able to wipe out a village with a few bombs."

"When I went back to the outer crust after the Great War that ended in 1918," said Innes, "I heard a lot about

7

the use of aeroplanes in war; but I also heard about a weapon which causes far more suffering and death than bombs."

"What was that?" demanded Perry, eagerly.

"Poison gas," said Innes.

"Ah, well," said Perry, "perhaps I shall put my mind to that later."

Dave Innes grinned. He knew that there was not a kinder hearted person living than Abner Perry. He knew that Perry's plans for slaughter were purely academic. Perry was a theoretician, pure and simple. "All right," he said, "let's have a look at your plane."

Perry led him to a small hangar—a strange anachronism in stone-age Pellucidar. "There!" he said, with pride. "There she is; the first aeroplane to fly the skies of Pellucidar."

"Is that an aeroplane?" demanded Innes. "It certainly doesn't look like one."

"That is because it utilizes some entirely new principles," explained Perry.

"It looks more like a parachute with a motor and a cockpit on top of it."

"Exactly!" said Perry. "You grasped the idea instantly —yet there is more to it than the eye perceives. You see one of the dangers of flying is, naturally, that of falling; now, by designing a plane on the principles of a parachute, I have greatly minimized that danger."

"But what keeps it in the air at all? What gets it up?"

"Beneath the plane is a blower, operated by the engine. This blows a strong current of air constantly straight up from beneath the 'wing'; and, of course, the air flow, while the ship is in motion supports it as is true in other, less advanced, designs; while the blower assists it in quickly attaining altitude."

"Are you going to try to go up in that thing?" demanded Innes.

"Why, no; I have been saving that honor for you. Think of it! The first man to have flown in the heavens of Pellucidar. You should be grateful to me, David."

Dave Innes had to smile; Perry was so naive about the whole thing. "Well," he said, "I don't want to disappoint you, Abner; and so I'll give the thing a trial—just to prove to you that it won't fly."

"You'll be surprised," said Perry. "It will soar aloft like a lark on the wing."

A considerable number of Sarians had gathered to inspect the plane and witness the flight. They were all skeptical, but not for the same reasons that David Innes was skeptical. They knew nothing about aeronautics, but they knew that man could not fly. Dian the Beautiful was among them. She is Dave Innes's mate.

"Do you think it will fly?" she asked Innes.

"No."

"Then why risk your life?"

"If it doesn't fly, there will be no risk; and it will please Abner if I try," he replied.

"There will be no honor," she said, "for it will not be the first aeroplane to fly over Pellucidar. The great ship that you called a dirigible brought a plane. Was it not Jason Gridley who flew it until it was brought down by a thipdar?"

They were walking around the plane examining it carefully. The frame of the single parachute-like wing was of bamboo: the "fabric" was fabricated of the peritoneum of a large dinosaur. It was a thin, transparent membrane well suited to the purpose. The cockpit was set down into the top of the wing; the motor stuck out in front like a sore thumb; and behind a long tail seemed to have been designed to counter-balance the weight of the engine. It carried the stabilizers, fin, rudder, and elevators.

The engine, the first gas engine built in Pellucidar,

was an achievement of the first magnitude. It had been built practically by hand by men of the stone age, under the direction of Perry, and without precision instruments.

"Will it run?" asked Innes.

"Of course it will run," replied Perry. "It is, I will concede, a trifle noisy; and is susceptible to some refinements, but a sweet thing nevertheless."

"I hope so," said Innes.

"Are you ready, David?" asked the inventor.

"Quite," replied Innes.

"Then climb into the cockpit and I'll explain the controls to you. You will find everything very simple."

Ten minutes later Innes said he knew all about flying the ship that he would ever know, and Perry climbed down to the ground.

"Everybody get out of the way!" he shouted. "You are about to witness the beginning of a new epoch in the history of Pellucidar."

A mechanic took his place at the propeller. It was so far off the ground that he had to stand on a specially constructed ladder. A man on either side stood ready to pull the blocks from beneath the wheels.

"Contact!" shouted Perry.

"Contact!" replied Innes.

The man at the propellor gave it a turn. The engine spluttered and died. "By golly!" exclaimed Innes. "It really fired. Try it again."

"Give her more throttle," said Perry.

The mechanic spun her again, and this time the engine took hold. The mechanic leaped from the ladder and dragged it away. David opened the throttle a little wider, and the engine almost leaped from its seat. It sounded as though a hundred men were building a hundred boilers simultaneously.

David shouted to the two men to pull the blocks, but

no one could hear him above the din of the motor. He waved and pointed and signalled, and finally Perry grasped what he wanted and had the blocks withdrawn. Everyone stood in wide-eyed silence as David opened the throttle wider. The engine raced. *The plane moved!* But it moved backward! It swung around and nearly crashed into the crowd of Sarians before Innes could cut the motor.

Perry approached, scratching his head. "What in the world did you do, David," he asked, "to make an aeroplane back up?"

Dave Innes laughed.

"What are you laughing at?" demanded Perry. "Don't you realize that we may have stumbled upon something sensational in aerodynamics? Just think of a fighter plane that could go either forward or backward! Just think of how it could dodge enemy planes! Think of its maneuverability! What *did* you do, David?"

"The honor is wholly yours, Abner," replied Innes. "You did it."

"But how did I do it?"

"You've reversed the pitch of your propeller blades. The plane cannot go in any other direction than backward."

"Oh," said Perry, weakly.

"But it does move," said Innes, encouragingly, "and the fault is easily remedied."

There being no such thing as time in Pellucidar, no one cared how long it took to effect a change in the propeller. Everyone except Perry and a couple of his mechanics lay down in the shade, under trees or under the plane until Perry announced that the propeller had been reversed.

Innes took his place in the cockpit, a mechanic spun the prop, the engine started, the blocks were yanked away. The engine roared and pounded and leaped. The plane almost jumped from the ground in harmony with the vibration. Innes was thrown about so violently in the cockpit that he could scarcely find the controls or keep his hands and feet on them.

Suddenly the plane started forward. It gained momentum. It rushed down the long, level stretch that Perry had selected on which to build his hangar. Innes struggled with the controls, but the thing wouldn't rise. It bounced about like a ship in a heavy sea until Innes was dizzy; and then, suddenly the fabric burst into flame.

Dave Innes discovered the flames as he was nearing the end of the runway. He shut off the motor, applied the brakes, and jumped. A moment later the gas tank burst, and Abner Perry's latest invention went up in smoke.

II

EVEN THOUGH Abner Perry's first gun powder would not burn, his aeroplane would not leave the ground, and his first ship turned bottomside up when it was launched, nevertheless he had achieved a great deal since Fate and the Iron Mole had deposited him at the center of the Earth.

He had discovered ores and smelted them; he had manufactured steel; he had made cement and produced a very good grade of concrete. He had discovered oil in Sari and refined it to produce gasoline; he had manufactured small arms and cannon. He had found and mined gold, silver, platinum, lead, and other metals. He was probably the busiest man in a whole world and the most useful. The great trouble was that the men of the stone age, or at least most of them, were not far enough advanced to appreciate what Perry had done and could do for them.

Often warriors armed with his rifles would throw them away in battle and go after the enemy with stone hatchets, or they would seize them by the muzzles and use them as clubs. He built a pumping plant near the village of Sari and pumped water through concrete pipes right into the village, yet many of the women still insisted upon walking half a mile to the spring and carrying water back in gourds balanced on the tops of their heads. Time meant nothing to them and carrying water on their heads gave them a fine carriage.

But Perry kept on just the same. He was never discouraged. He was almost perpetually good natured; and when he wasn't praying, he was swearing like a trooper. Dave Innes loved him, and so did Dian the Beautiful One and Ghak the Hairy One, who was King of Sari. In fact everyone who knew Abner Perry loved him. The young Sarians who worked for him looked up to him and worshipped him as though he were a god. And Abner Perry was very happy.

After the aeroplane failed, he started in on another invention that he had had in mind for some time. If he had known what was to come of it, he would probably have thrown away all his plans; but of course he could not know.

Dave Innes took a company of warriors and went on a tour of inspection of some of the other kingdoms of the loose confederation which constitutes the Empire of Pellucidar, of which he had been elected Emperor, following the incident of the aeroplane. He went first to Amoz, which is two hundred miles northeast of Sari on the Lural Az, a great uncharted, unexplored ocean. Six hundred miles northeast of Amoz lies Kali. Kali is the last of the kingdoms in this direction which still gives allegiance to the Empire. Suvi, four hundred miles westerly from Kali, dropped out of the confederation and made war upon Kali. The king of Suvi, whose name is Fash, had once held Dian the Beautiful prisoner; and that act had never been avenged.

Dave Innes had this in mind when he went North. It would be well to teach Fash a lesson and, perhaps, place on the throne of Suvi a man loyal to the Empire.

Sari is not on the sea coast; so the party marched to Greenwich, a hundred and fifty miles, and there took one of the ships of the Navy, which had been built under Perry's direction. Greenwich was established and named by Dave Innes and Abner Perry. Through it passes the prime meridian of Pellucidar, also an invention of Innes and Perry.

From Greenwich, they sailed to Amoz in the EPS *Sari*. The EPS is a conceit of Perry's. It means Empire of Pellucidar ship, like USS California. The Sari, like most of the ships of Pellucidar, was manned by red skinned Mezops from the Island of Anoroc, a seafaring race of fighting men. They had known only canoes until Perry and Innes introduced them to sails, but they soon mastered the new ships and learned what little of navigation Dave Innes could teach them—all dead reckoning, with only crude compasses to aid them.

Beneath a stationary sun, without the aid of stars or moon, there can be few navigational aids. The Mezops knew all there was to know about tides and currents in the coastal waters near their island. Innes and Perry gave them the compass, the log, and a chronometer which was never accurate and which could never be corrected; so it was seldom used. Their navigation was mostly b'guess and b'God, but they got places. They could always sail the most direct course toward home because of the marvellous homing sense which is common to all Pellucidarians, a Providential compensation for their lack of guiding celestial bodies.

Kander is King of Amoz. The title, like that of Emperor, was Perry's idea. Kander, like the other kings of the confederation, is chief of a tribe of cave men. He is about as far advanced in the scale of evolution and civilization as the Cro-Magnons of the outer crust were in their time; but like the Cro-Magnons, he is intelligent.

From him Innes learned that Fash was warring with Kali again and had boasted that he would move on down south and conquer Amoz and Sari, making himself Emperor of Pellucidar. Now Innes had brought but fifty warriors with him, but he decided to go on to Kali and learn first hand what was happening there. First he sent a runner back to Sari with a verbal message instructing Ghak to gather the fleet at Amoz and proceed to Kali with as many warriors as the ships would accommodate; then he got a detail of fifty warriors from Kander and sailed north for Kali, the hundred warriors straining the capacity of the EPS *Sari*.

Six hundred miles by water brought the Sari opposite Kali, which lies some forty miles inland; and from here he dispatched a runner to Oose, King of Kali. The runner was Hodon the Fleet One, a Sarian warrior of proven courage and loyalty; and it requires courage to carry a message across savage Pellucidar. Fierce beasts and fiercer reptiles are a constant menace, and hostile tribes may lie in ambush along the way.

All the forty miles to Kali, Hodon had good fortune with him. Once he met a tarag, the giant sabertooth tiger; and the beast charged him, but an experienced runner knows how best to safeguard himself. He does not run in a straight line across open plains, but from tree to tree, much after the manner of a merchant ship zigzagging to elude a submarine.

The sabertooth, which is a confirmed man-eater, may be aware of this strategy from much hunting of men; but, be that as it may, this particular beast timed its charge to a nicety and launched it at the moment that Hodon was farthest from any tree.

It was a thrilling race—for Hodon a race with Death; for few men have met and killed a tarag singlehanded. An occasional super-warrior may boast that he has done so with the long, stout spear which they usually carry; but Hodon, running light, carried no spear. He had only his speed upon which he might depend for his life, his speed and a stone knife.

The tarag covered the ground in great, bounding leaps which would quickly have overhauled an ordinary man; but Hodon is no ordinary man. He has not won the distinction of having Fleet One added to his name for nothing. And now he really ran.

The great beast was but a few yards behind him when Hodon sprang into the tree that was his goal and scrambled out of harm's way; then he sat upon a branch and spit down into the face of the tarag and called him all the vile names to which a Pellucidarian can lay his tongue, and they are many.

The tarag wasted no time waiting for Hodon to come down, as experience may have taught him that he would starve to death before any man-thing would come down to be eaten; so he made off in search of other prey.

A little farther on another tree saved Hodon from the talons of a thipdar, a huge pterodactyl such as winged the steaming skies of the Mesozoic. This mighty pteranodon, with a wing spread of twenty feet, hunted high in the air—a preposterous eagle or hawk, ready to swoop down upon any living thing. The only defense against it is the shelter of a tree, and once again Hodon reached this sanctuary just in time.

Hissing with rage, the reptile soared away; and when it was out of sight Hodon continued on to Kali, which he reached without further adventure.

The village of Kali consists mostly of caves in a limestone cliff, with a few rude, thatched shelters at its base, which are used for cooking, eating, and communal gatherings.

As Hodon approached the village he was met by a score of warriors, which was what he might have expected on approaching any well guarded village. They demanded his business there; and when he told them that he bore a message from the Emperor of Pellucidar to Oose, the King of Kali, they looked at one another; and some of them grinned behind his back.

"I will take word to the king," said one. "Wait here."

Presently the man returned and instructed Hodon to follow him, and all the warriors who had come to meet him accompanied them. It might have been a guard of honor, but Hodon had a feeling that it more nearly resembled the guard of a prisoner.

He was conducted to one of the thatched shelters, where a man sat upon a stool, surrounded by other warriors.

"What message do you bring to Oose, King of Kali, from the Emperor of Pellucidar?" demanded the man.

Now, Hodon had never before been to Kali, nor had he ever seen Oose; but it was evident to him that this man was the king. He thought that he was an ill-favored fellow, and he took an instinctive dislike to him.

"You are the king?" he asked, wishing to make sure before he delivered the message. "You are the king of Kali?"

"Yes," replied the man. "I am the king of Kali. What message do you bring?"

"The Emperor wishes you to know that his ship is anchored off the coast of Kali with a hundred warriors. He has heard that you are having trouble with Fash, the king of Suvi; and he wishes to talk the matter over with you, that an expedition may be sent against Fash to punish him for his treason to the Empire. I am to take

17

word back to him as to whether you will come to the coast to talk with him, or if you would prefer that he came here; for he knows that it is not always easy for a village to feed a hundred extra men."

"I will send a runner to the Emperor," said the king of Kali. "You will remain here and rest."

"My orders are to bring the message to the Emperor myself," replied Hodon.

"I give orders here," said the king; and then he spoke to the leader of the warriors who surrounded Hodon. "Take this man to a high cave and place a guard over him. See that he does not escape."

"What is the meaning of this?" demanded Hodon. "I am a Sarian and one of the Emperor's men. What you are doing is treason."

"Take him away," said the king.

Up rickety wooden ladders Hodon's guard forced him to climb to the highest level. Here a narrow ledge ran in front of several cave mouths. A guard of two warriors already squatted on the ledge near the top of the ladder; two others sat before the mouth of one of the caves. Into this cave Hodon was ordered, and at the same time the king of Kali dispatched a runner to the coast with a message for David Innes.

When Hodon's eyes became accustomed to the darkness of the interior of the cave, he saw that he was not alone. The cave was a large one, and fully fifty men squatted or lay upon the floor.

"Who are you?" demanded one of these, as Hodon groped his way in search of a place to sit down.

"I seem to be a prisoner," replied Hodon.

"We are all prisoners," said the man. "I did not recognize you as you came in. Are you a Kalian?"

"Are you?" asked Hodon.

"We are all Kalians."

"Then why are you prisoners in Kali?" demanded Hodon.

"Because the warriors of Suvi attacked and overcame the village while most of the men were on the hunt and as we returned they fell upon us from ambush, killing many and capturing the rest."

"Then the man sitting in the shelter at the foot of the cliff is not king of Kali?" asked Hodon.

"He calls himself King of Kali, because he has captured the village," replied the man; "but I am king of Kali."

"You are Oose?" demanded Hodon.

"I am Oose, and the man who calls himself King of Kali is Fash, the king of Suvi."

"Then I have given the Emperor's message to the Emperor's enemy," said Hodon, "but how was I to know."

"The message was for me?" asked Oose.

"For you," said Hodon, and then he repeated the message to Oose.

"It is bad," said Oose, "for now Fash is warned."

"How many warriors has he?" asked Hodon.

"I can count only to ten times the number of my fingers," said Oose. "We men of Kali are not wise like the men of Sari who had been taught many things by Innes and Perry, but if I counted all of my fingers ten times; then I should say that Fash has five times that many warriors."

Hodon shook his head. "I must escape," he said; "for when I do not return after a couple of sleeps, the Emperor will come after me; and he will be outnumbered five to one."

"You cannot escape," said Oose. "Four warriors squat upon the ledge, and many warriors are at the foot of the cliff."

"Are we allowed on the ledge?" asked Hodon.

"If you have a good reason you will be allowed to go to the little cave at the far end of the ledge."

"I have a good reason," said Hodon, and he went to the mouth of the cave and spoke to one of the warriors on guard there.

The fellow grunted surly permission, and Hodon came out upon the ledge and moved slowly toward the little cave at the far end. He did not look down; but always up, scanning the face of the cliff to its summit, which was only a few feet above his head.

A warrior came to the shore of the Lural Az. He saw a ship anchored in a little cove a short distance off shore, and he shouted until he had attracted attention of those on board. A small boat floated beside the ship, and presently a number of copper colored warriors dove from the deck of the ship and clambered into the small boat, which they paddled toward the shore. When they had come close, they shouted to the warrior and asked him who he was and what he wanted.

"I bring a message from the king of Kali to the Emperor of Pellucidar," the man replied; then the boat was brought to the shore, and the messenger taken aboard. A few moments later he was hauled to the deck of the Sari and brought before David Innes.

"You bring a message from the king of Kali?" asked Innes. "Why did my own warrior not return with it as I ordered?"

"He was ill; and he was very, very tired," replied the messenger. "That there might be no delay, the King sent me."

"What is the message?"

"The King asks that you come to Kali. He cannot leave Kali now because of the danger of attack."

"I understand," said Innes. "I shall come at once."

"I will go ahead and tell the King. He will be very

pleased. Will you come alone?"

"I will bring a hundred warriors with me," replied Innes.

So David Innes started for Kali, and the messenger of Fash went ahead to carry the word to his king.

Hodon walked slowly along the ledge, examining every inch of the cliff face above him until he came to the little cave at the far end. Here the cliff dipped downward, and its summit was scarcely four feet above Hodon's head. He turned and looked back along the ledge. One of the guards was watching him; so Hodon stooped and entered the little cave. He turned around immediately, waited a moment, and then looked out. The guard was still looking at him. Hodon retreated into the cave, remained there a short time, and then came boldly out. His heart sank—two members of the guard had their eyes on him. He knew that he must have just a moment while no one was looking in order to put his plan into successful operation. Now there was nothing to do but return to the prison cave.

Here he tried to think of some plan that would help him to carry out that which he had in mind, and finally he hit upon one. He moved over beside Oose, and sat down close to him; then he explained his plan in low whispers.

"We will do it," said Oose; "but do not forget what I told you—you cannot escape."

"I can try," said Hodon.

After a while—whether an hour, a day, or a week of outer Earthly time, who may know?—the guard upon the ledge was changed; then Hodon went immediately to the mouth of the cave and asked permission to go to the small cave at the end of the ledge. Again he was granted permission.

He walked along the ledge slowly. This time he looked

down. At the bottom of the cliff he saw women and children, but only a few warriors—perhaps just enough to guard the village. Where were the others? Hodon thought that he knew, and he chafed to make good his escape. If he did, would he be in time?

Just as he reached the little cave he heard shouts and yells behind him. They were muffled, as though they came from the interior of a cave. He glanced back, and saw the four guards running toward the prison cave. Hodon smiled.

III

AFTER DAVID INNES left for Kali, Abner Perry busied himself upon a new project. He was determined to have something worth while to show Innes when he returned, for he was still a little depressed over the signal failure of his aeroplane.

He sent hunters out to slay dinosaurs—the largest they could find—with orders to bring back only the peritonea of those they killed; and while they were gone he succeeded in capping a gas well which had been blowing millions of cubic feet of natural gas into the air of Pellucidar for—well, who knows for how long?

He had many women braiding rope, and others weaving a large basket—a basket four feet in diameter and three feet high. It was the largest basket the Sarians had ever seen.

While this work was going on, the messenger arrived from Innes instructing Ghak to set forth with many warriors. When they had departed there were few warriors left, and they had to remain in the village as a guard, except for a couple of hunters sent out daily for fresh meat. The village was full of women; but that did not interfere with Perry's plans, as the warriors had returned with more than enough peritonea.

The peritonea was stretched and dried and rubbed until they were thoroughly cured; then Perry cut them into strange shapes according to a pattern he had fashioned, and the women sewed them together with very fine stitches and sealed the seams with a cement that Perry thought would not be attacked by the constituents of natural gas.

When this work was complete, Perry attached the great bag to the basket with the ropes the women had braided; and to the bottom of the basket he attached a heavier rope that was five or six hundred feet long. No one in Sari had ever seen a rope like that, but they had long since ceased to marvel much at anything that Perry did.

With little ropes, many little ropes, Perry fastened the basket to the ground by means of pegs driven into the earth all around it; then he ran a clay pipe from the gas well into the opening at the small end of the bag. Perry had given birth to a balloon! To him it was the forerunner of a fleet of mighty dirigibles which could carry tons of high-explosive bombs, and bring civilization to countless underprivileged cliff dwellers.

Hodon smiled, just a fleeting little smile that vanished almost as it was born; then he stooped before the little cave at the far end of the ledge and leaped upward. Hodon was proud of his legs; so was all Sari. They were the best legs in the Empire of Pellucidar, so far as anyone knew to the contrary; and they were just as marvelous at jumping as they were at running. They easily carried Hodon upward until his fingers could seize the top of the cliff. It was solid limestone. Hodon had determined that when he first examined the cliff. Had there been top soil right up to the edge of the cliff, the thing would not have been so easy—it might, in fact, have been impossible of accomplishment; but there was no top soil, and the hard stone did not crumble. It held magnificently, doing its part to thwart the evil machinations of the wicked Fash.

Sometimes we are annoyed by the studied perversities of inanimate objects, like collar buttons and quail on toast; but we must remember that, after all, some of them are the best friends of man. Take the dollar bill, for instance—but why go on? You can think of as many as I can.

So Hodon the Fleet One clambered over the summit of the cliff of Kali, and no man saw him go. When he had come he had carried a stone knife, but they had taken that from him. Now he must go absolutely unarmed across perhaps forty miles of danger ridden terrain, but he was not afraid. Sometimes I think that the men of the old stone age must have been very brave. They must have had to be very brave, as otherwise they could not have survived. The coward might have survived for a while—just long enough for him to starve to death—but it took a brave man to go out and brave the terrific creatures he must have had to face to find food for himself and his family.

Hodon's only thought now was to reach David Innes before he ran into the ambush that he was sure Fash had laid for him. He moved swiftly, but he moved silently. Always every sense was alert for danger. His keen eyes ranged far ahead; his sensitive nostrils picked up every scent borne to them by each vagrant breeze. He was glad that he was running up wind, for now he could be warned of almost any danger that lay ahead.

Suddenly he caught a scent which brought a frown of puzzlement to his brow. It told him that there was a woman ahead of him—a lone woman—where there should not have been a woman. His judgment told him that there must be at least one man where there was a woman so far from a village, but his nostrils told him that there was no man.

He kept on in the direction of the woman, for that was the direction in which he was going. Now he went even more warily, if that were possible; and at last he saw her. Her back was toward him. She was moving slowly, looking in all directions. He guessed that she was afraid. She did not know that she was not alone until a hand fell upon her shoulder. She wheeled, a dagger in her hand—a slim dagger laboriously chipped from basalt—and as she wheeled, she struck a vicious blow at Hodon's breast.

Being a Pellucidarian, he had expected something like this; for one does not accost a strange lady with impunity in the stone age. So he was ready. He seized her wrist, and held it. Then she tried to bite him.

Hodon smiled down into her flashing eyes, for she was young and beautiful. "Who are you?" he demanded. "What are you doing out here so far from your village alone?"

"That is my business," she said. "Let me go! You cannot keep me, for if you do I'll surely kill you."

"I can't waste time on you," said Hodon, "but you are too young and good looking to be left for the first stray tarag to make a meal of. You may come along with me, if you wish. We have only your dagger, but I'll use it for you."

"Tell me who you are," she said, a trifle more amicably.

"I am Hodon of Sari," he said.

"A Sarian! They are the friends of my father's people. If you are a Sarian, you will not harm me."

"Who said I would. I *am* a Sarian. Now who are you?"

"I am O-aa, the daughter of Oose, King of Kali."

"And you are running away because Fash has conquered your people. Am I right?" He released his hold upon her wrist, and she returned her dagger to its sheath.

"Yes, you are right," she replied. "After Fash had conquered Kali, he took me for himself; but I escaped. It was well for Fash that I did; because I should have killed him. You see, I am the daughter of a king, and my mother was—"

"I have no time to listen to your life history," said Hodon. "Are you coming with me, or not?"

"Where are you going?"

He told her.

"I do not like your manner; and I shall probably not like you," said O-aa, "but I will come with you. You are better than nobody. Being the daughter of a king, I am accustomed to being treated with respect. All of my father's people—"

"Come!" said Hodon. "You talk too much," and he started off again in the direction of the coast.

O-aa trotted along at his side. "I suppose you will delay me," grumbled Hodon.

"I can run as fast and as far as you can. My mother's father was the fastest runner in all his country, and my brother—"

"You are not your mother's father nor are you your brother," said Hodon. "I am only interested in how fast and how far you can run. If you cannot keep up with me, you will be left behind. The fate of the Emperor is much more important than yours."

"You don't call this running, do you?" demanded O-aa, derisively. "Why, when I was a little girl I used to run down and capture the orthopi. Everyone marveled at my swiftness. Even my mother's father and my brother could not run down and capture the orthopi."

"You are probably lying," said Hodon, increasing his speed.

"For that, my brother will probably kill you," said

O-aa. "He is a mighty warrior. He—"

Hodon was running so fast now that O-aa had not the breath for both running and talking, which was what Hodon had hoped for.

Ghak the Hairy One, King of Sari, embarked a thousand warriors on two ships. They were much larger ships than the Sari which was the first successful ship that Perry had built and now practically obsolete. While the Sari had but two guns, one-pounders, one in the bow and the other in the stern, the newer ships had eight guns, four on each side on a lower deck; and they fired shells which occasionally burst when they were supposed to, but more often did not burst at all or prematurely. However, the cannon made a most satisfactory racket and emitted vast clouds of black smoke.

When Perry's first one-pounder was fired for the first time, the cannon ball rolled out and fell on the ground in front of the cannon. Innes said that this had its advantages, since there would be no waste of ammunition —they could just pick the balls up and use them over again; but Perry's new pieces hurled a shell a full mile. He was very proud of them. The trouble was that the ships never found anyone to shoot at. There was no other known navy in Pellucidar except that of the Korsars, and Korsar is five thousand miles from Sari by water.

As Ghak's expeditionary force beat up the coast toward Kali, David Innes and his hundred warriors marched inland toward the village. Half of Innes's men were armed with the Perry musket, a smooth bore, muzzle loading flintlock; the other half carried bows and arrows. All had knives, and many carried the short spear that all Pellucidarians prefer. It hung by a leather thong about their necks and swung down their backs.

These men were all veterans—the *corps elite* of the

Pellucidarian army. Perry had named them The Imperial Guard, and Innes had succeeded in inculcating some ideas of discipline upon their ruggedly individualistic egos. They marched now in a loose column of fours, and there were an advance guard and flankers. A hundred yards in front of the advance guard three warriors formed the point. Innes was taking no chance on an ambush.

They had covered about half the distance to Kali when the point halted at the summit of a little rise; then one of them turned and raced back toward the main body.

He came directly to Innes. "Many warriors are coming this way," he reported.

Innes disposed his men and advanced slowly. The musketeers were in the first line. As a rule the noise and smoke of one of their ragged volleys would frighten away almost any enemy; which was well; because they seldom hit anybody. After they fired, the archers moved up through their ranks and formed the first line while the musketeers reloaded.

But none of this was necessary now; as a messenger came racing back from the point to say that the force approaching them was friendly—Oose's warriors coming to welcome them to Kali and escort them to the village.

Innes went forward to investigate personally. At the top of the rise he found a hairy caveman waiting for him. Beyond, he saw a large force of warriors.

"Where is Oose?" he demanded.

"Oose is sick. He has a pain in his belly. He could not come; so he sent me to guide you to Kali."

"Why did he send so many warriors?"

"Because we are at war with Suvi, and Fash's warriors may be nearby."

Innes nodded. The explanation seemed reasonable. "Very well," he said, "lead the way."

His warriors advanced. Soon they were in contact with the warriors of the other party, and these offered them food. They seemed to wish to make friends. They moved among the warriors of The Imperial Guard, handing out food, passing rough jokes. They seemed much interested in the muskets, which they took in their hands and examined interestedly. Soon all the muskets of The Imperial Guard were in the hands of these friendly warriors, and four or five of them surrounded each member of the Guard.

Hodon had taken a short cut. He and O-aa had come over a hill through a forest, and now they halted at the edge of the forest and looked down into the little valley below. In the valley were hundreds of warriors. Hodon's keen eyes picked out David Innes among them; they saw the muskets of the musketeers. Hodon was puzzled. He knew that most of those warriors were the warriors of Fash of Suvi, but there was no battle. The men appeared to be mingling in peace and friendship.

"I cannot understand it," he said. He was thinking out loud.

"I can," said O-aa.

"What do you understand?" asked Hodon. "Tell me in a few words without any genealogical notes."

O-aa bridled. "My brother—" she began.

"Oh, bother your brother!" cried Hodon. "Tell me what you think you understand. You can tell me while we are walking down there to join David Innes."

"You would be fool enough to do that," the girl sneered.

"What do you mean?"

"That is one of Fash's tricks. Wait and see. If you go down, you will soon be back in the prison cave—if they do not kill you instead; which would be good riddance."

She had scarcely ceased speaking, when the leader of the friendly warriors voiced a war whoop and, with several of his men, leaped upon David Innes and bore him to the ground. At the signal, the rest of the friendly warriors leaped upon the members of The Imperial Guard whom they had surrounded. There was some resistance, but it was futile. A few men were killed and a number wounded, but the outcome was inevitable. Inside of five minutes the survivors of The Imperial Guard had their hands tied behind their backs.

Then Fash came from behind a bush were he had been hiding and confronted David Innes. "You call yourself Emperor," he said with a sneer. "You would like to be Emperor of all Pellucidar. You are too stupid. It is Fash who should be Emperor."

"You may have something there," said David Innes— "at least for the time being. What do you intend doing with us?"

"Those of your men who will promise to obey me shall live; I will kill the others."

"For every one of my men you kill, five Suvians shall die."

"You talk big, but you can do nothing. You are through, David Innes. You should have stayed in that other world you are said to have come from. It does not pay to come to Pellucidar and meddle. As for you, I do not know. Perhaps I shall kill you; perhaps I shall hold you and trade you for ships and guns. Now that I am also King of Kali, I can make use of ships with which to conquer the rest of Pellucidar. Now I am Emperor! I shall build a city on the shore of the Lural Az and all Pellucidar shall soon know who is Emperor."

"You have a big mouth," said Innes. "Perhaps you are digging your grave with it."

"I have a big fist, too," growled Fash, and with that, he knocked David Innes down.

At word from Fash, a couple of warriors yanked Innes to his feet. He stood there, the blood running from his mouth. A shout of anger rose from the men of The Guard.

David Innes looked straight into the shifty eyes of Fash, the king of Suvi. "You had better kill me, Fash," he said, "before you unbind my wrists."

Hodon looked on in consternation. There was nothing that he could do. He moved back into the forest, lest some of Fash's warriors see him. Not that they could have caught him, but he did not wish them to know that their act had been witnessed by a friend of David Innes.

"You were right," he said to O-aa. "It was a trick of Fash's."

"I am always right," said O-aa. "It used to make my brother very angry."

"I can well understand that," said Hodon.

"My brother—"

"Yes, yes," said Hodon; "but haven't you any other relatives than a brother and a mother's father?"

"Yes, indeed," cried O-aa. "I have a sister. She is very beautiful. All the women in my mother's family have always been very beautiful. They say my mother's sister was the most beautiful woman in Pellucidar. I look just like her."

"So you have a mother's sister!" exclaimed Hodon. "The family tree is growing. I suppose that will give you something more to talk about."

"That is a peculiar thing about the women of my family," said O-aa; "they seldom talk, but when they do—"

"They never stop," said Hodon, sadly.

"I could talk if I had some one of intelligence to listen to me," said O-aa.

IV

THE GAS BAG of Perry's balloon filled rapidly. It billowed upon the ground and grew larger. It rose above its basket. The eyes of the Sarians grew wide in astonishment. It grew fat stretching its envelope. It tugged at the guy ropes.

Perry shut off the gas. There were tears on the old man's cheeks as he stood there fondling the great thing with his eyes.

"It is a success!" he murmured. "The very *first* time it is a success."

Dian the Beautiful came and slipped her arm through his. "It is wonderful, Abner," she said; "but what is it for?"

"It is a balloon, my dear," explained Perry. "It will take people up into the air."

"What for?" asked Dian the Beautiful.

Perry cleared his throat. "Well, my dear, for many reasons."

"Yes?" inquired Dian. "What, for instance?"

"Come, come," said Perry; "you wouldn't understand."

"How could they get down again?" she asked.

"You see that big rope? It is attached to the bottom of the basket. The other end of the rope passes around the drum of this windlass we have built. After the balloon has ascended as high as we wish it to we turn the windlass and pull it down."

"Why would anyone wish to go up there?" asked Dian. "There is nothing up there but air and we have plenty of air down here."

"Just think of all the country you could see from way up there," said Perry. "You could see all the way to the

Lural Az. With my binoculars, you might see all the way to Amoz."

"Could I see David, if he were coming back?"

"You could see his ships on the Lural Az a long way off," said Perry, "and you could see a large body of marching men almost as far as Greenwich."

"I shall go up in your balloon, Perry," said Dian the Beautiful. "Go and let your bi-bi—whatever you called them, that I may look through them and see if David is returning. I have slept many times and we have had no word from him since his messenger came summoning Ghak."

"I think that we had better test it first," said Perry. "There might be something wrong with it. There have been isolated instances where some of my inventions have not functioned entirely satisfactorily upon their initial trial."

"Yes," agreed Dian the Beautiful.

"I shall put a bag of earth of more than twice your weight in the basket, send it up, and haul it down. That should prove an entirely adequate test."

"Yes," said Dian, "and please hurry."

"You are sure you are not afraid to go up?" asked Perry.

"When was a woman of Sari ever afraid?" demanded Dian.

Hodon retraced his steps to the summit of the cliff above Kali. He had a plan, but it all depended upon Fash's imprisoning David Innes in the cave on the upper ledge of the village.

Just before he reached the summit of the cliff, he stopped and told O-aa to remain hidden among some bushes. *And do not talk!* he commanded.

"Why?" asked O-aa. "Who are you to tell me that I cannot talk?"

"Never mind about that," said Hodon, "and don't start telling me about any of your relations. They make me sick. Just remember this: if you talk, one of the warriors on guard may hear you and then there will be an investigation. And remember one more thing: if you talk before I come back here, I'll cut your throat. Can you remember that?"

"Wait until my brother—"

"Shut up!" snapped Hodon and walked away toward the top of the cliff.

As he neared it he got down on his belly and crawled. He wormed his way forward like an Apache Indian; and like an Apache Indian he carried a little bush in one hand. When he was quite close to the cliff edge, he held the little bush in front of his face and advanced but an inch at a time. At last he could peer over the edge and down upon the village of Kali. Once in position he did not move. He waited, waited with the infinite patience of primitive man.

He thought of David Innes, for whom he would have gladly laid down his life. He thought of O-aa and he smiled. She had spirit and the Sarians liked women with spirit. Also she was undeniably beautiful. The fact that she knew it detracted nothing from her charm. She would have been a fool if she hadn't known it, and a hypocrite if she had pretended that she did not know that she was beautiful. It was true that she talked too much, but a talkative woman was better than a sullen one.

Hodon thought that O-aa might be very desirable but he knew that she was not for him—she had too frankly emphasized her dislike of him. However one sometimes took a mate against her will. He would give the matter thought. One trouble with that was that David Innes did not approve of the old fashioned method of knocking a lady over the head with a club and dragging her off to one's cave. He had made very strict laws on the subject. Now no man could take a mate without the girl's consent.

As these thoughts were passing through his mind he saw warriors approaching the village. They kept coming into view from an opening in the forest. Yes, it was the Suvians with their prisoners. He saw David Innes walking with his head up, just as he always walked in paths of peace or paths of war. No one ever saw David Innes' chin on his chest. Hodon was very proud of him.

There was a brief halt at the foot of the cliff, and then some of the prisoners were herded toward the cliff and up the ladders. Would David Innes be one of these? So much depended on it that Hodon felt his heart beating a little faster.

All the prisoners could not be accommodated in the prison cave on the upper ledge. Some of them would have to be confined elsewhere or destroyed. Hodon was sure that no member of The Imperial Guard would accept Fash's offer and prove a traitor to the Empire.

Yes! At last here came David Innes! The guards were particularly cruel to him. They prodded him with spears as he climbed the rickety ladders. They had removed the bonds from his wrists, but they had seen that he was at a safe distance from Fash before they did so.

Up and up he climbed. At last he was on the topmost ladder. Inwardly, Hodon whooped for joy. Now there was a chance. Of course his plan was full of bugs, but there was one chance in a hundred that it might succeed —one wild chance.

Just one little hour of night would have simplified things greatly but Hodon knew nothing of night. From the day of his birth he had known only one long, endless day, with the stationary sun hanging perpetually at zenith. Whatever hé did now, as always, would have to be done in broad daylight among a people who had no set hours for sleeping; so that at least a half of them could be depended upon to be awake and watchful at all times.

He watched until he saw David Innes enter the prison cave; then he crawled back to O-aa. She was fast asleep! How lovely she looked. Her slim, brown body was almost naked, revealing the perfection of its contours. Hodon knelt beside her. For a moment he forgot David Innes, duty, honor. He seized O-aa and lifted her in his arms. He pressed his lips to hers. She awakened with a start. With the speed and viciousness of a cat, she struck—she struck him once across the mouth with her hand, and then her dagger sprang from its sheath.

Hodon leaped quickly back, but not quite quickly enough; the basalt blade ripped a six-inch slash in his chest. Hodon grinned.

"Well done," he said. "Some day you are going to be my mate, and I shall be very proud of you."

"I would as soon mate with a jalok," she said.

"You will mate with me of your own free will," said Hodon, "and now come and help me."

V

"You think you understand perfectly what you are to do?" asked Hodon a few minutes later, after carefully explaining his plan to O-aa.

"You are bleeding," said O-aa.

"It is nothing but a flesh wound," said Hodon.

"Let me get some leaves and stop it."

"Later," said Hodon. "You are sure you understand?"

"Why did you want to kiss me?" asked O-aa. "Was it just because I am so beautiful?"

"If I tell you, will you answer my question?"

"Yes," said O-aa.

"I think it was just because you are O-aa," said Hodon.

O-aa sighed. "I understand all that I am to do," she said. "Let us commence."

Together they gathered several large and small pieces of sandstone from a weathered outcropping, and inched them up to the very edge of the cliff. One very large piece was directly over the ladder which led to the next ledge below; others were above the mouth of the prison cave.

When this was accomplished, Hodon went into the forest and cut several long lianas and dragged them close to the cliff; then he fastened an end of each of them to trees which grew a few yards back.

"Now!" he whispered to O-aa.

"Do not think," she said, "because I have helped you and have not slipped my dagger between your ribs, that I do not hate you. Wait until my brother—"

"Yes," said Hodon. "After we have finished this you may tell me all about your brother. You will have earned the right. You have been splendid, O-aa. You will make a wonderful mate."

"I shall make a wonderful mate," agreed O-aa, "but not for you."

"Come on," said Hodon, "and keep your mouth shut— if you can."

She gave him a venomous look, but she followed him toward the edge of the cliff. Hodon looked over to be sure that everything was as he hoped it would be. He nodded his head at O-aa, and grinned.

He pushed the great stone nearer the edge, and O-aa did the same with some of her smaller ones. She watched Hodon very closely, and when she saw him pushing his over the edge, she stood up and hurled one of hers down.

The big stone struck the two guards squatting at the top of the ladder, carrying them and the ladder crashing down from ledge to ledge, carrying other ladders with them.

Hodon ran to the rocks that O-aa was hurling down, and O-aa ran to the lianas and dropped them over the edge. Hodon was calling David Innes by name. One of the other two guards had been hit and had fallen over the cliff; then David Innes and some of the other prisoners ran from the cave.

Only one guard opposed them. Neither O-aa or Hodon had been able to strike him with a rock. David Innes rushed him, and the guard met him on the narrow ledge with his short spear. As he lunged at Innes, the latter seized the weapon and struggled to wrench it from the Suvian's grasp. The two men wrestled for the weapon on the brink of eternity. At any moment either of them might be precipitated to the foot of the cliff. The other prisoners seemed too stunned or too anxious to escape to go to Innes' assistance, but not Hodon. Sensing the danger to his chief, he slid down one of the lianas and ran to Innes' side. With a single blow he knocked the Suvian over the edge of the cliff; then he pointed to the lianas.

"Hurry!" he said. "They are already starting up the canyon to climb the cliff and head us off."

Each on a different liana, the two men clambered to the summit. Already most of the Kalians had disappeared into the forest. Innes had been the only Sarian confined on the upper ledge. Oose had not run away. He and another Kalian were talking with O-aa. Oose's companion was a squat, bearded fellow with a most unprepossessing countenance. He looked like a throwback to a Neanderthal type. As Hodon and Innes approached the three, they heard O-aa say, "I will not!"

"Yes, you will," snapped Oose. "I am your father and your king. You will do as I tell you. Blug is a mighty hunter, a mighty fighter. He will make a fine mate. He has a large cave and three other women to lighten your labors."

O-aa stamped a sandalled foot. "I tell you I will not. I would just as soon mate with a Sagoth."

Now, the Sagoths are those half human gorilla men who did the strong arm work for the Mahars, the reptiles who dominated Pellucidar before David Innes drove them away—at least away from that portion of the inner world of which he was Emperor. O-aa could scarcely have voiced a more comprehensive insult.

Blug growled angrily. "Enough!" he said. "I take her." He reached for O-aa, but Hodon stepped between them and struck Blug's hand away.

"You do not take her," he said. "O-aa chooses her own mate."

Blug, being more or less of an inarticulate low-brow, with a short temper, replied to words with action. He swung a terrific blow at Hodon that might well have felled a bos, had there been a bos there and had the blow landed; but there was no bos and the blow did not land. Hodon ducked under it, picked Blug up and hurled him heavily to the ground.

Blug was surprised and so was Oose, for Hodon looked like no match for the massive Blug. Hodon's muscles rolled smoothly beneath his bronzed skin—deceptively. They had great strength and they possessed agility. Blug had only strength; but he had courage, too —the courage of stupidity. He scrambled to his feet and charged Hodon—charged like a wild bull. And this time Hodon struck him full in the mouth and dropped him in his tracks.

"Enough of this!" snapped David Innes. "If you stand here fighting, we shall all be captured."

"Enough," said Oose to Blug.

"I shall kill him later, then," said Blug.

"What—again?" asked Hodon. He looked about him.

"Where is O-aa?" he asked.

O-aa had fled. While the two men fought, she had run away. Maybe she thought, as Blug and Oose had thought, that Blug would easily kill Hodon.

"I did not see her go," said Oose. "When I find her, I shall beat her and give her to Blug."

"Not if I'm around," said Hodon.

"You should not interfere in the affairs of others, Hodon," counselled David.

"It is my affair," said Hodon.

Innes shrugged. "Very well," he said; "but if it's your own funeral, too, do not say that I did not warn you. Now we must get away from here."

"There are some caves farther up the coast," said Oose, "that we have used at other times that Kali has been invaded. My people have probably gone there. We had better go there also."

"I shall remain near here," said Innes. "Many of my warriors are prisoners here. I cannot desert them."

"I will stay with you," said Hodon.

Oose and Blug moved away into the forest. "If you are around here when I come back," said the latter to Hodon, "I will kill you. I will bring my mate back to see me do it. I shall find O-aa at the other caves, and there I shall take her."

"You have a big mouth," said Hodon. "It fills so much of your head that there is no room for brains."

Blug did not retort. He could think of nothing to say, his powers of repartee being limited; so he disappeared into the forest wrapped in the gloomy cloak of anger.

"I hear the Suvians coming," said Innes.

"Yes," replied Hodon. "Come with me. I have become a little familiar with parts of this land, and I know where we can find a hiding place."

"I do not like to hide," said David Innes.

"Nor I; but two men cannot fight five hundred."

"You are right," said Innes. "Lead the way. I will follow you."

They moved away very quietly, Hodon trying to find rocks to step on wherever he could and Innes stepping always in the exact spots that Hodon stepped. When they came to a little stream, Hodon entered it and walked up its bed. It would take an excellent tracker to follow them at all.

VI

PERRY BEAMED with satisfaction, and Dian the Beautiful clapped her hands ecstatically. Many other Sarians, mostly women and children, stood open mouthed and goggle eyed. Every head was tilted back, every eye looked straight aloft to where a great gas bag partially eclipsed the eternal noonday sun. The balloon was a success.

Its basket loaded with rock, it had risen at the end of its rope, as four stalwart Sarians payed out on the windlass. Everyone was surprised, none more so than Abner Perry; for this was the first one of his "inventions" that functioned on its initial trial. He would not have been greatly surprised had it instead of going up bored itself into the ground.

"This is a great day for Pellucidar, Dian," he said. "Won't David be surprised!"

True enough David was due for a big surprise.

As those who had been left behind in Sari watched the swaying balloon, like little children with a new toy, Ghak the Hairy One and his thousand fighting men sailed on toward Kali.

And Hodon led David Innes to a little canyon into the head of which tumbled a mountain brook in a waterfall of exquisite beauty. Continually watered by the spray and warmed by the never failing sun, lush vegetation swarmed up the side of the cliff and spread out on the floor of the valley. Great sprays of orchids trailed down the rocky face of the cliff, gorgeous corsages pinned to the breast of the mountain. Flowers that withered and died forever on the outer crust eons ago challenged the beauty of the orchids, and hidden behind this mass of greenery and blooms was a little cave —a cave that could be defended by a single warrior against an army of stone age men.

"Beautiful!" exclaimed Innes, "and not far from Kali. We can stay here until Ghak comes. We will take turns watching for him. Really, we should watch by the sea; but I want to be where I can also watch Kali; here my warriors are imprisoned. Perhaps an opportunity will come for us to get them out of the prison caves."

Fruit and nuts grew in abundance on the trees and shrubs of the little canyon; but fighting men require meat; and one must have weapons to have meat. These two had not even a stone knife between them, but the first men had no weapons originally. They had to make them.

Innes and Hodon went into the little stream and hunted around until they found a large mussel. They pried it open with a sharp stone, and each took a half shell. With these they cut two pieces of bamboo-like arborescent grass to form the hafts of two spears. Searching again they collected a number of stones: soft stones, hard stones, flat stones, stones with sharp edges; and with some of these they chipped and scraped at others until they had fashioned two spear heads and a couple of crude knives. While Hodon was finding the toughest fibers with which to bind the spear heads to the hafts, Innes made a bow and some arrows, for this was one of his favorite weapons.

How long all this took, of course there was no way of

telling, other than that they ate several times and slept once. All in all, it may have taken them a week of outer earthly time, or half a day, or a year. Occasionally one of them would go to a high point in the hills and look out across the country toward the coast always hoping to see Ghak the Hairy One and his warriors.

Hodon was hunting. He had gone out northeast of Kali a little farther this time than usual; for his luck had not been good. He had seen some game—red deer and orthopi the little primitive three toed horse that once ranged the outer crust—but something had always happened to frighten them away before he could get within spear range.

Of a sudden he heard a terrific roaring, and the crash of a heavy body coming through the undergrowth of the forest. Hodon looked for a tree that could be easily and swiftly scaled. He knew the author of that roar. It was a cave lion and the less business he had with a cave lion the happier he would be and the longer he would live.

He had just found a nice tree when he saw something burst from the underbrush in the direction from which the roaring was coming, but it was not a cave lion. It was O-aa. She was running like a scared rabbit and right behind her was the cave lion.

Hodon forgot the tree. The lion was not making as good progress through the underbrush as was O-aa. She was leaping as lightly and almost as swiftly as a springbok. Hodon ran to meet her.

"Go back!" she cried. "It is Ta-ho."

Hodon could see that it was Ta-ho, but he didn't go back. As O-aa passed him, he knelt and jambed the butt of his spear into the ground, holding the haft at an angle, the stone point ahead of him.

The spear was a little short for the purpose for which he was using it. With a long spear some great hunters had killed the cave lion and the sabertooth tiger thus; but with a short spear such as his, one would be almost sure to be mauled to death before death came to the beast. However, Hodon had never hesitated from the moment that he had seen O-aa.

The great lion rose snarling above him, its face a hideous mask of savagery; and then its momentum hurled it upon the spear point. Instantly Hodon leaped to one side and drew his puny stone knife; then he threw himself upon the back of the pain maddened beast tangling the fingers of one hand in its mane while with the other he plunged his knife through the thick hide into the beast's side.

The lion threw itself from side to side. It turned to seize the man-thing. It rolled upon the ground to dislodge him; and then, quite suddenly, it rolled over on its side. The spear had pierced its heart.

Hodon stood up and looked around him, searching for O-aa. She was nowhere in sight. He called her by name, but there was no answer. So, he had risked his life for her and she had run away from him! At that moment Hodon almost became a misogynist.

He started out to look for her with the intention of giving her a good beating when he found her. Being an excellent tracker it did not take him long to pick up her trail. He followed it as silently as though he were stalking the wariest of game for that he knew she would be.

Beyond the edge of the forest he saw her. Evidently she thought that she had eluded him, for she was walking along quite nonchalantly. The sight of her impertinent little back goaded Hodon to fury. He decided that a beating was far from adequate punishment; so he drew his stone knife from its scabbard and ran quietly after her determined to cut her throat.

After all, Hodon the Fleet One was only a cave man

of the stone age. His instincts were primitive and direct, but they were sometimes faulty—as in this instance. He thought that the feeling that he harbored for O-aa was hate, when, as a matter of fact, it was love. Had he not loved her, he would not have cared that she ran away from him while he was risking his life for her. There are few sentiments more closely allied and inextricably intermingled than love and hate, but of this Hodon was not aware. At that moment he hated O-aa with utter singlemindedness and abandon.

He caught up with O-aa and seized her by the hair, spinning her around so that he looked down into her upturned face. That was a mistake, if he really wished to kill her. Only a man with a stone where his heart should have been could have slit O-aa's throat while looking into her face.

O-aa's eyes were very wide. "You are going to kill me?" she asked. "When my brother—"

"Why did you run away from me?" demanded Hodon. "I might have been killed."

"I did not run away until I saw Ta-ho roll over dead," said O-aa.

"Why did you run away then?" Hodon's knife hand hung at his side, and he loosened his grasp on O-aa's hair. Hodon's rage was oozing out through his eyes as they looked into the eyes of O-aa.

"I ran away because I am afraid of you. I do not wish to mate with you or any other man until I am ready. I am not ready. No man has won me yet."

"I have fought for you," Hodon reminded her. "I have killed Ta-ho in your defense."

"Ta-ho is not a man," said O-aa, as though that settled the whole matter.

"But I fought Blug for you. Every time I fight for you you run away. Why do you do that?"

"That time, I was running away from Blug. I thought

he would kill you and then come after me; and anyway, fighting Blug was nothing—you didn't kill him. I saw Blug and my father afterward, but they did not see me."

"So, I shall have to kill a man before you will mate with me?" demanded Hodon.

"Why, of course. I think you will have to kill Blug. I do not understand why he did not kill you when you fought. If I were you I should keep out of Blug's way. He is a very great fighter. I think he would break you in two. I should like to see that fight."

Hodon looked at her for a long minute; then he said, "I think you are not worth having for a mate."

O-aa's eyes flashed. "It is a good thing for you that my brother did not hear you say that," she said with asperity.

"There you go," said Hodon, "dragging in your family again. I am sick and tired of hearing of your family all the time."

As they talked, unconscious of any but themselves, six strange looking creatures crept toward them through the underbrush.

VII

THE FOUR Sarians at the windlass wound the balloon down to earth, and held it there while others removed the stone ballast. Everyone clustered around, examining it and heaping praise on Abner Perry. And Perry was so proud and happy that he felt like doing a little dance.

"And now," said Dian, "I shall go up."

"Perhaps you had better wait until David comes," counselled Perry. "Something might happen."

"It took all that rock up," argued Dian, "and I do not weigh as much as the rock."

"That is not the point," said Perry. "It would take you up, all right; but I don't think you should go until after David gets back. As I said before, something *might* happen."

"Well, I am going," said Dian.

"What if I forbade it?" asked Perry.

"I should go anyhow. Am I not Empress of Pellucidar?" She smiled as she said it; but Perry knew that, Empress of Pellucidar or not, Dian the Beautiful would go up in the balloon if she wished to.

"Very well," he said; "I'll let you go up a little way."

"You'll let me go up to the end of the rope," she said. "I want to see if David is coming home."

"Very well," said Perry, resignedly. "Get in."

The other Sarians clustered around Dian as she clambered into the basket. Here was a new experience far beyond anything that they had ever imagined, and Dian the Beautiful was about to have it. They all envied her. They made little jokes and told her what to look for when she got up to the sun. They asked her all the questions outer Earth people might have asked under similar circumstances—all but one: nobody asked her if she were afraid. One does not ask a Sarian if he is afraid.

Perry signalled to the four men at the windlass and the balloon commenced to rise. Dian the Beautiful clapped her hands happily. "Faster!" she called to the four men at the windlass.

"Slower!" said Perry. "Take it easy."

Up and up went the great gas bag. A little breeze caught it, and it swayed to and fro. Dian felt very small up there all alone with that huge thing billowing above her.

"Can you see David?" some one shouted.

"Not yet," shouted Dian, "but I can see the Lural Az. Send me up higher!"

Soon almost all the rope was out, and Perry was glad;

for then he could start pulling the balloon down. He was anxious to see Dian the Beautiful on terra firma again. Perhaps Perry had a premonition.

The terrible creatures crept closer and closer to Hodon and O-aa. They were men, naked black men with long, prehensile tails. Their brows protruded above small, close-set eyes; and there was practically no head above the brows. Short, stiff black hair grew straight out from their skulls; but their outstanding feature was a pair of tusks that curved down from the upper jaw to below the chin.

"I wish," O-aa was saying, "that you would go away and leave me alone. I do not like you. If my brother—"

It was then that the creatures charged, roaring like beasts. With hands and tails, they seized Hodon and O-aa; and the two were helpless in their grasp. Chattering and jabbering among themselves they dragged their prisoners off into the forest.

Hodon tried to talk to them; but they did not understand him, nor could he understand them. They were very rough, slapping and cuffing their captives without provocation.

"Now we shall die," said O-aa.

"What makes you think so?" asked Hodon. "If they had intended to kill us, they could have done so when they attacked us."

"Do you not know what they are?" asked O-aa.

"No," said Hodon. "I have never seen nor heard of such creatures before."

"They are the sabertooth men," she said. Of course she did not use the word saber. What she said was, roughly, the taragtooth men—the tarag being the sabertooth tiger. "They are man eaters," she added for good measure.

"You mean they are taking us home to eat?" demanded Hodon.

"Exactly," said O-aa.

"If you had come with me long ago, this would not have happened to you," said Hodon.

"Oh, there are worse things than being eaten by a saber-tooth man," rejoined O-aa.

"Maybe you are right," agreed Hodon; "having to hear about your family, for instance."

"My brother is a mighty fighter," said O-aa. "He could break you in two, and my sister is very beautiful. You have no women in Sari so beautiful as my sister. She is almost as beautiful as I. My mother's father was so strong that he could carry the carcass of a full grown bos on his back."

"Now, I know you are lying," said Hodon. "Why must you lie so much, and always about your family? I am not interested in your family. I am only interested in you."

"My father is a king," said O-aa.

"He can be a Sagoth, for all I care. I do not wish to mate with your father."

"Now you will never mate with anybody," said O-aa. "Instead, you will be eaten by a sabertooth man and his mate."

"Maybe the same man will eat us both," said Hodon, grinning. "Then we shall be truly mated."

"If he does that to me I will give him a pain in his belly," said O-aa.

"You do not like me very well," said Hodon.

"You are very stupid, if you have only just discovered that," replied O-aa.

"I do not understand why you don't like me. I am not bad to look at. I would be kind to you, and I can certainly protect you."

"This looks like it," said O-aa.

Hodon subsided.

Two of the sabertooth men each had his tail wrapped around the neck of one of the captives. Thus they dragged them along, while other sabertooth men pushed, and slapped, and kicked their prisoners from the rear. The grotesque blacks kept jabbering. They reminded Hodon of the little hairy men who lived in the trees of the forests.

The cliff of Kali is the last rampart of a range of mountains that extended toward the northeast, parallel with the coast of the Lural Az. It was into these mountains that O-aa and Hodon were being dragged. The terrain became rougher as they ascended, the limestone formation giving way to volcanic rock. Extinct volcanos were visible on either hand. The vegetation was sparse and poor. It was a rough country.

Buffeted and bruised, the prisoners were dragged at last to a yawning hole in the side of a mountain. Inside it was dark as a pocket, but the sabertooth men did not even pause on the threshold. Still jabbering, they entered the cavern and raced along as though in broad daylight. Neither O-aa nor Hodon could see a thing. They felt the smooth surface of the rock beneath their sandals and they could tell that they were ascending. Presently the ascent became so steep that they would have fallen back had not their captors supported them. Up and up they went, dragged by their necks. In the grip of the choking tails they were gasping for breath.

At last the ascent became absolutely perpendicular and here were long lianas depending from above, and there was daylight. Above them they could see a round opening into which the sun shone, and they could see that they were ascending a circular shaft. They did not know it, but they were in a volcanic tube.

The sabertooth men swarmed up the lianas, dragging O-aa and Hodon with them; and when they reached the top of the tube both their prisoners were unconscious. Then they released them, and the two lay as though dead where they had fallen.

Dian the Beautiful looked out across forest and rolling hills and fertile plains. She saw great herds of bos and red deer and herbivorous dinosaurs feeding on the lush vegetation. She saw the Lural Az curving upward, like Professor Einstein's time and space, until it was simply lost in the distance; for there is no horizon in Pellucidar. She saw Anoroc Island, where the copper colored Mezops dwell in their tree houses; and beyond Anoroc, the Luana Islands. She could have seen Greenwich had it been more than an imaginary spot on an imaginary map. But she saw no sign of David Innes, though she strained her eyes until the tears came to them.

The four men at the windlass kept letting out more and more rope, their eyes on the balloon and not on the drum. Perry was watching the balloon, too. He felt that Dian the Beautiful had gone high enough and had been up long enough to have seen all that there was to see; so he turned to the men at the windlass to order them to haul the balloon down. What he saw brought a scream of horror from his throat.

At the same time, David Innes stood upon a promontory above Kali and looked out toward the Lural Az. He was looking for Ghak the Hairy One, but his search was no more successful than had Dian's been. Slowly he made his way back to the hidden canyon. Hodon would have returned with meat, he thought; and they would feast, but Hodon was not there.

David went into the cave and slept, and when he awoke there was still no sign of Hodon. So David went out and made a kill himself. He ate many times and slept twice more, and still Hodon had not returned. Now David became worried, for he knew that Hodon would have returned had all been well with him. He determined to go and search for him, though he knew that it would be like searching for a needle in a hay stack.

He found Hodon's almost obliterated tracks, and he came upon the carcass of the cave lion. The dagger wounds in the beast's side and the spear wound in its breast told a graphic story. Then he discovered the prints of O-aa's little sandals.

What he read when he came to the spot at which the two had been captured by the sabertooth men filled him with apprehension. He saw great splayed, manlike footprints, and the trail of the party leading away to the northeast. For the most part, the spoor of O-aa and Hodon was obliterated by that of their captors; but David Innes saw enough to know that a party of creatures unknown to him had captured O-aa and Hodon.

There was but one thing to do: he must follow. This he did until the trail entered the dark mouth of the volcanic tube. He went in a short distance, but he could neither see nor hear anything; he felt a strong wind sucking in past him toward the interior of the cave. He came out and examined the terrain. Above him lay the slope of an extinct volcano. He could see the rim of the crater sharply defined against the blue of the sky. Suddenly he had an inspiration, and he commenced the ascent of the mountain.

When Hodon and O-aa regained consciousness they were still lying where they had fallen. All around them rose the walls of a volcanic crater, the level floor of which was covered with verdure. In the center was a small lake of blue water. Rude shelters were dotted about.

They found themselves surrounded by sabertooth

people—men, women, and children. There was much jabbering in the strange, monkey-like language of these hideous people. They snarled and growled at one another and occasionally one of them would try to grab either O-aa or Hodon with a long, prehensile tail. Three or four large males stood close to the captives, and every time one of their fellows tried to seize either of them, he would be set upon and chased away. It was apparent to Hodon that they were being guarded, but why?

After they regained consciousness, these guards jerked them to their feet and led them away toward one of the shacks—an open structure with a flimsy grass roof. Here a large male squatted on the ground, and beside him was the strangest looking human being either Hodon or O-aa had ever seen. He was a little, wizened old man with a white beard that almost concealed the rest of his features. He had no teeth, and his eyes were the eyes of a very old man.

"Well," he said, looking them over, "you're certainly in a fix. Back in Cape Cod, we'd say you was in a Hell of a fix; but we ain't back in Cape Cod, and you never heard of Hell, unless this here place is it, which I sometimes believe; for doesn't the Good Book tell us that people go *down* to Hell? or doesn't it? Well, I dunno; but I came *down* to get to this here place, an' I don't believe Hell could be much worse." He spoke in Pellucidarian with a Cape Cod accent. "Well," he continued, taking a breath, "here you are. Do you know what's goin' to happen to you?"

"No," said Hodon; "do you?"

"Well, they'll probably fatten you up and eat you. That's what they usually do. They might keep you a long time. They're funny that way. You see they ain't no such thing as time down here; so how's a body to know how long it will be before you get fat or before they eat you? God only knows how long I been here. I had black hair and a good set o' teeth when I come, but look at me now! Maybe they'll keep you until your teeth fall out. I hope so, because I get danged lonesome for company down here. These here things aren't very good company."

"Why haven't they eaten you?" asked Hodon.

"Well, that there's a long story. I'll tell you all about it—if they don't eat you too quick."

The large sabertooth man sitting beside the old man now commenced to jabber at him, and the old man jabbered back in the same strange tongue; then he turned to Hodon.

"He wants to know where you come from and if there's more like you real handy. He says that if you'll guide his people to your village, he won't have you killed right away."

"Tell him I've got to rest first," said Hodon. "Maybe I can think of a village where the people are all nice and fat."

The old man turned and translated this to the sabertooth man, who replied at some length.

"He says that's all right, and he'll send some of his people with you right away."

"Tell him I've got to rest first," said Hodon.

After some further conversation between the sabertooth man and the old man, the latter said: "You can come with me now. I'm to look after you until you have rested."

He got up, and Hodon and O-aa followed him to another shelter, which was much more substantially built than the others.

"This is my cabin," said the old man. "Sit down and make yourselves at home. I built this myself. Got all the comforts of home." The comforts of home were a bunk filled with dried grass, a table, and a bench.

"Tell me how you got here, and why they don't eat you," said Hodon.

"Well, the reason they don't eat me, or rather the reason they didn't eat me at first, was because I saved the life of that fellow you seen sitting beside me. He's chief. I think about the only reason they don't eat me now is because I'm too damned old and tough.

"Now, as to how I got here, I come from a place you never even heard of in a world you never heard of. You don't know it, but you're living in the center of a round ball; and on the ouside is another world, entirely different from this one. Well, I come from that other world on the outside.

"I was a seafarin' man up there. Used to go whalin' up around the Arctic. Last time I went was an awful open summer up there. We went farther north than we'd ever been before, and no ice—just a great open polar sea as far as the eye could reach.

"Well, everything was lovely till we run into the worst dod-blasted storm you ever see; and the Dolly Dorcas was wrecked. The Dolly Dorcas was my ship. I dunno what become of the others, but there was eight of us in the boat I was in. We had food an' water an' a compass an' sails as well as oars; but still it didn't look very good. We was way up in the Arctic Ocean an' winter comin' on. We could just about kiss ourselves goodby.

"We sailed what we thought was south for a long time, and all the time the compass kept acting stranger an' stranger. You'd thought the dod-blasted thing had gone crazy. Then we ran out o' food, an' the fust thing you knowed we commenced to eat one another—startin' in on the weakest fust. Then some of 'em went crazy; an' two jumped overboard, which was a dirty trick when they knew we craved meat so bad.

"Well, to make a long story short, as the feller said, finally they wasn't nobody left but me; and then, dod-blast it, if the weather didn't commence to get warmer, and pretty soon I sighted land and found fruits and nuts and fresh water. Believe me, it was just in time too; for I was so doggone hungry I was thinkin' of cuttin' off one of my legs an' eatin' it."

O-aa sat wide eyed and wondering, drinking in every word. Hodon had never known her to be silent for so long. At last she had met her match.

"What's become of your brother and your mother's father?" asked Hodon.

"Eh! What's that?" demanded the old man.

"I was speaking to O-aa," said Hodon.

"Well, don't interrupt me. You talk too much. Now, where was I? You got me all confused."

"You were thinking of eating your leg," said O-aa.

"Yes, yes. Well, to make a long story short, as the feller said, I was in Pellucidar. How I ever lived, I'll be doggone if I know; but I did. I got in with one tribe after another, an' none of 'em killed me for one reason or another. I learned the language an' how to hunt with spears. I made out somehow. Finally I stole a canoe an' set sail on the biggest doggone ocean you ever seen. My beard was a yard long when I landed near here an' got captured by these things.

"Well, I better start feedin' you an' fattenin' you up. I reckon this gal will be pretty tasty eatin' right soon." He reached out and pinched O-aa's flesh. "Yum!" he exclaimed. "She's just about right now."

"Do you eat human flesh?" demanded Hodon.

"Well, you see I sort o' acquired a taste for it after the Dolly Dorcas was wrecked. Ole Bill was a mite tough an' rank, but there was a Swede I et who was just about the nicest eatin' you ever see. Yes, I eat what the Lord furnishes. I reckon I'm goin' to enjoy both of you."

"I thought you said you hoped they wouldn't eat us, because you would like to have our company," said O-aa.

"Yes, I'm sort o' torn between two loves, as the feller said: I loves to eat an' I loves to talk."

"We like to listen," said Hodon.

"Yes," agrees O-aa; "we could listen to you forever."

What Perry had seen that had brought the scream to his lips was the end of the rope slipping from the drum. He had forgotten to have it made fast! He sprang forward and seized at the rope, but the free balloon leaped upward carrying the rope's end far above him. Of course his gesture was futile, as a dozen men could not have held the great gas bag that Perry had made.

The old man looked up at the great balloon, rapidly growing smaller as it rose; then he sat down, and, covering his face with his hands, commenced to sob; for he knew that Dian the Beautiful was already as good as dead. No power on earth or within it could save her now.

How high she would be carried he could not even guess, nor how far from Sari. She would doubtless die from lack of oxygen, and then her body would be carried for a thousand miles or more before the bag would lose sufficient gas to bring it down.

He loved Dian the Beautiful as he would have loved a daughter, and he knew that David Innes worshipped her. Now he had killed Dian and wrecked David's life— the two people he loved most in the world. His silly inventions had done a little good and some harm, but whatever good they had accomplished had been wiped out by this. Worst of all, he realized, was his criminal absent-minded carelessness.

Dian felt the sudden upward rush of the balloon. She looked down over the edge of the basket and instantly realized what had happened. Everything was growing smaller down there. Soon she could no longer distinguish people. She wondered what would become of her. Perhaps she would be carried up to the sun and incinerated. She saw that the wind was carrying the balloon in a south-westerly direction.

She did not realize the greatest error of all that Perry had made; neither did Perry. He had arranged no rip cord on the gas bag. With that, Dian could have let gas out of the bag gradually and made a landing within a comparatively few miles from Sari. Perry was always leaving some essential thing off of everything he built. His first musket had no trigger.

Dian the Beautiful guessed that she was as good as dead. She cried, but not because she was afraid to die. She cried because she would never see David again.

And David, far away, reached the rim of the crater and looked over. Below him, scarcely a hundred feet, he saw a round valley, green with verdure. He saw a little lake and grass thatched shelters and people. He saw Hodon and O-aa. His surmise had been correct.

He saw the strange sabertooth people. There were a couple of hundred of them. How could he, single handed, rescue Hodon and O-aa from such an overwhelming number of enemies?

David Innes was resourceful; but the more he cudgeled his brains, the more hopeless a solution of his problem appeared. It would profit them nothing if he went down into the crater. That would mean simply his own capture; then he could do nothing for them.

He examined the crater closely. The inside walls were perpendicular and unscalable in all but a single place. There the wall had crumbled inward, the rubble forming an incline that reached to the top of the rim that was little more than fifty feet above the floor of the crater at that point. There was an avenue of escape, but how could he call Hodon's attention to it. How could he create a diversion that would take the attention of their captors from them long enough for them to make a break for freedom. Suddenly he recalled the wind rushing past him as he had stood in the darkness of the cavern that was the entrance to the crater. He turned and started down the mountainside.

The old man had been talking constantly. Even O-aa could not get a word in edgewise, but at last he paused for a moment, probably to refresh his mind concerning the past, in which he lived.

Hodon seized upon this moment to voice a suggestion that had been in his mind for some time. "Why don't you escape?" he asked the old man.

"Eh? What? Escape? Why—er—I haven't thought of it since before my last bicuspid dropped out. But of course I couldn't escape."

"I don't see why not," said Hodon. "I don't see why the three of us couldn't escape. Don't you see that low place there? We could run up there in no time if you could find some way to get their attention somewhere else."

"M-m-m," murmured the old man thoughtfully. "Sometimes many of them are asleep at the same time. It might be done, but I doubt it. Anyway, what good would it do me to escape? I'd only be killed by the first tribe that captured me if some of the beasts didn't get me before."

"No," said Hodon. "I would take you to Sari. They would treat you well there. You might meet some old friends. There are two men from Hartford, Connecticut there."

The old man became instantly alert. "What do you know about Hartford, Connecticut?" he demanded.

"Nothing," said Hodon, "but these men do. I have heard them speak of it many times."

"How did they get down here? That must be a story like mine. I'll bet they'd like to hear my story."

"I know they would," said O-aa, who was nobody's fool. "I think you ought to come with us."

"I'll think it over," said the old man.

David Innes made his way to the entrance to the tube. He gathered dry wood and leaves and green grass, and he piled it far into the tube, with the grass on top. Then he made fire and lighted it. As soon as he saw that it was burning freely, he ran from the tube and started up the side of the mountain as fast as he could go.

When he reached the top and looked over he saw smoke rising from the opening into the tube. Already a jabbering crowd of sabertooth men were gathering about it. Others were joining them. David was just about to risk everything by shouting to Hodon to run for the low place in the rim, when he saw O-aa, Hodon, and another walking toward it. He saw that the third member of the party was not one of the natives; so he assumed it must be another prisoner.

The diversion that Hodon had hoped for had occurred almost miraculously, and the three lost no time in taking advantage of it.

"You are sure, are you, that these men from Hartford, Connecticut, are where we are going?" demanded the old man. "Dod-burn you, if they ain't, I'll eat you the first chance I get."

"Oh, they're there all right," said O-aa. "I saw them just before we left."

Hodon looked at her in amazement not unmixed with admiration. "We may see one of them before we get to Sari," he said. "He was with me just before we were captured."

"I hope so," said the old man. "I'd sure like to see some one from Hartford. By gum, I'd even like to see some one from Kansas."

"Oh," said O-aa with a shrug. "We know lots of people from Kansas. You can see all you want."

Hodon's expression turned to one of awe, but now they were at the base of the shelving rubble. He looked back. Every single sabertooth was gathered around the smoking vent; not an eye was turned in their direction. "Start up slowly," he cautioned. "Do not start to hurry unless they discover what we are doing; then you'll really have to climb. Once on the outside you and I, O-aa, can outdistance any of them, but I don't know about the old man."

"Listen, son," said that worthy. "I can run circles around you and all your family. Why, when I was a young man they used to race me against race horses. I'd give 'em two lengths start and beat 'em in a mile."

Hodon didn't know what a horse was; but he had an idea that whatever it was the old man was lying; so he said nothing. He was thinking that between O-aa and the old man it was a toss-up.

They reached the summit without being detected; and as they started down, Hodon saw David coming toward him. He hurried forward to meet him. "It was you who started the fire that made the smoke, wasn't it? But how did you know we were in the crater?"

"Is this one of the men from Hartford?" demanded the little old man.

"Yes," said Hodon, "but don't start telling him the story of your life now. Wait until we get out of reach of your friends."

Dian was surprised to discover that the nearer the sun she got the colder she was. She was also mystified by the noises she heard in her ears and the difficulty she had in breathing; but even so, she gave little thought to her own danger. She could think only of David—David whom she would never see again.

The balloon was drifting now at an even altitude. It would rise no higher. Eventually it would commence to drop lower; but before it came to earth, Dian the Beautiful might be dead of hunger and exhaustion. Being practically naked, except for a most sketchy loin cloth she was already chilled through and shivering.

A hunting party far below saw the strange thing floating toward them; and they ran and hid beneath trees, thinking it some new and terrible reptile. Dacor the Strong One, Dian's brother, was in the party. Little did he dream that his sister floated there high above him. He and his companions would tell of the awful creature they had seen; and the story would grow in the telling, but nothing which they could fabricate could equal the truth, if they could have known it.

The sabertooth people are not very bright, but they do know what a volcano is; because there is an intermittently active one in the mountains not far from their own crater; so, putting two and two together, they assumed that their own volcano was about to become active. Had they been just a little bit more intelligent, they would have reasoned that wood smoke does not come from a volcano; but all they knew was that it was smoke and smoke meant fire; and they were afraid.

The best thing to do, then, was to get out of the crater; so they turned to the low point in the crater's rim. It was then that they discovered that their prisoners had escaped.

As they swarmed out of the crater, they were not only frightened but angry. No prisoner had ever escaped before, and they didn't purpose letting these prisoners get away with it. Being good trackers capable of moving with great speed, they had no doubt but that they would soon overhaul the fugitives. The latter however, were also fleet of foot; and they had two advantages: they did not have to watch for spoor to follow, and they were fleeing for their lives. There is no greater spur to honest and concentrated effort than this. Even the old man revealed amazing possibilities as he scampered in the wake of the others.

David and Hodon, being congenitally opposed to flight, hated the position in which they found themselves; but what were they to do? David alone was armed. He carried his crude bow and arrow and a stone knife but these were not enough to repel an attack by a numerically greater force of savage beasts such as the sabertooth men.

While they did not yet know that they were being followed, they assumed that they would be; and the old man had assured them that they would.

"I been there since before my teeth began falling out," he said, "an' you can lay to it that they'll follow us all the way to hell an' gone, for they ain't no prisoner ever escaped from 'em in my time."

Hodon, who was leading, guided them toward the little canyon where he and David had found sanctuary; and they succeeded in reaching its mouth before the first of the pursuers came within sight. It was just after they entered it that a chorus of savage roars told them that the sabertooth men had overtaken them.

David glanced back. Racing toward him were three or four of the swiftest males and strung out behind them were other bucks and shes and young—the whole tribe was on their heels!

"Get the others into the cave, Hodon!" he called. "I'll hold them up until you're all in."

Hodon hesitated. He wanted to come back and fight at David's side.

"Go on!" shouted the latter. "We'll all be lost if you don't," then Hodon raced on toward the cave with O-aa and the old man.

David wheeled about and sent an arrow into the breast of the leading savage. The fellow screamed and clutched at the shaft; then he spun around like a top and crashed to earth. A second and a third arrow in quick succession found their marks, and two more saber-tooth warriors writhed upon the ground. The others paused.—David fitted another arrow to his bow and backed away toward the cave.

The sabertooths jabbered and chattered among themselves. Finally a huge buck charged. Hodon and O-aa were in the cave; and the former, reaching down, grasped the hand of the old man and dragged him up. David was still backing toward the cave, holding his fire. His supply of arrows would not last forever; so he must not miss.

The great brute was almost upon him before he loosed his shaft. It drove straight through the heart of the buck, but there were others coming behind him. Not until he had dropped two more in rapid succession did the others pause momentarily; then David turned and raced for the cave. At his heels came the whole tribe of sabertooths, roaring and screaming. They came in mighty leaps and bounds, covering the ground twice as rapidly as David.

Hodon stood in the mouth of the cave. "Jump!" he cried to David. He leaned out and down, extending his hand. As David leaped upward toward the cave mouth, a sabertooth at his heels reached out to seize him; but simultaneously a bit of rock struck the fellow full between the eyes, and he stumbled forward on his face. O-aa, grinning, brushed the dust from her hands.

Hodon pulled David into the cave. "I never thought you'd make it," he said.

There were extra spears and arrows in the cave and a little food. The waterfall dropped so close that they could reach out and catch water in a cupped hand. They would not suffer from thirst. One man with a spear could defend the entrance against such ill-armed brutes as the sabertooths. Altogether, they felt rather secure.

"These brutes won't stay here forever," said David. "When they find they can't get us, they'll go away."

"You don't know 'em," said the old man. "They'll stick around here 'till Hell freezes over, but the joke's goin' to be on them."

"What do you mean?" asked David.

"Why, instead of gettin' four of us, they're only goin' to get one," explained the old man.

"How's that?" inquired David.

"We can't get no food in here," said the old man; "so we gotta eat each other. I reckon I'll be the last man. I'm too dod-burned old and tough to eat. Even the sabertooths wouldn't eat me. This here'll make a tender morsel. I reckon we'll start on her."

"Shut up!" snapped David. "We're not cannibals."

"Well, neither was I back at Cape Cod. I would have reared up on my hind legs an' fit anybody then that had said I'd ever eat man, woman, or child; but then I hadn't never nearly starved to death, nor I didn't know what good eatin' some people can be after you get used to it. Before you come along I was tellin' these other two about that sweet Swede I et once."

"You also said," interposed O-aa, "that after you'd eaten all your friends you were about to cut your leg off and start eating yourself."

"Yes," admitted the old man, "that's plumb right."

"Then," said O-aa, "when you get hungry, you'd better start eating yourself; because you're not going to eat any of us."

"That's what I calls plumb selfish," said the old man. "If we don't eat each other, the sabertooths are goin' to eat us; an' I'd think you'd rather be eaten by a friend than by one of them criters."

"Look here—er—what is your name, anyway?" David spoke with marked asperity.

The old man puckered his brow in thought. "Dod-burn it!" he exclaimed at last. "What the dickens is my name? I'll be dod-burned if I ain't plumb forgot. You see I ain't heard it since I was a young man."

"I think," said O-aa to David, "that his name is Dolly Dorcas."

"Well, never mind," said David; "but get this straight: there's to be no more talk of eating one another. Do you understand?"

"Wait until you get good *an'* hungry," said the old man; "then it won't be a matter of talking about it."

David rationed out what food there had been stored in the cave—mostly nuts and tubers; as these would not spoil quickly. Each had his share. They took turns watching, while the others slept, if they cared to; and as there was nothing else to do, they slept a great part of the time. It is a custom of Pellucidarians. They seem to store up energy thus, so that they need less sleep afterward. Thus they prepare themselves for long journeys or arduous undertakings.

Some of the sabertooths remained in the canyon at all times. They made several attempts to storm the cave; but after being driven off easily, they gave up. They would starve their quarry out.

The food supply in the cave dwindled rapidly. David presently suspected that it dwindled fastest while the old man was on watch and the others slept; so once he feigned sleep and caught the old man taking a little food from the supply of each of the others and hiding it in a crevice in the back of the cave.

He awoke the others and told them, and O-aa wanted to kill the old man at once. "He deserves to die," said David, "but I have a better plan than that of killing him ourselves. We'll drop him down to the sabertooths."

The old man whimpered and begged, and promised never to do it again; so they let him live, but they did not let him stand watch alone again.

At last their food was all gone, and the sabertooths were still in the canyon. The besieged were ravenous. They drank quantities of water to allay the craving for food. They were getting weaker and weaker, and David realized that the end was near. They slept a great deal, but fitfully.

Once, when O-aa was standing watch, David awoke with a start; and was horrified to see the old man sneaking up behind her with a spear. His intentions were all too obvious. David called a warning and leaped for him—but just in time.

Hodon awoke. The old man was grovelling on the floor of the cave. O-aa and David were looking down at him.

"What has happened?" demanded Hodon.

They told him. Hodon came toward the old man. "This time he dies," he said.

"No! No!" shrieked the terrified creature. "I was not going to keep it all for myself. I was going to share it with you."

"You beast!" exclaimed Hodon, picking up the spear the old man had dropped.

Screaming the latter leaped to his feet; and, running to the mouth of the cave, sprang out.

A hundred sabertooths were in the canyon. Straight toward them the old man ran, screaming at the top of his voice, his eyes wild with terror, his toothless mouth contorted.

The sabertooths fell aside, shrinking from him; and through the lane they made the old man fled and disappeared in the forest beyond the end of the canyon.

Ghak the Hairy One, with a thousand warriors, marched up to Kali. He did not know that Fash, the king of Suvi, had conquered it; so he was surprised when his advance guard was attacked as they neared the cliff. However, it made no difference to Ghak the Hairy One whether he fought Suvian or Kalian.

Fash had thought that the advance guard constituted the whole force with which he had to deal, as it was his own custom to hold all his warriors in one body when he attacked. He did not know that David Innes had taught the Sarians a different method of warfare, which was unfortunate for Fash.

When Ghak's main body came up, Fash's men scattered in all directions. A number retreated to the caves of Kali. The Sarians swarmed up after them before they could remove the ladders. Men fought hand to hand on the narrow ledges all the way up to the highest ledge. Here, cornered Suvians leaped to their death; and at last Ghak the Hairy One stood victorious above the caves of Kali.

Then the Sarian prisoners came from their prison caves and for the first time Ghak learned that David's little force had been either killed or made prisoner and that David was missing. All agreed that he must be dead.

Ghak's force rested and fed at the Kali cliff; and then victorious but sad, started back to their ships waiting on the Lural Az. They had scarcely left the cliff when a strange figure of a man came dashing out of the forest— a toothless little old man with an enormous white beard. His beard was stained with juice of berries and the pulp of fruit. He jibbered and yammered like the little hairy men who live in the trees of the forest.

The warriors of Sari had never seen a creature like this before; so they captured him, as they might have captured any strange animal and took him to show to Ghak.

"Who are you?" demanded Ghak.

"Are you going to kill me?" The old man was whimpering, the tears rolling down his cheeks.

"No," Ghak assured him. "Tell me who you are and what you are doing here."

"My name is *not* Dolly Dorcas," said the old man, "and I was going to divide O-aa with the others; but Hodon wanted to kill me."

"Hodon!" exclaimed Ghak. "What do you know of Hodon?"

"I know that he was going to kill me, but I ran away."

"Where is Hodon?" demanded Ghak.

"He and David and O-aa are in the cave. The sabertooth men are waiting to eat them."

"What cave? Where is it?" asked Ghak.

"If I told you, you'd take me back there and Hodon would kill me," said the old man.

"If you lead us to where David and Hodon are, no one will kill you. I promise you that," Ghak assured him.

"And you'll see that I get plenty to eat?"

"All you can hold."

"Then follow me, but look out for the sabertooths; they will eat you all unless you kill them."

O-aa looked very wan and weak. Hodon looked at her and tears almost came to his eyes; then he spoke to David.

"David," he said, "perhaps I have done wrong. I have hoarded my ration of food, eating only half of it."

"It was yours to do with as you wished," said David. "We shall not take it from you."

"I do not want it," said Hodon. "I saved it for O-aa, and now she needs it."

O-aa looked up and smiled. "I hoarded mine too, Hodon," she said. "I saved it for you. Here it is." She took a little package of food wrapped in the large leaves that grew over the mouth of the cave and handed it to Hodon.

David walked to the mouth of the cave and looked out down the little canyon; but everything was blurred, as though he were looking through a mist.

Hodon knelt beside O-aa. "A woman would do that only for the man she loved," he said.

O-aa nodded and crept into his arms. "But I have not killed Blug," said Hodon.

O-aa drew his lips down to hers.

"What will your brother and sister say?" asked Hodon.

"I have no brother or sister," said O-aa.

Hodon held her so tight that she gasped for breath. Presently the mist cleared, and David could see quite plainly. He saw sabertooths who had been outside the canyon running in. They were jabbering excitedly. Then he saw human warriors approaching, warriors who carried muskets. There were many of them. When the sabertooths charged them, they were mowed down by a ragged volley. The noise was terrific, and clouds of black smoke filled the mouth of the canyon.

At the noise of the muskets, O-aa and Hodon ran to the mouth of the cave.

"Ghak has come," said David. "Now everything is all right."

It was well that he was to have a brief interlude of happiness before he returned to Sari.

PART II

MEN OF THE BRONZE AGE

I

WHEN THE LAST of the sabertooth men had been killed or had fled, David, Hodon, and O-aa joined Ghak and his warriors. Immediately, Hodon espied the little old man and advanced upon him.

"I kill," said Hodon.

The little old man screamed and hid behind Ghak. "You promised that you would not let Hodon kill me," he whimpered, "if I guided you here."

"I shall keep my promise," said Ghak. "Leave the man alone, Hodon! What has he done that you should want to kill him?"

"He tried to kill O-aa; so that he could eat her," replied Hodon.

"I was not going to keep her all for myself," whined the old man; "I was going to share her with Hodon and David."

"Who is this old man," demanded Ghak, "who says that his name is *not* Dolly Dorcas?"

"He was a prisoner of the sabertooth men," said David. "I think he is a little crazy."

"He led me here," said Ghak; "so you have him to thank for your rescue. Do not harm him. What does he mean by saying his name is not Dolly Dorcas?"

"He told us," explained David, "that he was wrecked

on a ship named the Dolly Dorcas near the North Pole of the outer world from which I come; then, in a small boat, he drifted through the North Polar Opening into Pellucidar. O-aa got things a little mixed and thought his name was Dolly Dorcas."

"He ate all the men that were in the boat with him," said O-aa; "and he said that when they were all gone, he was about to cut off one of his own legs and eat that, when he found food. He is a very hungry man."

"I do not see how he could eat anybody," said Ghak; "he has no teeth."

"You'd be surprised," said the little old man.

"Well, you— What is your name anyway, if it isn't Dolly Dorcas?" demanded Ghak.

"I don't remember," said the old man.

"Well, then, we shall just call you Ah-gilak; and that will be your name." (Ah-gilak means in Pellucidarian, old man.)

"Well," said the litle old man, "at least Ah-gilak is a better name for a man than Dolly Dorcas."

"And remember this, Ah-gilak," continued Ghak, "if you ever try to eat anybody again, I'll let Hodon kill you."

"Some of them were very good eating," sighed Ah-gilak, reminiscently, "especially that Swede."

"Let us go the village of Kali now," said David. "O-aa, Hodon, and I must have food. We nearly starved to death in that cave. Then I shall send a runner north to the caves where Oose and the remnants of his people are hiding, after which we will go down to the Lural Az, where your ships lie, Ghak, and embark for home; if you feel that you have taught the Suvians their lessons sufficiently well."

Between the canyon and the village of Kali, they saw a party of men coming from the north. At sight of so many armed warriors, these people turned to flee; but

O-aa called to them, "Come back! It is all right; these are our friends;" then she said to Ghak, "those are my people; I recognized my father, the king of Kali."

When the newcomers approached more closely, Hodon saw that Blug was with Oose; and he went and put his arm around O-aa. When Blug saw that, he ran forward.

"I told you that if you were around here when I came back, I'd kill you," he shouted.

"Go away!" said O-aa. "Hodon is my mate."

"What is that?" demanded Oose, her father. "I told you you were to mate with Blug, and I meant it; Blug shall have you."

"I kill!" shouted Blug, as he bore down on Hodon.

The Sarian met him with a clean right to the chin, and Blug dropped in his tracks. The Sarian warriors yelled in delight; but Blug was up in an instant, and this time he managed to clinch. The two men fell to the ground, fighting like a couple of wild cats. It was not a pretty fight, as the Marquis of Queensberry was entirely unknown to these men of the Stone Age. They gouged and bit and scratched, as Blug tried to fasten his teeth in Hodon's jugular.

They were both covered with blood, and one of Blug's eyes was hanging out on his cheek, when Hodon espied a rock lying near at hand. He happened to be on top for the moment; and, seizing the rock, he raised it high and brought it down with all his strength full on Blug's face.

Blug had never been beautiful; but without any features to speak of left, and those scrambled, he was something of a sight. Hodon raised the rock and struck again; the third time, Blug relaxed and lay still; but Hodon did not stop striking him until his whole head was a jelly; then he stood up.

He looked at Oose. "O-aa is my mate," he said.

Oose looked down at Blug. "Blug is not much good any more," he said. "If O-aa wants you she may have you."

They looked around, then, for O-aa. She had disappeared. "It has always been thus," said Hodon. "Three times I have fought for her, and three times she has run away while I was fighting."

"When you catch her, you should beat her," said Oose.

"I will," said Hodon.

He searched for O-aa for a long time, but he did not find her; then he came to the village of Kali, where his fellow Sarians were eating and resting.

When David Innes had rested sufficiently, the Sarians bid the Kalians farewell and departed for their ships, which lay off the coast forty miles away.

Hodon went with them. He was very sad, for he thought that O-aa had run away from him because she did not really wish to be his mate.

And O-aa? When she had seen Blug get his arms around Hodon, and the two men had fallen to the ground, she had known that Hodon would be killed; so she had run away, rather than remain and mate with Blug. She started south, intending to find Sari, which lay eight hundred miles away. She knew that she had a long journey before her and that the chances were quite remote that she would survive all the innumerable dangers of the way; but, with Hodon dead, she did not care much.

She was a cave girl, and death was such a familiar occurrence in her life that she did not fear it particularly. Early man must have been a fatalist; otherwise he would have gone crazy from fear. O-aa was a fatalist. She said to herself, "If the tarag, or the thipdar, or Ta-ho happened to meet me at just the right time and place, I shall be killed. Whatever they and I are doing now must lead up to that moment when we meet or do not meet; nothing can change it." That is the way she felt; so she did not worry—but she kept her eyes and her ears open, just the same.

O-aa had never been to Sari, but she knew that it lay inland from the Lural Az and that between Kali and Sari there were a few tribes which belonged to the Federation and would be friendly to her. She would follow along the shore of the Lural Az until she found one of these tribes, and then she could get better directions for the remainder of her journey.

She knew that David Innes and the other Sarians would soon be going down to the sea and their ships, but she wanted to avoid them for fear that they would send her back to her father and Blug; so she went quite a distance south before she turned toward the east and the Lural Az, that great body of uncharted water, teeming with giant saurians, such as ruled the Cretaceous seas in the Mesozoic period of the outer crust. O-aa was a hill girl and was afraid of the great sea, but no less terrible were the dangers that threatened her on land.

And as O-aa came down to the sea of which she was so afraid, eyes watched her from the concealment of bushes that she was approaching.

Abner Perry was a broken man; he could neither eat nor sleep, for he knew that it was his own culpable carelessness that had tossed Dian the Beautiful to the mercy of the winds on high. He had dispatched three runners to try to follow the course of the drifting balloon; but he held too little hope that, should they find it when it came to earth, they would find Dian alive: cold, hunger, and thirst would long since have taken their grim toll of her strength. For the first time in his life, Abner Perry seriously considered taking his own life.

Dian the Beautiful had been mildly surprised by the

sudden upward rush of the balloon, but she had not guessed what it portended until she looked down over the edge of the basket and saw the end of the rope which had secured the balloon to the windlass dangling high above the village of Sari.

Dian the Beautiful is a cave girl of the Stone Age. She knew nothing about balloons other than what she had gathered from Abner Perry while he was building this one. Only in a vague way did she know what made it go up in the air. She knew nothing about ripcords, and so she did not realize that once again Perry had blundered; he had neglected to equip the balloon with this safety device.

Had she known more about balloonery, she would have known that she might have climbed the suspension lines to the net and cut a hole in the gas bag with her dagger, letting the gas escape. But Dian the Beautiful did not know this; and so she watched her friends shrink to tiny dots far below; and eventually, with the village of Sari, disappear in the distance.

Dian knew that the sun was a ball of fire; and so she was surprised to discover that the closer she got to the sun, the colder she became. It didn't make sense, and it upset a theory that was as old as the human race in Pellucidar. But then the balloon upset some long-standing theories, too. She knew that the basket and the peritonea of dinosaurs, of which the gas bag was fabricated, were far too heavy to sail up into the air. Why they should do so was beyond her; so she decided that it was because Perry could do anything.

The prevailing winds of Pellucidar blow, generally, from the north to south for half the outer-Earthly year and from south to north the other half, depending upon whether it is winter at one Pole or the other. The wind that carried Dian away from Sari was blowing in a southwesterly direction and bearing her toward Thuria,

The Land of Awful Shadow.

Beneath the eternal noonday sun, the surface temperature of Pellucidar is usually high, requiring of her inhabitants a minimum of clothing; so Dian's costume was scanty to a degree. A bit of skin, caught with a rawhide throng across one shoulder, hung gracefully and becomingly in a long point to below her knees in one place, leaving one well-shaped leg entirely bare almost to her waist. It had been designed with as much subtlety as the finest creation of a French couturier, to accentuate and reveal, to hide and intrigue; but it had not been designed for great altitudes. Dian was cold.

Dian was hungry and thirsty, too; but there were neither food nor drink in this new world into which she had soared; so she did what Pellucidarians usually do when they are hungry and cannot obtain food—she lay down and slept. This conserves energy and prolongs life; it also gives one some respite from the gnawing of hunger and the pangs of thirst.

Dian did not know how long she slept, but when she awoke she was over The Land of Awful Shadow. She was in shadow herself, and now it was very cold. Above her was the Dead World, as the Pellucidarians call it, that tiny satellite of Pellucidar's sun that, revolving coincidentally with the rotation of the Earth, remained constantly in a fixed position above that part of the inner world known as The Land of Awful Shadow. Below her was Thuria, which lies partially within the shadow, and, to her right, the Lidi Plains where the Thurians graze and train their gigantic saddle animals, the huge diplodocuses of the Upper Jurassic, which they call lidi.

The greater cold had awakened Dian, and now she was suffering from that and from hunger and from thirst. Hope had left her, for she knew that she must soon die; and she thought that her dead body would continue to float around above Pellucidar forever.

When the balloon emerged again into sunlight, Dian lay down and slept; and, from exhaustion, she must have slept a long time, for when she awoke she was above the nameless strait that extends for a thousand miles or more and connects the Sojar Az with the Korsar Az. She knew what it was, for it bounds the southwestern portion of the continent on which Sari lies—beyond it was the *terra incognita* of her people, and no man knew what lay in that land of mystery.

The strait is about two hundred miles wide at the point at which Dian was crossing it; and the land, curving gently upaward around her, gave her such a range of vision that she could see the opposite shore.

Even in her hopelessness she could not but be impressed by the fact that she was looking upon a new world, the first of all her people to set eyes upon it. It gave her a little thrill, in which, possibly, was something of terror.

Her absorption was broken in upon by a hissing sound that came from above and behind her. Turning and looking up, she saw that terror of the Pellucidarian skies—a giant thipdar circling above the gas bag. The body of this huge pterodactyl measures some forty feet in length, while its bat-like wings have a spread of fully thirty feet. Its mighty jaws are armed with long, sharp teeth and its claws are equipped with horrible talons.

As a rule it attacks anything in sight. If it attacked the gas bag and ripped it open, Dian would be plummeted into the water below. She was helpless; she could only watch the terrible creature circling about the balloon and listen to its angry hisses.

The gas bag had the thipdar baffled. It paid no attention to him, but floated on serenely; it neither tried to escape nor give battle. What was the thing, anyway? He wondered if it were good to eat; and to find out, he gave it a tentative nip. Instantly some foul smelling stuff blew into his nostrils. He hissed angrily, and flew off a short distance; then he wheeled and came screaming toward the gas bag again.

Dian tried to think only of David, as one might concentrate on prayer who knew the end was near.

II

O-AA, ALWAYS ALERT to danger, nevertheless was not aware of the man hiding in the bushes. He was a large man with broad shoulders, a deep chest, and mighty forearms and biceps. He wore a loin cloth made of the feathers of birds—yellow feathers with two transverse bars of red feathers. It was artistic and striking. He had rings in his ears; they were made of fish bone. A few strands of his hair were braided and made into a small knot at the top of the back of his head; into this knot were stuck three long, yellow feathers barred with red. He carried a stone knife and a spear tipped with the tooth of a huge shark. His features were strong and regular; he was a handsome man, and he was suntanned to a golden bronze.

As O-aa came opposite him, he leaped from his concealment and seized her by the hair; then he started to drag her through the bushes down toward the beach. He soon found that that was not so easy as he had hoped. Dragging O-aa was like dragging a cat with hydrophobia; O-aa didn't drag worth a cent. She pulled back; she bit; she scratched; she kicked; and when she wasn't biting, she was emitting a stream of vitriolic vituperation that would have done credit to Pegler when on the subject of Mr. Brown.

Cave people of the Stone Age are of few words and short tempers; the prehistoric Adonis who was dragging

O-aa along by the hair was no exception that proved the rule; he was wholly orthodox. After a couple of bites, he raised his spear and clunked O-aa on the head with the haft of it; and O-aa took the full count. Then he swung her across one shoulder and trotted down to the beach, where a canoe was drawn up on the sand. He dumped O-aa into it and then pulled it out into the water.

He held it against the incoming rollers; and at precisely the psychological moment, he leaped in and paddled strongly. The light craft rose on the next roller, dove into the trough beyond, and O-aa was launched upon the great sea she so greatly feared.

When she recovered consciousness her heart sank. The canoe was leaping about boisterously, and land was already far away. The man sat upon the deck of the tapering stern and paddled with a very broad, flat paddle. O-aa appraised him furtively. She noted and appreciated his pulchritude at the same time that she was seeking to formulate a plan for killing him.

She also examined the canoe. It was about twenty feet long, with a three foot beam; it was decked over fore and aft for about six feet, leaving an eight foot cockpit; transverse booms were lashed across it at each end of the cockpit, protruding outboard about four feet on either side; lashed to the underside of the ends of these booms was a twenty foot length of bamboo, about six inches in diameter, running parallel with the craft on each side, the whole constituting a double out-rigger canoe. It was a clumsy craft to handle, but it was uncapsizable; even O-aa, who knew nothing about boats or seas, could see that; and she felt reassured. She would have been even more reassured had she known that the compartments beneath the two decks were watertight and that in addition to this, they held fresh water in bamboo containers and a quantity of food.

The man saw that she had regained consciousness. "What is your name?" he asked.

"My name is O-aa," she snapped; "I am the daughter of a king. When my mate, my father, and my seven brothers learn of this, they will come and kill you."

The man laughed. "My name is La-ak," he said. "I live on the Island of Canda. I have six wives; you will be the seventh. With seven wives I shall be a very important man; our chief has only seven. I came to the mainland to get another wife; I did not have to look long, did I?" Again he laughed.

"I will not mate with you," O-aa snapped.

Once again La-ak laughed. "You will be glad to," he said, "after my other six wives teach you how to behave —that is, you will if you live through it; they will not stand for any foolishness. They have already killed two women whom I brought home, who refused to become my wives. In my country no man may take a mate without her consent. I think it is a very foolish custom; but it is an old one, and we have to abide by it."

"You had better take me back to the mainland," said O-aa, "for I will not mate with you; and I shall certainly kill some of your wives before they kill me; then you will be worse off than you are now."

He looked at her for a long time before he spoke again, "I believe you," he said; "but you are very beautiful, and I do not intend to be cheated of you entirely. What happens in this canoe, no one in Canda will ever know, for I'll throw you overboard before we get there;" then he laid down his paddle and came toward her.

David Innes, Hodon, and the little old man, Ah-gilak, boarded the ship of Ghak the Hairy One; and when all of the other warriors had boarded this and the other ships, the fleet set sail.

Ah-gilak looked around him with a critical and contemptuous eye. "Dod-burn it!" he ejaculated. "What dod-burned landlubber built this tub? There ain't a gol-durned thing right about her. I reckon as how she'd sail sidewise just as well as she would ahead! *an'* a lateen sail!" he added, disgustedly. "Now, you should have saw the Dolly Dorcas; there was a sweet ship."

Ghak the Hairy One glared at him with a dangerous gleam in his eye, for Ghak was proud of every ship in the Navy of the Empire of Pellucidar. They were the first ships he had ever seen and they carried the first sails; to him they were the last word in perfection and modernity. Abner Perry had designed them; did this little, toothless runt think he could do better than Abner Perry? With a great, hairy hand Ghak seized Ah-gilak by the beard.

"Wait!" cautioned David. "I think Ah-gilak knows what he is talking about. He sailed ships on the outer Earth. Perry never did. Perry did the best he could down here, with no knowledge of ship design and no one to help him who had ever seen a ship before. He would be the first to welcome some one who could help us build a better navy. I think we can use Ah-gilak after we get home."

Ghak reluctantly released Ah-gilak's beard. "He talks too much," he said; and, turning, walked away.

"If I hadn't been wrecked in the Arctic and washed down into this dod-burned world," said Ah-gilak, "I would probably have commanded the fastest clipper ship in the world today. I was aimin' for to build it just as soon as I got back to Cape Cod."

"Clipper ship!" said David. "There aren't any more clipper ships. I don't suppose there's been one built in more than fifty years."

"Why, dod-burn you," exclaimed Ah-gilak; "they hadn't been building 'em more'n five year when the

Dolly Dorcas went down—let's see; that was 1845."

David Innes looked at him in amazement. "Are you sure of that date?" he demanded.

"Sure as I am that I'm standin' here, as the feller said," replied Ah-gilak.

"How old were you when the Dolly Dorcas was lost?" asked David.

"I was forty years old. I can always remember, because my birthday was the same as President Tyler's. He would have been fifty-five on March 29th, 1845, if he lived; an' I was just fifteen years younger than him. They was talkin' about a feller named Polk runnin' for President when we sailed."

"Do you know how old you are now?" asked David.

"Well, I sort o' lost track o' time down here in this dod-burned world; but I reckon I must be close to sixty."

"Not very close," said David; "you're a hundred and fifty-three."

"Well, of all the dod-burned liars, you sure take the cake! A hundred an' fifty-three! God an' Gabriel! Do I look a hundred an' fifty-three?"

"No," said David; "I'd say that you don't look a day over a hundred and fifty."

The old man looked at David disgustedly. "I ain't mentionin' no names," he said; "but some folks ain't got no more sense than a white pine dog with a poplar tail, as the feller said"; then he turned and walked away.

Hodon had been listening to the conversation; but he knew nothing about years or ages, and he wondered what it all meant. Anyway, he would not have been much interested, had he; for he was thinking of O-aa, and wondering where she was. He was sorry now that he had not stayed on shore and searched for her.

The flag ship of the little fleet of three ships was called Amoz in honor of Dian the Beautiful, who came from the land of Amoz. It was crowded with five hundred warriors. It had eight guns, four on a side, on a lower deck. There were solid shot, chain shot, and shells for each of the guns, all of which were muzzle loading. They had to be run back on crude wooden tracks to load, and then run forward again, with their muzzles sticking out of port holes, to fire; they were the pride of the Navy.

The sailors who manned the Amoz and the other ships were copper colored Mezops from the Anoroc Islands; and the Admiral of the Fleet was Ja, King of Anoroc. The lateen sail of the Amoz was enormous; it required the combined strength of fifty husky Mezops to raise it. Like the gas bag of Perry's balloon and the fabric of his late aeroplane, it was made of the peritonea of dinosaurs. This was one of Perry's prime discoveries, for there were lots of dinosaurs and their peritonea were large and tough. Habitually, they objected to giving them up; so it was quite an exciting job collecting peritonea, for dinosaurs such as carry A-1 peritonea are large, ferocious, and ill-mannered.

The fleet had been under way for but a short time, when Ah-gilak, casting a weather eye about from long habit, discovered a cloud astern. "We're a-goin' to have a blow," he said to Ja, and pointed.

Ja looked and nodded. "Yes," he said, and gave orders to shorten sail.

The cloud was not very large when it was first discovered, but it was undeniably a wind cloud. As it came closer, it grew in extent; and it became black. Ragged shreds of it whipped ahead. Around the ship was a sudden, deadly calm.

"We're a-goin' to have more 'n a gale. That there looks like a dod-burned hurricane."

Now there was a sudden gust of wind that made the sagging sail flap angrily. Ja had ordered it close reefed;

and the Mezops were battling with the whipping peritonea, as the wind increased in violence.

And now the storm was upon them. Rolling black clouds shut out the eternal sun, lightning flashed, and thunder roared; rain began to fall—not in drops or sheets, but in solid masses. The wind wailed and shrieked like some ferocious demon of destruction. Men clung to the ship's rails, to one another, to anything that they could lay hands on to keep from being blown overboard.

David Innes went among them, ordering them below; at last only the Mezop sailors and a few Sarians remained on the upper deck—they and the little old man, Ah-gilak. Innes and Ghak and Hodon clustered behind Ja and Ah-gilak. The little old man was in his element.

"I bin wrecked seven times," he shrieked above the storm, "an' I can be wrecked again, as the feller said; an' dod-burn it if I don't think I'm goin' to be."

The sea had risen, and the waves were growing constantly in immensity. The clumsy, overloaded ship wallowed out of one great sea only to be half swallowed by another.

So dark was it and so thick the rain that neither of the other ships could be seen. David was fearful for the safety of the little Sari; in fact, he was fearful for the fate of all three of the ships if the storm did not abate soon or if it increased in violence. As though possessed of sardonic humor, the hurricane raged even more violently while the thought was yet in David's mind.

The Amoz rose upon the crest of a watery mountain to plunge into a watery abyss. The men clung to whatever they could as the ship buried its nose deep in the sea; and a huge, following wave combed over the stern, submerging them.

David thought it was the end. He knew that the ship would never rise again from beneath those tons of raging water, yet still he clung to the thing he had seized. Slowly, ponderously, like some gigantic beast trying to drag itself from quick-sand, the Amoz, staggered up, shaking the water from its deck.

"Dod-burne me!" screamed Ah-gilak; "but this is a sweet ship. It didn't take half that sea to swamp the Dolly Dorcas, and I thought she was a sweet ship. Well, live and learn, as the feller said."

There were not as many men on the deck as there had been. David wondered how many of the poor devils had been lost. He looked at those about him; Ghak, and Ja, and Hondon, and Ah-gilak were all there.

David looked up at the waves as they towered above the ship, and he looked down into the abysses as the ship started down from the crest. "Seventy feet," he said, half to himself; "a good seventy feet."

Suddenly Ah-gilak yelled, "Make fast there an' say your prayers!"

David glanced astern. The most stupendous wave he had ever seen trembled above them—hundreds of tons of water poised to crush the ship; then it came!

Dian the Beautiful awaited the end with supreme indifference; she had reached the limit of human endurance; but she was not afraid. In fact, she was just a little fascinated by the situation, and wondered whether the screaming thipdar winging toward her was coming for her or the gas bag—not that it would make much difference to her in the end.

Suddenly the giant pterodactyl veered to one side, and rushed past. Dian watched it as it soared away, waiting for it to turn and renew the attack; but it did not return. It had finally discovered something of which it was afraid.

Dian looked down over the edge of the basket. She could see the land beyond the strait quite plainly now;

she seemed to be much lower, and wondered. She did not know that the gas was leaking from the balloon where the thipdar had nipped it.

It was some time before she realized the truth—that the balloon was actually descending; and now she had something more to worry about: would it reach the shore, or would it come down in the water? If the latter, she would make food for some saurian; or for a horde of them that would tear her to pieces.

And on the land a short distance back from the shore she saw an amazing sight for Pellucidar—a city, a walled city. She would not have known what it was had David not told her of the cities of his world. Well, she might be about as well off among the saurians as among strange human beings. There was little choice, but upon reflection she hoped that the ballon reached the land before it came down.

It was quite low now, and the land was still a good half mile away. She tried to gauge the relation between its drop and its horizontal progress toward the land. She looked down over the edge of the basket and saw that the rope was already dragging in the water. The rope was five hundred feet long. After a part of the rope was submerged the balloon didn't seem to drop any more; but its progress toward land was also retarded, as it dragged the submerged rope through the water. However, it appeared now that it would reach the land first.

Dian was congratulating herself on this as she peered down into the strait when she saw the head of a creature which she knew as an aztarag, or tiger of the sea, break the water near the trailing rope.

She was congratulating herself upon the fact that she was not down there, when she creature seized the rope in its mighty jaws and started for the center of the strait.

This was too much! Tired, hungry, thirsty, and exhausted, though no longer cold, Dian almost broke down. With an effort she kept back the tears for now there was no hope.

But was there one! If she could cut the rope, the balloon would be freed; and would continue on toward shore. Relieved of the weight of five hundred feet of heavy rope, it would certainly drift far inland before it came down. But she couldn't reach the rope; it was fastened to the underneath side of the basket.

There must be some way! She drew her stone knife and commeced to hack at the wickerwork of the basket's floor. At last she had a hole large enough to get her arm through. Feeling around, she found the large rope. It was attached to the basket by many smaller ropes which ran to the periphery of the basket's bottom.

Dian commenced to saw on these smaller ropes. She could see through the hole in the bottom of the basket, and she saw that the ballon was being rapidly dragged toward the water—the aztarag had sounded and was pulling the balloon down behind it!

The girl worked frantically, for once the basket was submerged she would be lost—the sea beneath her was alive with hungry creatures. She saw a gigantic shark just below her; it thrust its snout out of water; and she could almost touch it, as the last rope parted.

Instantly the balloon leaped into the air, and once more started its precarious and seemingly endless journey toward the mysterious world beyond the nameless strait.

III

As O-aa saw La-ak coming toward her she stood up. "Go back to your paddle," she said, "or I will jump overboard."

La-ak hesitated; for he guessed, rightly, that the girl meant what she said; furthermore, he knew that eventually she must sleep; then he could overpower her. "You are a fool," he said, as he resumed his paddle; "one lives but once."

"O-aa lives in her own way," retorted the girl.

She sat facing the stern; so that she might watch La-ak. She saw his spear lying beside him; she saw the dagger at his hip. These were instruments of escape, but she could not get them. She glanced around over the great sea that she so feared. Very, very dimly, through the haze of distance, she thought that she could see the mainland; elsewhere there was no sign of land—just the vast expanse of blue water rolling gradually upward in the distance to merge with the blue sky that arched over them and down again to merge with the blue water again on the opposite side. To her left she saw a little cloud, far away. It meant nothing to O-aa, who was a hill girl and consequently less cloud conscious than those who live much upon the sea.

Astern, she saw something else—a long, slender neck toppled by a hideous head with great-fanged jaws. Occasionally she caught a glimpse of a sleek, seal-like body rising momentarily above the slow ground swells. She knew this thing as a ta-ho-az, or a sea lion. It was not the harmless, playful creature that sports in the waters of our own Pacific Ocean; but a terrible engine of destruction whose ravenous appetite was never satisfied.

The fearsome creature was gliding smoothly through the water toward the canoe. That long neck would arch over the gunwale and snatch either La-ak or herself, probably both; or the creature would place a giant flipper on the craft and capsize or swamp it. O-aa thought quickly. She wished to be saved from La-ak, but not at the risk of her own life, if that comfortable circumstance could be avoided.

She stood up and pointed, taking a couple of steps toward La-ak as she did so. "Look!" she cried.

La-ak turned to look behind him, and as he did so O-aa sprang forward and seized his spear; then she thrust it with all her strength into the body of La-ak beneath his left shoulder.

With a scream of agony and rage, La-ak tried to turn upon her; but O-aa held to the end of the spear's haft; and when La-ak turned, the sharp shark's tooth with which the spear was tipped, tore into his heart. Thus died La-ak of the Island of Canda.

O-aa looked back at the ta-ho-az. It was approaching, but leisurely; as though it was quite sure that its quarry could not escape, and consequently saw no occasion for haste.

O-aa looked at the pretty yellow and red feather loin cloth on the body of La-ak and at the feathers in his hair. These she had admired greatly; so she removed them, after jerking the spear from the dead man; and then she rolled the naked body of La-ak over the stern of the canoe, after which she picked up the paddle; and with strong, if clumsy, strokes sent the craft ahead.

She glanced back often to see what the ta-ho-az was doing; and at last, to her relief, she saw that it was doing what she had hoped it would do—it had stopped to devour the body of La-ak. This, she guessed, would occupy it for some time; since, though its jaws were enormous, its neck was slender; and it must necessarily nibble rather than gulp.

O-aa had never handled a paddle before, which is not strange, since never before had she been in a boat of any description; but she had watched La-ak; and now she did remarkably well, considering her ignorance and clumsiness of the craft.

She was hungry, thirsty, and sleepy, and, as now she had lost sight of all land and had no idea in which direction to paddle, she decided that it would be foolish to paddle at all; since, there being so many different directions, and the nearest land being in one direction only, the chances were all in favor of her paddling in a wrong direction. It would be much pleasanter just to drift with the wind.

Of course she was endowed with that homing instinct that is the common heritage of all Pellucidarians to compensate them for lack of heavenly bodies to guide them, but out here on this vast expanse of water in an environment so totally unfamiliar, for the first time in her life she did not trust it.

The little cloud that she had seen had grown to a big cloud, and was coming nearer. O-aa looked at it and thought that it was going to rain, for which she would be thankful; since it would give her water to drink; then she turned her attention to other things.

She had noticed that there was one plank in the after deck where La-ak had sat that didn't seem to fit as well as the others; and though it was a trivial thing, she had wondered at it. It had suggested something to her—that no one would come out upon this great ocean without food or water. Now she investigated; for O-aa, as you may have gathered, was no fool; and she found that the board, skillfully grooved on both edges, pulled out, revealing a large compartment beneath. In this compartment were extra weapons, fishhooks, lines, nets, bamboo water containers, and smoked meats and dried fruits and vegetables.

O-aa ate and drank her fill; then she lay down to sleep, while the great, black cloud billowed toward her, and the lightning flashed and the thunder boomed. O-aa slept the dreamless sleep of utter exhaustion plus a full and contented stomach.

David was sure that the Amoz was doomed, as he saw the giant wave curling above her stern; then it broke over them, crushing them to the deck, tearing at them to break their holds on the supports to which they clung, driving the prow of the ship deep into the sea.

Not a man there but knew she could never recover from this blow; but she did. Rolling and wallowing she slowly emerged; and as the water sluiced from her deck, David saw the little old man going with it toward the bow, and he lunged after him.

The mast had gone, leaving only a stump, around which was tangled cordage and a section of the sail, that had fouled and ripped away. Just as he reached this, David caught the little old man by one ankle; then, as he himself was being washed toward the stern, he managed to seize hold of the cordage and retain his hold until the last of the water had gone over the side.

He thought that a man one hundred and fifty-three years old could never recover from such a shock; and he was about to pick him up and carry him back, when Ah-gilak scrambled to his feet.

"Dad-burn it!" ejaculated the old man, "I durn near got my feet wet that time, as the feller said."

"Are you all right?" David asked.

"Never felt so fit in my life," replied Ah-gilak. "Say, you come after me, didn't you? Why, you dod-burned fool, you might have been washed overboard." That was all he ever said about it.

That last wave marked the height of the storm. The wind continued to blow a gale, but the hurricane was past. The sea still ran high, but was diminishing. After what the Amoz had withstood, she seemed safe enough now. With no headway, she wallowed in the trough of the sea; often standing on her beam ends, but always righting herself.

"It'd take a dod-burned act of Congress to upset this tub," said Ah-gilak. "You can't sail her, an' you can't steer her; but, by gum, you can't wreck her; an' if I'd a-had her instead o' the Dolly Dorcas I wouldn't be down here now in this dod-burned hole-in-the-ground, but back in Cape Cod, probably votin' for John Tyler again, or some other good Democrat."

David went below, at the risk of life and limb, to see how the men there had fared. With the coming of the storm, they had closed all ports, and fastened the guns down more securely. Fortunately, none of them had broken loose; and there were only a few minor casualties among the men, from being thrown about during the wild pitching of the ship.

The Mezop sailors above had not fared so well; all but twenty-five of them had been washed overboard. All the boats were gone, the mast was gone, and most of the sail. The Amoz was pretty much of a derelict. Neither of the other ships was in sight; and David had given them both up for lost, especially the little Sari.

Their situation looked rather hopeless to these men of the Stone Age. "If the boats hadn't been lost," said Ghak, "some of us could get ashore."

"Why can't we break up the deck and build a raft— several of them?" suggested Hodon. "We could paddle rafts to shore, but we couldn't ever paddle the Amoz."

"You dod-burned landlubbers give me a pain," snorted Ah-gilak. "We got the stub of a mast, part of the sail, and plenty cordage; we can jury rig the gol-durned tub, an' get to shore twice as fast an' ten times as easy as buildin' rafts an' paddlin'. Give me some hands, an' I'll have her shipshape in two shakes of a dead lamb's tail, as the feller said. How fer is to port?"

David shrugged. "That depends on how far the hurricane carried us and in what direction. We may be fifty miles from port, or we may be five hundred. Your guess would be better than mine."

"How's the fresh water?" demanded Ah-gilak.

"We've enough for many sleeps," said Ja.

"Dod-burn it!" cried the old man; "how in tarnation's

a fellow goin' to do any figurin' with a bunch of land-lubbers that ain't never knowed what time it was since they was born."

"On the contrary," said David, "they always know what time it is."

"How come?" demanded Ah-gilak.

"It is always noon."

Ah-gilak snorted. He was in no mood for persiflage. "Well," he said, "we'll do the dod-burndest best we can. We may run short of water, but we got plenty food," he cast his eyes on the warriors coming up from the lower deck.

O-aa was awakened by the pitching of the canoe, and opened her eyes to see a wall of water towering above her. She lay in a watery canyon, with another wall of water hemming her in on the other side. This was a harrowing situation that was quite beyond her experience; nothing could save her; one of the walls would topple over on her. But nothing of the kind happened. Instead, the wall came down; and the canoe was lifted to the summit of one just like it. Here, O-aa could see a tumbling mass of wind torn water as far as the eye could reach. The sky was black with angry, rolling clouds, that were split by vivid flashes of lightning to the accompaniment of peals of earth shaking thunder. The wind howled and shrieked in a fury of malign hate. Then the canoe sank into another canyon.

This went on and on; there seemed to be no end to it. The cockpit was half full of water; but La-ak had built well—the canoe could neither capsize nor sink and it was so light that it rode the crest of even the most mountainous waves; nothing short of a bolt of ligthning could destroy it. This, however, O-aa did not know; she thought that each wave would be the last, as far as she was concerned; but as wave after wave lifted her upon its crest and then dropped her into a new abyss that was exactly like the last one, she took courage; until presently she was enjoying the experience. O-aa had never been on a roller coaster; but she was getting the same sort of thrill out of this experience; and it lasted much longer, and she didn't have to buy any tickets.

The Sari, being a lighter ship than either of the other two, was blown along before the hurricane much faster; also, as it carried a much smaller sail, its mast did not go by the board as quickly as had that of the Amoz. The third ship had lost its mast even before that of the Amoz had gone; so when the wind abated a little, the Sari, while also by this time a demasted derelict, was far ahead of her sister ships.

Having but a single, open deck, she had lost most of her complement; but she was still staunch of frame and timber—for Perry and David had built her well, much better than the first ship Perry had designed, and for which she was named, which had turned bottomside up at its launching.

The continuing gale, which persisted after the worst of the hurricane had past, was blowing the Sari merrily along to what fate or what destination no man knew. The survivors were only glad that they were alive; like most men of the Stone Age, they had no questions to ask of the future, the present being their only immediate concern; though, belying that very assertion, they did catch what rain water they could to augment the supply already aboard.

The deck of the Sari was still a more or less precarious resting place, when one of the Mezops sighted something floating dead ahead. He called his companions' attention to it, and several of them worked their way around the rail to have a look at what he had discovered.

Now, anything floating on this lonely sea was worthy of remark; it was not like the waters off the coast of California, where half the deck loads of Oregon lumbermen bob around to menace navigation and give the Coast Guard the jitters.

"It's a canoe," said Ko, the big Mezop who had discovered it.

"Is there anyone in it?" asked Raj, the captain of the Sari and a chief among the Mezops.

"Wait until it comes up again," said Ko.

"It must be a wonderful canoe, to have lived through such a storm," said Raj.

"It had a most peculiar look," said Ko. "Here it comes again! I think I see someone in it."

"It is a strange canoe," said Raj. "There are things sticking out from its sides."

"I once saw one like it," said another Mezop; "perhaps many thousand sleeps ago. It was blown to our island with a man who said that he came from an island called Canda, far out on the Lural Az. The canoe had bamboo floats on either side of it. It could not capsize. It had watertight compartments; so it could not sink. We killed the man. I think this canoe is from Canda."

Presently the Sari, which presented a larger surface to the wind than the canoe, overhauled it. O-aa was watching it. Having heard about the great ships of the Sarians from Hodon and David, she guessed that this must be one of them; and she was not afraid. Here was rescue, if she could get aboard. She waved to the men looking over the rail at her.

"It is a girl," said Raj. "Get a rope; we will try to get her aboard."

"She is from Canda," said the sailor who had seen the man from Canda, "she wears the same feather loin cloth that the man from Canda wore. We had better let her drown."

"No," said Raj; "she is a girl." Just what were the implications of this statement, you may guess as well as I. Raj was a man of the Stone Age; so, in many respects he was probably far more decent than men of the civilized outer world; but he was still a man.

One of the outriggers of the canoe bumped against the side of the Sari just as Ko threw a rope to O-aa. The girl seized it as the ship heeled over to starboard and rose on another wave while the canoe dropped into the trough, but O-aa held on. She was jerked from the canoe and banged against the side of the ship; but she clambered up the rope like a monkey—cave girls are that way, probably from climbing inadequate and rickety ladders and poles all their lives.

As she clambered over the side, Raj took her by the arm. "She is not only a girl," he said, "but she is beautiful; I shall keep her for myself."

O-aa slapped him in the face, and jerked away. "I am the daughter of a king," she said. "My mate, my father, and my nine brothers will find you out and kill you if you harm me."

A man from Thuria, who was searching for a herd of lidi which had strayed, followed them to the end of the world which is bounded by the nameless strait. There a shadow passed across him. He looked up, thinking to see a thipdar; but there was a tree close by, and he was not afraid. What he saw filled him with amazement and not a little awe. A great round thing, to the bottom of which something seemed to be attached, was floating high in the air out across the nameless strait. He watched it for a long time, until it was only a speck; then he went on searching for his lost lidi which he never found.

He thought a great deal about this remarkable experience as he made his way back to Thuria on his giant lidi. What could the thing have been? He was sure that it was not alive, for he had seen no wings nor any movement of any kind; the thing had seemed just to drift along on the wind.

Being a Stone Age man living in a savage world, he had had so many exciting adventures that he didn't even bother to mention most of them after he got home; unless he hadn't had any adventures at all and hadn't killed any one or anything, nor hadn't been nearly killed himself; then he told his mate about that, and they both marvelled.

But this thing that he had seen above the nameless strait was different; this was something really worth talking about. No one else in the world had ever seen anything like that, and the chances were that nobody would believe him when he told about it. He would have to take that chance, but nothing could change the fact that he had seen it.

As soon as he got home, he commenced to talk about it; and, sure enough, no one believed him, his mate least of all. That made him so angry that he beat her.

"You were probably off in that village of Liba with that frowzy, fat, she-jalok; and are trying to make me believe that you went all the way to the end of the world," she had said; so perhaps he should have beaten her.

He had been home no great time, perhaps a couple of sleeps, when a runner came from Sari. Everybody gathered around the chief to hear what the runner had to say.

"I have run all the way from Sari," he said "to ask if any man of Thuria has seen a strange thing floating through the air. It is round—"

"And it has something fastened to the bottom of it," fairly shouted the man whom no one would believe.

"Yes!" cried the runner. "You have seen it?"

"I have seen it," said the man.

His fellow Thurians looked at him in amazement; after all he had told the truth—that was the amazing part of it. His mate assumed an air of importance and an I-told-you-so expression as she looked around at the other women.

"Where did you see it?" demanded the runner.

"I had gone to the end of the world in search of my lost lidi," explained the man, "and I saw this thing floating out across the nameless strait."

"Then she is lost," cried the runner.

"Who is lost?" demanded the chief.

"Dian the Beautiful who was in the basket which hung from the bottom of the great round ball that Perry called a balloon."

"She will never be found," said the chief. "No man knows what lies beyond the nameless strait. Sometimes, when it is very clear, men have thought that they saw land there; that is why it is called a strait; but it may be an ocean bigger than the Sojar Az, which has no farther shore as far as any man knows."

IV

RELIEVED OF THE weight of the rope, the balloon soared aloft much higher than it had been when the rope first started to drag in the waters of the nameless strait. Soon it was over the land and the city. Dian looked down and marvelled at this wondrous thing built by men.

It was a mean little city of clay houses and narrow winding streets, but to a cave girl of the Stone Age who had never before seen a city, it was a marvelous thing. It impressed her much as New York City impresses the outlanders from Pittsburgh or Kansas City, who see it for the first time.

The balloon was floating so low now that she could see the people in the streets and on the roofs of the buildings. They were looking up at her in wonder. If Dian had never seen a city, she had at least heard of them; but these people had not only never before seen a balloon, but they had never heard of such a thing.

When the balloon passed over the city and out across the country beyond, hundreds of people ran out and followed it. They followed it for a long way as it slowly came closer and closer to the ground.

Presently Dian saw another city in the distance, and when she came close to this second city she was quite close to the ground—perhaps twenty feet above it; then she saw men running from the city. They carried shields and bows and arrows, and for the first time she noticed that those who had followed her all the way from the first city were all men and that they, too, carried shields and bows and arrows.

Before the basket touched the ground the men from the two cities were fighting all around it. At first they fought with bows and arrows, but when they came to close quarters they drew two bladed short-swords from scabbards that hung at their sides and fought hand-to-hand. They shouted and screamed at one another, and altogether made a terrible din.

Dian wished that she could make the balloon go up again, for she did not wish to fall into the hands of such ferocious people, but down came the balloon right in the midst of the fighting. Of course the gas bag dragged it, bumping and jumping along the ground, closer and closer to the second city. Warriors of both sides seized the edge of the basket and pulled and hauled, the men from the first city trying to drag it back and those of the second city trying to haul it on toward their gates.

"She is ours!" cried one of the latter. "See! She tries

to come to Lolo-lolo! Kill the infidels who would steal our Noada!"

"She is ours!" screamed the men of the first city; "we saw her first. Kill the infidels who would cheat us of our Noada!"

Now the basket was near the gates of the city, and suddenly a dozen men rushed forward, seized hold of Dian, lifted her from the basket, and carried her through the gates, which were immediately slammed on friend and foe alike.

Relieved of the weight of Dian, the balloon leaped into the air, and drifted across the city. Even the fighters stopped to watch the miracle.

"Look!" exclaimed the warrior of the second city, "it has brought us our Noada, and now it returns to Karana."

Lolo-lolo was another city of clay houses and winding, crooked streets through which Dian the Beautiful was escorted with what, she realized, was deepest reverence.

A warrior went ahead, shouting, "Our Noada has come!" and as she passed, the people, making way for her little cortege, knelt, covering their eyes with their hands.

None of this could Dian understand, for she knew nothing of religion, her people being peculiarly free from all superstition. She only knew that these strange people seemed friendly, and that she was being received more as an honored guest than as a prisoner. Everything here was strange to her; the little houses built solidly along both sides of the narrow streets; the yellow skins of the people; the strange garments that they wore—leather aprons, painted with gay designs, that fell from their waists before and behind; the leather helmets of the men; the feather headdress of the women. Neither men nor women wore any garment above the waist, while the children and young people were quite naked.

The armlets and anklets and other metal ornaments of both men and women, as well as the swords, the spear heads, and the arrow tips of the warriors were of a metal strange to Dian. They were bronze, for these people had passed from the Stone Age and the Age of Copper into the Bronze Age. That they were advancing in civilization was attested by the fact that their weapons were more lethal than those of the Stone Age people —the more civilized people become, the more deadly are the inventions with which they kill one another.

Dian was escorted to an open square in the center of the village. Here the buildings were a little larger, though none was over one story in height. In the center of one side of the quadrangle was a domed building, the most imposing in the city of Lolo-lolo; although to describe it as imposing is a trifle grandiloquent. It was, however, remarkable, in that these people could design and construct a dome as large as this one.

The shouting warrior who had preceded the escort had run ahead to the entrance of this building, where he shouted, "Our Noada comes!" repeating it until a number of weirdly costumed men emerged. They wore long leather coats covered with painted ornamentation, and the head of each was covered by a hideous mask.

As Dian approached the entrance to the building, these strange figures surrounded her; and, kneeling, covered the eye holes of their masks with their hands.

"Welcome, our Noada! Welcome to your temple in Lolo-lolo! We, your priests welcome you to The House of the Gods!" they chanted in unison.

The words welcome, priests, and gods were new words to Dian; she did not know what they meant; but she was bright enough to know that she was supposed to, and to realize that they thought her somebody she was not and that this belief of theirs was her best safe-guard; so she merely inclined her head graciously and waited for what might come next.

The square behind her had filled with people, who now began to chant a weird pagan song to the beating of drums, as Dian the Beautiful was escorted into The House of the Gods by the priests of Noada.

Under the expert direction of Ah-gilak, the men of the Amoz set up a jury rig; and once more the ship moved on its journey. A man from Amoz was the compass, sextant, chronometer, and navigator; for the navel base of Pellucidar was the little bay beside which were the cliffs of Amoz. Guided by his inherent homing instinct, he stood beside the wheelsman and pointed toward Amoz. His relief was another Amozite, and the period of his watch was terminated when he felt like sleeping. The arrangement was most satisfactory, and the results obtained were far more accurate than those which might have been had by use of compass, sextant, and chronometer.

The wind had not abated and the seas were still high; but the EPS Amoz wallowed and plowed along toward port, which all aboard were now confident it would reach eventually.

"Dod-burn the old hooker," said Ah-gilak; "she'll get there some day, as the feller said."

When O-aa said to Raj, "I am the daughter of a king," the Mezop cocked an ear, for the word had been grafted onto the language of Pellucidar by Abner Perry, and those who had a right to the title were the heads of "kingdoms" that belonged to the federation known as the Empire of Pellucidar. If the girl was just any girl, that was one thing; but if her people belonged to the Federation, that was something very different indeed.

"Who is your father?" demanded Raj.

"Oose, King of Kali," she replied; "and my mate is Hodon the Fleet One, of Sari. My nine brothers are very terrible men."

"Never mind your nine brothers," said Raj; "that you are a Kalian, or that your mate is Hodon of Sari is enough. You will be well treated on this ship."

"And that will be a good thing for you," said O-aa, "for if you hadn't treated me well, I should have killed you. I have killed many men. My nine brothers and I used to raid the village of Suvi all alone, and I always killed more men than any of my brothers. My mother's brother was also a great killer of men, as are my three sisters. Yes, it will be very well for you if you treat me nicely. I always—"

"Shut up," said Raj, "you talk too much and you lie too much. I shall not harm you, but we Mezops beat women who talk too much; we do not like them."

O-aa stuck her chin in the air, but she said nothing; she knew a man of his word when she met one.

"If you are not from Canda," said the sailor who had once seen a man from Canda, "where did you get that feather loin cloth?"

"I took it from La-ak, the Candian, after I had killed him," replied O-aa, "—and *that* is no lie."

The Sari was blown along before the gale, and at the same time it was in the grip of an ocean current running in the same direction; so it was really making excellent headway, though to O-aa it seemed to be going up and down only.

When they came opposite the Anoroc Islands, the Mezops became restless. They could not see the islands; but they knew exactly the direction in which they lay, and they didn't like the idea of being carried past their home. The four boats of the Sari had been so securely lashed to the deck against the rail that the storm had not been able to tear them away; so Raj suggested to the Sarians that he and his fellow Mezops take two of the boats and paddle to Anaroc, and that the Sarians take the other two and make for shore, since the ship was also opposite Sari.

The high seas made it extremely difficult and dangerous to launch the boats; but the Mezops are excellent sailors, and they finally succeeded in getting both their boats off; and with a final farewell they paddled away over the high seas.

O-aa looked on at all of this with increasing perturbation. She saw the frail boats lifted high on mighty waves only to disappear into the succeeding trough. Sometimes she thought that they would never come up again. She had watched the lowering of the boats and the embarkation of the Mezops with even greater concern; so, when the Sarians were ready to launch their boats, she was in more or less of a blue funk.

They told her to get into the first boat, but she said that she would go in the second—she wanted to delay the dread moment as long as possible. What added to her natural fear of the sea, was the fact that she was quite aware that the Sarians were not good sailors. Always they have lived inland, and had never ventured upon the sea until David and Perry had decreed that they become a naval power, and even then they had always gone as cargo and not as sailors.

O-aa watched the lowering of the first boat in fear and trepidation. They first lowered the boat into the sea with two men in it; these men tried to hold it from pounding against the side of the ship, using paddles for the purpose. They were not entirely successful. O-aa expected any minute to see it smashed to pieces. The other Sarians who were to go in the first boat slid down ropes; and when they were all in the boat, the Sari suddenly heeled over and capsized it. Some of the men succeeded in seizing the ropes down which they had slid, and these were hauled to the deck of the Sari; for the others there was no hope. O-aa watched them drown.

The remaining Sarians were dubious about lowering the second boat; no one likes to be drowned in a high sea full of ravenous reptiles. They talked the matter over.

"If half the men had taken paddles and held the boat away from the Sari, instead of trying to paddle before the ship rolled away from them, the thing would not have happened," said one. Others agreed with him.

"I think we can do it safely," said another. O-aa didn't think so.

"If we drift around on the Sari, we shall die of thirst and starvation," said a third; "we won't have a chance. Once in the boat, we will have a chance. I am for trying it." Finally the others agreed.

The boat was lowered successfully, and a number of men slid down into it to hold it away from the ship's side.

"Down you go," said a man to O-aa, pushing her toward the rail.

"Not I," said O-aa. "I am not going."

"What! You are going to remain on board the Sari alone?" he demanded.

"I am," said O-aa; "and if you ever get to Sari, which you won't, and Hodon is there, tell him that O-aa is out on the Lural Az in the Sari. He will come and get me."

The man shook his head, and slid over the side. The others followed him. O-aa watched them as they fended the boat from the side of the ship until it rolled away from them; then they drove their paddles into the water and stroked mightily until they were out of danger. She watched the boat being tossed about until it was only a speck in the distance. Alone on a drifting derelict on a storm-tossed ocean, O-aa felt much safer than she would have in the little boat which she was sure would never reach land.

O-aa had what she considered an inexhaustible supply of food and water, and some day the Sari would drift ashore; then she would make her way home. The greatest hardship with which she had to put up was the lack of some one with whom to talk; and, for O-aa, that was a real hardship.

The wind blew the ship toward the southwest, and the ocean current hastened it along in the same direction. O-aa slept many times, and it was still noon. The storm had long since abated. Great, smooth swells lifted the Sari gently and gently lowered it. Where before the ocean had belabored the ship, now it caressed her.

When O-aa was awake she was constantly searching for land, and at last she saw it. It was very dim and far away; but she was sure that it was land, and the Sari was approaching it—but, oh, so slowly. She watched until she could no longer hold her eyes open, and then she slept. How long she slept no man may know; but when she awoke the land was very close, but the Sari was moving parallel with it and quite rapidly. O-aa knew that she could never reach the land if the ship kept on its present course, but there was nothing that she could do about it.

A strong current runs through the nameless strait from the Sojar Az, into which the Sari had drifted, to the Korsar Az, a great ocean that bounds the western shore of the land mass on which Sari is located. None of this O-aa knew, nor did she know that the land off the port side of the Sari was that dread terra incognita of her people.

The wind, that had been blowing gently from the east, changed into the north and increased, carrying the Sari closer inshore. Now she was so close that O-aa could plainly discern things on land. She saw something that aroused her curiosity, for she had never seen anything like it before; it was a walled city. She had not the slightest idea what it was. Presently she saw people emerging from it; they were running down to the shore toward which the Sari was drifting. As they came closer, O-aa saw that there were many warriors.

O-aa had never seen a city before, and these people had never seen a ship. The Sari was drifting in bow on, and O-aa was standing on the stump of the bowsprit, a brave figure in her red and yellow feather loincloth and the three feathers in her hair.

The Sari was quite close to shore now and the people could see O-aa plainly. Suddenly they fell upon their knees and covered their eyes with their hands, crying, "Welcome, our Noada! The true Noada has come to Tanga-tanga!"

Just then the Sari ran aground and O-aa was pitched head-foremost into the water. O-aa had learned to swim in a lake above Kali, where there were no reptiles; but she knew that these waters were full of them; she had seen them often; so when she came to the surface she began swimming for shore as though all the saurians in the world were at heels. Esther Williams would not have been ashamed of the time in which the little cave girl of Kali made the 100 meters to shore.

As she scrambled ashore, the awe-struck warriors of Tanga-tanga knelt again and covered their eyes with their hands. O-aa glanced down to see if she had lost her loin-cloth, and was relieved to find that she had not.

V

O-AA LOOKED AT the kneeling warriors in amazement; the situation was becoming embarrassing. "What are you doing that for," she demanded. "Why don't you get up?"

"May we stand in your presence?" asked a warrior.

O-aa thought quickly; perhaps this was a case of mistaken identity, but she might as well make the best of it. If they were afraid of her, it might be well to keep them that way.

"I'll think it over," she said.

Glancing around, she saw some of the warriors peeking at her; but the moment she looked at them they lowered their heads. Even after they had looked at her, O-aa discovered, they still didn't realize their mistake. She saw that they were yellow men, with painted leather aprons, and strange weapons, they wore helmets that O-aa thought were very becoming.

After she had taken her time looking them over, she said, "Now you may stand;" and they all arose.

Several of the warriors approached her. "Our Noada," one of them said, "we have been waiting for you for a long time—ever since the first Xexot learned that only with your help can we hope to reach Karana after we die; perhaps that was a million sleeps ago. Our priests told us that some time you would come. Not so many sleeps ago one came out of the air whom we thought was our Noada, but now we know that she was a false Noada. Come with us to Tanga-tanga, where your priests will take you into your temple."

O-aa was puzzled. Much that the man had said to her was as Greek to a Hottentot; but little O-aa was smart enough to realize that she seemed to be sitting pretty, and she wasn't going to upset the apple cart by asking questions. Her greatest fear was that they might start asking her questions.

Dian the Beautiful had learned many things since she had come to the city of Lolo-lolo; and she had learned them without asking too many questions, for one of the first things she had learned was that she was supposed to know everything—even what people were thinking.

She had learned that this race of yellow men called themselves Xexots; and that she had come direct from a place called Karana, which was up in the sky somewhere, and that if they were good, she would see that they were sent there when they died; but if they were bad, she could send them to the Molop Az, the flaming sea upon which Pellucidar floats.

She already knew about the Molop Az, as what Pellucidarian does not? The dead who are buried in the ground go there; they are carried down, piece by piece, to the Molop Az by the wicked little men who dwell there. Everyone knows this, because when graves are opened it is always discovered that the bodies have been partially or entirely borne off. That is why many of the peoples of Pellucidar place their dead in trees where the birds may find them and carry them bit by bit to the Dead World that hangs above the Land of Awful Shadow. When people killed an enemy, they always buried his body in the ground; so that it would be sure to go to Molop Az.

She also discovered that being a Noada, was even more important than being an empress. Here in Lololo, even the king knelt down and covered his eyes when he approached her; nor did he arise again until she had given him permission.

It all puzzled Dian a great deal, but she was learning. People brought her presents of food and ornaments and leather and many, many little pieces of metal, thin and flat and with eight sides. These the priests, who eventually took most of the presents, seemed to value more than anything else; and if there were not a goodly supply left in the temple every day, they became very angry and scolded the people. But no matter how puzzled she was, Dian dared not ask questions; for she was intuitively aware that if they came to doubt that she was allwise, they would doubt that she was really a Noada; and then it would go hard with her. After they had worshipped her so devoutly, they might tear her to pieces if they discovered that she was an imposter.

The king of Lolo-lolo was called a go-sha; his name was Gamba. He came often to worship at the shrine of the Noada. The high priest, Hor, said that he had never come to the temple before except on feast days; when he could get plenty to eat and drink and watch the dancing.

"You are very beautiful, my Noada," said Hor; "perhaps that is why the go-sha comes more often now."

"Perhaps he wants to go to Karana when he dies," suggested Dian.

"I hope that that is all he wants," said Hor. "He has been a very wicked man, failing to pay due respect to the priesthood and even deriding them. It is said that he does not believe in Karana or Molop Az or the teachings of Pu and that he used to say that no Noada would ever come to Lolo-lolo because there was no such thing as a Noada."

"Now he knows better," said Dian.

Shortly after this conversation, Gamba came to the temple while Hor was asleep; he knelt before Dian and covered his eyes with his hands.

"Arise, Gamba," said Dian.

She was seated on a little platform upon a carved stool covered with painted leather and studded with bronze; she wore a soft leather robe fastened at the waist with a girdle. The robe was caught over one shoulder, leaving the other bare, and on one side it was slit to her hip and fastened there with a bronze disc. Around her neck were eight strands of carved ivory beads, each strand of a different length, the longest reaching below her waist. Bronze bracelets and anklets adorned her limbs, while surmounting this barbaric splendor was a headdress of feathers.

Dian the Beautiful, who had never before worn more than a sketchy loin cloth, was most uncomfortable in all this finery, not being sufficiently advanced in civilization to appreciate the necessity for loading the feminine form with a lot of useless and silly gew-gaws. She knew that Nature had created her beautiful and that no outward adornment could enhance her charms.

Gamba appeared to be in hearty accord with this view, as his eyes seemed to ignore the robe. Dian did not like the look in them.

"Did the go-sha come to worship?" inquired Dian the Goddess.

Gamba smiled. Was there a suggestion of irony in that smile? Dian thought so.

"I came to visit," replied Gamba. "I do not have to come here to worship you—that I do always."

"It is well that you worship your Noada," said Dian; "Pu will be pleased."

"It is not the Noada I worship," said Gamba, boldly; "it is the woman."

"The Noada is not pleased," said Dian, icily; "nor is Pu; nor will Hor, the high priest, be pleased."

Gamba laughed. "Hor may fool the rest of them; but he doesn't fool me, and I don't believe that he fools you. I don't know what accident brought you here, nor what that thing was you came in; but I do know you are just a woman, for there is no such thing as a Noada; and there are a lot of my nobles and warriors who think just as I do."

"The Noada is not interested," said Dian, "the go-sha may leave."

Gamba settled himself comfortably on the edge of the

dais. "I am the go-sha," he said; "I come and go as I please. I please to remain."

"Then *I* shall leave" said Dian, rising.

"Wait," said Gamba. "If you are as wise as I think you are, you will see that it is better to have Gamba for a friend than an enemy. The people are dissatisfied; Hor bleeds them for all he can get out of them; and since he has had you with whom to frighten them, he has bled them worse. His priests threaten them with your anger if they do not bring more gifts, especially pieces of bronze; and Hor is getting richer, and the people are getting poorer. They say now that they have nothing left with which to pay taxes; soon the go-sha will not have the leather to cover his nakedness."

"Of these things, you should speak to Hor," said Dian.

"By that speech you convict yourself," exclaimed Gamba, triumphantly, "but yours is a difficult role; I am surprised that you have not tripped before."

"I do not know what you mean," said Dian.

"The Noada is the representative of Pu in Pellucidar, according to Hor; she is omnipotent; she decides; she commands—not Hor. When you tell me to speak to Hor of the things of which the people complain, you admit that it is Hor who commands—not you."

"The Noada does command," snapped Dian; "she commands you to take your complaints to Hor; just as the common people take their complaints to the lesser priests—they do not burden their Noada with them, nor should you. If they warrant it, Hor will lay them before me."

Gamba slapped his thigh. "By Pu!" he exclaimed, but you are a bright girl. You slipped out of that one very cleverly. Come! let us be friends. We could go a long way together in Lolo-lolo. Being the wife of the go-sha would not be so bad, and a lot more fun than being a Noada cooped up in a temple like a prisoner—which you are. Yes, you are a prisoner; and Hor is your jailer. Think it over, Noada; think it over."

"Think what over?" demanded a voice from the side of the room.

They both turned. It was Hor. He came and knelt before Dian, covering his eyes with his hands; then he rose and glared at Gamba, but he spoke to Dian. "You permit this man to sit upon this holy spot?" he demanded.

Gamba eyed Dian intently, waiting for her reply. It came: "If it pleases him," she said, haughtily.

"It is against the laws that govern the temple," said Hor.

"I make the laws which govern the temple," said Dian; "and I make the laws which govern the people of Lololo," and she looked at Gamba.

Hor looked very uncomfortable. Gamba was grinning. Dian rose. "You are both excused," she said, and it sounded like a command—it was a command. Then Dian stepped down from the dais and walked toward the door of the temple.

"Where are you going?" demanded Hor.

"I am going to walk in the streets of Lolo-lolo and speak with my people."

"But you can't," cried Hor. "It is against the rules of the temple."

"Didn't you just hear your Noada say that she makes the temple laws?" asked Gamba, still grinning.

"Wait, then," cried Hor, "until I summon the priests and the drums."

"I wish no priests and no drums," said Dian. "I wish to walk alone."

"I will go with you." Gamba and Hor spoke in unison, as though the line had been rehearsed.

"I said that I wished to go alone," said Dian; and with that, she passed through the great doorway of the temple out into the eternal sunlight of the square.

"Well," said Gamba to Hor, "you got yourself a Noada, didn't you?" and he laughed ironically as he said it.

"I shall pray Pu to guide her," said Hor, but his expression was more that of an executioner than a suppliant.

"She'll probably guide Pu," said Gamba.

As the people saw their Noada walking alone in the square, they were filled with consternation; they fell upon their knees at her approach and covered their eyes with their hands until she bade them arise. She stopped before a man and asked him what he did.

"I work in bronze," said the man. "I made those bracelets that you are wearing, Noada."

"You make many pieces for your work?" Dian had never known a money system before she came to Lololo; but here she had learned that one could get food and other things in exchange for pieces of bronze, often called "pieces" for short. They were brought in quantities to the temple and given to her, but Hor took them.

"I get many pieces for my work," replied the man, "but—" He hung his head and was silent.

"But what?" asked Dian.

"I am afraid to say," said the man; "I should not have spoken."

"I command you to speak," said Dian.

"The priests demand most of what I make, and the go-sha wants the rest. I have barely enough left to buy food."

"How much were you paid for these bracelets that I am wearing?" demanded Dian.

"Nothing."

"Why nothing?"

"The priests said that I should make them and give them as an offering to the Noada, who would forgive my sins and see that I got into Karana when I died."

"How much are they worth?"

"They are worth at least two hundred pieces," said the man; "they are the most beautiful bracelets in Lololo."

"Come with me," said Dian, and she continued across the square.

On the opposite side of the square from the temple was the house of the go-sha. Before the entrance stood a number of warriors on guard duty. They knelt and covered their eyes as Noada approached, but when they arose and Dian saw their faces she saw no reverence there—only fear and hate.

"You are fighting men," said Dian. "Are you treated well?"

"We are treated as well as the slaves," said one, bitterly.

"We are given the leavings from the tables of the go-sha and the nobles, and we have no pieces with which to buy more," said another.

"Why have you no pieces? Do you fight for nothing?"

"We are supposed to get five pieces every time the go-sha sleeps, but we have not been paid for many sleeps."

"Why?"

"The go-sha says that it is because the priests take all the pieces for you," said the first warrior, boldly.

"Come with me," said Dian.

"We are on guard here, and we cannot leave."

"I, your Noada, command it; come!" said Dian, imperiously.

"If we do as the Noada commands us," said one, "she will protect us."

"But Gamba will have us beaten," said another.

"Gamba will not have you beaten if you always obey

me. It is Gamba who will be beaten if he harms you for obeying me."

The warriors followed her as she stopped and talked with men and women, each of which had a grievance against either the priests or the go-sha. Each one she commanded to follow her; and finally, with quite a goodly procession following her, she returned to the temple.

Gamba and Hor had been standing in the entrance watching her; now they followed her into the temple. She mounted the dais and faced them.

"Gamba and Hor," she said, "you did not kneel as your Noada passed you at the temple door. You may kneel now."

The men hesitated. They were being humiliated before common citizens and soldiers. Hor was the first to weaken; he dropped to his knees and covered his eyes. Gamba looked up defiantly at Dian. Just the shadow of a smile, tinged by irony, played upon her lips. She turned her eyes upon the soldiers standing beside Gamba.

"Warriors," she said, "take this—" She did not have to say more, for Gamba had dropped to his knees; he had guessed what was in her mind and trembling on her lips.

After she had allowed the two to rise, she spoke to Hor. "Have many pieces of bronze brought," she said.

"What for?" asked Hor.

"The Noada does not have to explain what she wishes to do with her own," said Dian.

"But Noada," sputtered Hor; "the pieces belong to the temple."

"The pieces and the temple, too, belong to me; the temple was built for me, the pieces were brought as gifts for me. Send for them."

"How many?" asked Hor.

"All that six priests can carry. If I need more, I can send them back."

With six priests trailing him, Hor left the apartment, trembling with rage; but he got many pieces of bronze, and he had them brought into the throne room of the temple.

"To that man," said Dian, pointing at the worker in bronze, "give two hundred pieces in payment for these bracelets for which he was never paid."

"But, Noada," expostulated Hor, "the bracelets were gift offerings."

"They were forced offerings—give the man the pieces." She turned to Gamba. "How many times have you slept since your warriors were last paid?"

Gamba flushed under his yellow skin. "I do not know," he said, surlily.

"How many?" she asked the warriors.

"Twenty-one times," said one of them.

"Give each of these men five pieces for each of the twenty-one sleeps," directed Dian, "and have all the warriors come immediately to get theirs"; then she directed the payment of various sums to each of the others who had accompanied her to the temple.

Hor was furious; but Gamba, as he came to realize what this meant, was enjoying it, especially Hor's discomfiture; and Dian became infinitely more desirable to him than she had been before. What a mate she would be for a go-sha!

"Now," said Dian, when all had received their pieces, "hereafter, all offerings to your Noada will be only what you can afford to give—perhaps one piece out of every ten or twenty; and to your go-sha, the same. Between sleeps I shall sit here, and Hor will pay to everyone who comes the number of pieces each has been forced to give. Those who think one piece in ten is fair, may return that amount to Hor. If you have any other grievances, bring them to your Noada; and they will be corrected. You may depart now."

They looked at her in wonder and adoration, the citizens and the warriors whose eyes had first been filled with fear and hatred of her; and after they had kneeled, they paid to Hor one piece out of every ten they had received. Laughing and jubilant, they left the temple to spread the glad tidings through the city.

"Pu will be angry," said Hor; "the pieces were Pu's."

"You are a fool," said Dian, "and if you don't mend your ways I shall appoint a new high priest."

"You can't do that," Hor almost screamed, "and you can't have any more of my pieces of bronze!"

"You see," said Gamba to Dian, "that what I told you is true—Hor collects all the pieces for himself."

"I spoke with many people in the square before the temple," said Dian, "and I learned many things from them—one of them is that they hate you and they hate me. That is why I called you a fool, Hor; because you do not know that these people are about ready to rise up and kill us all—the robbed citizens and the unpaid warriors. After I return their pieces that have been stolen from them, they will still hate you two; but they will not hate me; therefore, if you are wise, you will always do what I tell you to do—and don't forget that I am your Noada."

VI

DIAN SLEPT. Her sleeping apartment was darkened against the eternal noonday sun. She lay on a leather couch—a tanned hide stretched over a crude wooden frame. She wore only a tiny loin cloth, for the apartment was warm. She dreamed of David.

A man crept into her apartment on bare feet, and

moved silently toward the couch. Dian stirred restlessly; and the man stopped, waiting. Dian dreamed that a tarag was creeping upon David; and she leaped up, awake, to warn him; so that she stood face to face with one of the lesser priests who carried a slim bronze dagger in one hand.

Face to face with Death in that darkened chamber, Dian thought fast. She saw that the man was trembling, as he raised the dagger to the height of his shoulder—in a moment, he would leap forward and strike.

Dian stamped her foot upon the floor. "Kneel!" she commanded, imperiously.

The man hesitated; his dagger hand dropped to his side, and he fell to his knees.

"Drop the dagger," said Dian. The man dropped it, and Dian snatched it from the floor.

"Confess!" directed the girl. "Who sent you here? but do I need ask? It was Hor?"

The priest nodded. "May Pu forgive me, for I did not wish to come. Hor threatened me; he said he would have me killed if I did not do this thing."

"You may go now," said Dian, "and do not come again."

"You will never see me again, my Noada," said the priest. "Hor lied; he said you were not the true Noada, but now I know that you are—Pu watches over and protects you."

After the priest had left the apartment, Dian dressed slowly and went to the temple throne room. As usual, she was ushered in by priests to the accompaniment of drums and chants. The priests, she noticed, were nervous; they kept glancing at her apprehensively. She wondered if they, too, had been commissioned to kill her.

The room was filled with people—priests, citizens, warriors. Gamba was there and Hor. The latter dropped to his knees and covered his eyes long before she was near him. There seemed to be considerable excitement among all those who were present. By the time she took her place upon the dais everyone in the room was kneeling. After she had bidden them arise, they pressed forward to lay their grievances at her feet. She saw the priests whispering excitedly among themselves.

"What has happened, Hor?" she asked. "Why is everyone so excited?"

Hor cleared his throat. "It was nothing," he said; "I would not annoy my Noada with it."

"Answer my question," snapped Dian.

"One of the lesser priests was found hanging by his neck in his room," explained Hor. "He was dead."

"I know," said Dian; "it was the priest called Saj."

"Our Noada knows all," whispered one citizen to another.

After the people had aired their grievances and those who felt that they had been robbed were reimbursed, Dian spoke to all those assembled in the temple.

"Here are the new laws," she said: "Of all the pieces of bronze which you receive, give one out of ten to the go-sha. These pieces will be used to keep the city clean and in repair and to pay the warriors who defend Lolololo. Give the same number of pieces for the support of my temple. Out of these pieces the temple will be kept in repair, the priests fed and paid, and some will be given to the go-sha for the pay of his warriors, if he does not have enough, for the warriors defend the temple. You will make these payments after each twenty sleeps. Later, I will select an honest citizen to look after the temple pieces.

"Now, one thing more. I want fifty warriors to watch over me at all times. They will be the Noada's Guard. After every sleep that your Noada sleeps, each warrior will receive ten pieces. Are there fifty among you who would like to serve on the Noada's guard?"

Every warrior in the temple stepped forward, and from them Dian selected the fifty largest and strongest.

"I shall sleep better hereafter," she said to Hor. Hor said nothing.

But if Hor said nothing, he was doing a great deal of thinking; for he knew that if he were ever to regain his power and his riches, he must rid himself of the new Noada.

While the temple was still jammed with citizens and warriors, alarm drums sounded outside in the city; and as the warriors were streaming into the square, a messenger came running from the city gates.

"The Tanga-tangas have come!" he cried; "they have forced the gates and they are in the city!"

Instantly all was confusion; the citizens ran in one direction—away from the gates—and the warriors ran in the other to meet the raiding Tanga-tangas. Gamba ran out with his warriors, just an undisciplined mob with bronze swords. A few had spears, but the bows and arrows of all of them were in their barracks.

The fifty warriors whom Dian had chosen remained to guard her and the temple. The lesser priests fell to praying, repeating over and over, "Our Noada will give us victory! Our Noada will save us!" But Hor was more practical; he stopped their praying long enough to have them close the massive temple doors and bar them securely; then he turned to Dian.

"Turn back the enemy," he said; "strike them dead with the swords of our warriors, drive them from the city, and let them take no prisoners back into slavery. Only you can save us!"

Dian noticed an exultant note in Hor's voice, but she guessed that he was not exulting in her power to give victory to the Lolo-lolos. She was on a spot, and she knew it.

They heard the shouting of fighting men and the clash of weapons, the screams of the wounded and the dying. They heard the battle sweep into the square before the temple; there was clamoring before the temple doors and the sound of swords beating upon them.

Hor was watching Dian. "Destroy them, Noada!" he cried with thinly veiled contempt in his voice.

The massive doors withstood the attack, and the battle moved on beyond the temple. Later it swept back, and Dian could hear the victory cries of the Tanga-tangas. After a while the sounds died away in the direction of the city gates; and the warriors opened the temple doors, for they knew that the enemy had departed.

In the square lay the bodies of many dead; they were thick before the temple doors—mute evidence of the valor with which the warriors of Lolo-lolo had defended their Noada.

When the results of the raid were finally known, it was discovered that over a hundred of Gamba's warriors had been killed and twice that number wounded; that all the Tanga-tangan slaves in the city had been liberated and that over a hundred men and women of Lolo-lolo had been taken away into slavery; while the Lolo-loloans had taken but a single prisoner.

This prisoner was brought to the temple and questioned in the presence of Dian and Gamba and Hor. He was very truculent and cocky.

"We won the great victory," he said; "and if you do not liberate me the warriors of our Noada will come again, and this time they will leave not a single Lolo-loloan alive that they do not take back into slavery."

"You have no Noada," said Gamba. "There is only one Noada, and she is here."

The prisoner laughed derisively. "How then did we win such a glorious victory?" he demanded. "It was with the help of our Noada, the true Noada—this one here is a false Noada; our victory proves it."

"There is only one Noada," said Hor, but he didn't say which one.

"You are right," agreed the prisoner; "there is only one Noada, and she is in Tanga-tanga. She came in a great temple that floated upon the water, and she leaped into the sea and swam to the shore where we were waiting to receive her. She swam through the waters that are infested with terrible monsters, but she was unharmed; only Pu or a Noada could do that—and now she has given us this great victory."

The people of Lolo-lolo were crushed; scarcely a family but had had a member killed, wounded, or taken into slavery. They had no heart for anything; they left the dead lying in the square and in the streets until the stench became unbearable, and all the time the lesser priests, at the instigation of Hor, went among them, whispering that their Noada was a false Noada, or otherwise this catastrophe would never have befallen them.

Only a few came to the temple now to worship, and few were the offerings brought. One, bolder than another, asked Dian why she had let this disaster overwhelm them. Dian knew that she must do something to counteract the effects of the gossip that the lesser priests were spreading, or her life would not be worth a single piece of bronze. She knew of the work of Hor and the priests, for one of the warriors who guarded her had told her.

"It was not I who brought this disaster upon you," she answered the man; "it was Pu. He was punishing Lolo-lolo because of the wickedness of those who robbed and cheated the people of Lolo-lolo."

It was not very logical; but then the worshippers of Pu were not very logical, or they would not have worshipped him; and those who heard her words, spread them through the city; and there arose a faction with which Hor and the lesser priests were not very popular.

Dian sent for Gamba and commanded him to have the dead removed from the city and disposed of, for the stench was so terrible that one could scarcely breathe.

"How can I have them removed?" he asked; "no longer have we any slaves to do such work."

"The men of Lolo-lolo can do it, then," said Dian.

"They will not," Gamba told her.

"Then take warriors and compel them to do it," snapped the Noada.

"I am your friend," said Gamba, "but I cannot do that for you—the people would tear me to pieces."

"Then *I* shall do it," said Dian, and she summoned her warrior guard and told them to collect enough citizens to remove the dead from the city; "and you can take Hor and all the other priests with you, too," she added.

Hor was furious. "I will not go," he said.

"Take him!" snapped Dian, and a warrior prodded him in the small of the back with his spear and forced him out into the square.

Gamba looked at her with admiration. "Noada or not," he said, "you are a very brave woman. With you as my mate, I could defy all my enemies and conquer Tanga-tanga into the bargain."

"I am not for you," said Dian.

The city was cleaned up, but too late—an epidemic broke out. Men and women died; and the living were afraid to touch them, nor would Dian's guard again force the citizens to do this work. Once more the lesser priests went among the people spreading the word that the disasters which had befallen them were all due to the false Noada.

"Pu," they said, "is punishing us because we have received her."

Thus things went from bad to worse for Dian the Beautiful; until, at last, it got so bad that crowds gathered in the square before the temple, cursing and reviling her; and then those who still believed in her, incited by the agents of Gamba, fell upon them; and there was rioting and bloodshed.

Hor took advantage of this situation to spread the rumor that Gamba and the false Noada were planning to destroy the temple and rule the city, defying Pu and the priests; and that when this happened, Pu would lay waste the city and hurl all the people into the Molop Az. This was just the sort of propaganda of terror that would influence an ignorant and superstitious people. Remember, they were just simple people of the Bronze Age. They had not yet reached that stage of civilization where they might send children on holy crusades to die by thousands; they were not far enough advanced to torture unbelievers with rack and red hot irons, or burn heretics at the stake; so they believed this folderol that more civilized people would have spurned with laughter while killing all Jews.

At last Gamba came to Dian. "My own warriors are turning against me," he told her. "They believe the stories that Hor is spreading; so do most of the citizens. There are some who believe in you yet and some who are loyal to me; but the majority have been terrified into believing that Hor speaks the truth and that if they do not destroy us, Pu will destroy them."

"What are we to do?" asked Dian.

"The only chance we have to live, is to escape from the city," replied Gamba, "and even that may be impossible. We are too well known to escape detection—your white skin would betray you, and every man, woman, and child in Lolo-lolo knows his go-sha."

"We might fight our way out," suggested Dian. "I am sure that my warriors are still loyal to me."

Gamba shook his head. "They are not," he said. "Some of my own warriors have told me that they are no longer your protectors, but your jailers. Hor has won them over by threats and bribery."

Dian thought a moment, and then she said, "I have a plan—listen." She whispered for a few minutes to Gamba, and when she had finished, Gamba left the temple; and Dian went to her sleeping apartment—but she did not sleep. Instead, she stripped off her robe of office and donned her own single garment that she had worn when she first came to Lolo-lolo; then she put the long leather robe on over it.

By a back corridor she came to a room that she knew would be used only before and after ceremonies; in it were a number of large chests. Dian sat down on one of them and waited.

A man came into the temple with his head so bandaged that only one eye was visible; he had come, as so many came, to be healed by his Noada. Unless they died, they were always healed eventually.

The temple was almost deserted; only the members of the Noada's Guard loitered there near the entrance. They were there on Hor's orders to see that the Noada did not escape, Hor having told them that she was planning to join Gamba in his house across the square, from which they were arranging to launch their attack against the temple.

The man wore the weapons of a common warrior, and he appeared very tired and weak, probably from loss of blood. He said nothing; he just went and waited before the throne, waited for his Noada to come—the Noada that would never come again. After a while he commenced to move about the throne room, looking at different objects. Occasionally he glanced toward the warriors loitering near the door. They paid no attention to him. In fact they had just about forgotten him when he slipped through a doorway at the opposite side of the room.

The temple was very quiet, and there were only a few people in the square outside. The noonday sun beat down; and, as always, only those who had business outside were in the streets. Lolo-lolo was lethargic; but it was the calm before the storm. The lesser priests and the other enemies of Gamba and the Noada were organizing the mob that was about to fall upon them and destroy them. In many houses were groups of citizens and warriors waiting for the signal.

Two priests came into the throne room of the temple; they wore their long, leather robes of office and their hideous masks; they passed out of the temple through the group of warriors loitering by the door. Once out in the square, they commenced to cry, "Come, all true followers of Pu! Death to the false Noada! Death to Gamba!" It was the signal!

Warriors and citizens poured from houses surrounding the square. Some of them ran toward the house of the go-sha, and some ran for the temple; and they were all shouting, "Death! Death to Gamba! Death to the false Noada!"

The two priests crossed the square and followed one of the winding streets beyond, chanting their hymn of death; and as they passed, more citizens and warriors ran screaming toward the square, thirsting for the blood of their quarry.

The survivors of the Amoz had finally brought the ship into the harbor beneath the cliffs of Amoz. David and Hodon and Ghak the Hairy One and the little old man whose name was not Dolly Dorcas had at last completed the long trek from Amoz and come again to Sari.

David found the people saddened and Perry in tears. "What is the matter?" he demanded. "What is wrong? Where is Dian, that she has not come to meet me?"

Perry was sobbing so, that he could not answer. The headman, who had been in charge during their absence, spoke: "Dian the Beautiful is lost to us," he said.

"Lost! What do you mean?" demanded David; then they told him, and David Innes's world crumbled from beneath him. He looked long at Perry, and then he went and placed a hand upon his shoulder. "You loved her, too," he said; "you would not have harmed her. Tears will do no good. Build me another balloon, and perhaps it will drift to the same spot to which she was carried."

They both worked on the new balloon; in fact everyone in Sari worked on it, and the work gave them relief from sorrowing. Many hunters went out, and the dinosaurs which were to furnish the peritonea for the envelope of the gas bag were soon killed. While they were out hunting, the women wove the basket and braided the many feet of rope; and while this was going on, the runner returned from Thuria.

David was in Sari when he came, and the man came at once to him. "I have news of Dian the Beautiful," he said. "A man of Thuria saw the balloon floating across the nameless strait at the end of the world, high in the air."

"Could he see if Dian was still in it?" asked David.

"No," replied the runner, "it was too high in the air."

"At least we know where to look," said David, but his heart was heavy; because he knew that there was little chance that Dian could have survived the cold, the hunger, and the thirst.

Before the second balloon was finished the survivors

of the Sari returned to the village; and they told Hodon all that they knew of O-aa. "She told us to tell you," said one, "that she was adrift in the Sari on the Lural Az. She said that when you knew that, you would come and get her."

Hodon turned to David. "May I have men and a ship with which to go in search of O-aa?" he asked.

"You may have the ship and as many men as you need," replied David.

VII

CHANTING THEIR horrid song of death, the two priests walked through the narrow streets of Lolo-lolo all the way to the gates of the city. "Go to the great square," they shouted to the guard. "Hor has sent us to summon you. Every fighting man is needed to overcome those who would defend the false Noada and Gamba. Hurry! We will watch the gates."

The warriors hesitated. "It is Hor's command," said one of the priests; "and with Gamba and the Noada dead, Hor will rule the city; so you had better obey him, if you know what's good for you."

The warriors thought so, too; and they hurried off toward the square. When they had gone, the two priests opened the gates and passed out of the city. Turning to the right, they crossed to a forest into which they disappeared; and as soon as they were out of sight of the city, they removed their masks and their robes of office.

"You are not only a very brave girl," said Gamba, "but you are a very smart one."

"I am afraid that I shall have to be a whole lot smarter," replied Dian, "if I am ever to get back to Sari."

"What is Sari?" asked Gamba.

"It is the country from which I came."

"I thought you came from Karana," said Gamba.

"Oh, no you didn't," said Dian, and they both laughed.

"Where is Sari?" asked Gamba.

"It is across the nameless strait," replied Dian. "Do you know where we might find a canoe?"

"What is a canoe?" asked Gamba.

Dian was surprised. Was it possible that this man did not know what a canoe was? "It is what men use to cross the water in," she replied.

"But no one ever crosses the water," protested Gamba. "No one could live on the nameless strait. It is full of terrible creatures; and when the wind blows, the water stands up on end."

"We shall have to build a canoe," said Dian.

"If my Noada says so, we shall have to build a canoe," said Gamba, with mock reverence.

"My name is Dian," said the girl; so the man who had been a king and the woman who had been a goddess went down through the forest toward the shore of the nameless strait.

Beneath the long robes of the priests, they had brought what weapons they could conceal. They each had a sword and a dagger, and Gamba had a bow and many arrows.

On the way to the shore. Dian looked for trees suitable for the building of a canoe. She knew that it would be a long and laborious job; but if the Mezops could do it with stone tools, it should be much easier with the daggers and swords of bronze; and then, of course there was always fire with which to hollow out the inside.

When they came to the shore of the nameless strait, they followed it until Gamba was sure there would be no danger of their being discovered by the people of Lolo-lolo or the people of Tanga-tanga.

"They do not come in this direction much," he said, "nor often so far from the cities. The hunters go more in the other direction or inland. There are supposed to be dangerous animals here, and there is said to be a tribe of wild savages who come up from below to hunt here."

"We should have an interesting time building the canoe," commented Dian.

At last the second balloon was completed. It was just like the first, except that it had a rip cord and was stocked with food and water, David's extra weight and the weight of the food and water being compensated for by the absence of the heavy rope which had been attached to the first balloon.

When the time came to liberate the great bag, the people of Sari stood in silence. They expected that they would never see David Innes again, and David shared their belief.

"Dod-burn it!" exclaimed the little old man whose name was not Dolly Dorcas, "there goes a *man,* as the feller said."

Ope, the high priest of the temple at Tanga-tanga, had acquired a Noada; but she was not at all what he had imagined Noada should be. At first she had been docile and tractable, amenable to suggestion; that was while O-aa was learning the ropes, before she learned that she was supposed to be all-wise and all-powerful, deriving her omniscience and omnipotence from some one they called Pu who dwelt in a place called Karana.

Later on, she became somewhat of a trial to Ope. In the first place, she had no sense of the value of pieces of bronze. When they were brought as offerings to her, she would wait until she had a goodly collection in a large bowl which stood beside her throne; then, when the temple was filled with people, she would scoop handfuls of the pieces from the bowl and throw them to the crowd, laughing as she watched them scramble for them.

This made O-aa very popular with the people, but it made Ope sad. He had never had such large congregations in the temple before, but the net profits had never been so small. Ope spoke to the Noada about this—timidly, because, unlike Hor of Lolo-lolo, he was a simple soul and guileless; he believed in the divinity of the Noada.

Furp, the go-sha of Tanga-tanga, was not quite so simple; but, like many an agnostic, he believed in playing safe. However, he talked this matter over with Ope, because it had long been the custom for Ope to split the temple take with him, and now his share was approaching the vanishing point, so he suggested to Ope that it might be well to suggest to the Noada that, while charity was a sweet thing, it really should begin at home. So Ope spoke to the Noada, and Furp listened.

"Why," he asked, "does the Noada throw away the offerings that are brought to the temple?"

"Because the people like them," replied O-aa. "Haven't you noticed how they scramble for them?"

"They belong to the temple."

"They are brought to *me*," contradicted O-aa. "Anyway, I don't see why you should make a fuss over some little pieces of metal. I do not want them. What good are they?"

"Without them we could not pay the priests, or buy food, or keep the temple in repair," explained Ope.

"Bosh!" exclaimed O-aa, or an expletive with the same general connotation. "The people bring food, which we can eat; and the priests could keep the temple in repair in payment for their food; they are a lazy lot, anyway. I have tried to find out what they do besides going around frightening people into bringing gifts, and wearing silly masks, and dancing. Where I come from, they would either hunt or work."

Ope was aghast. "But you come from Karana, Noada!" he exclaimed. "No one works in Karana."

O-aa realized that she had pulled a boner, and that she would have to do a little quick thinking. She did. "How do you know?" she demanded. "Were you ever in Karana?"

"No, Noada," admitted Ope.

Furp was becoming more and more confused, but he was sure of one point, and he brought it out. "Pu would be angry," he said, "if he knew that you were throwing away the offerings that the people brought to his temple, and Pu can punish even a Noada."

"Pu had better not interfere," said O-aa; "my father is a king, and my eleven brothers are very strong men."

"What?" screamed Ope. "Do you know what you are saying? Pu is all-powerful, and anyway a Noada has no father and no brothers."

"Were you ever a Noada?" asked O-aa. "No, of course you never were. It is time you learned something about Noadas. Noadas have a lot of everything. I have not one father only, but three, and besides my eleven brothers, I have four sisters, and they are all Noadas. Pu is my son, he does what I tell him to. Is there anything more you would like to know about Noadas?"

Ope and Furp discussed this conversation in private later on. "I never before knew all those things about Noadas," said Ope.

"Our Noada seems to know what she's talking about," observed Furp.

"She is evidently more powerful than Pu," argued Ope, "as otherwise he would have struck her dead for the things she said about him."

"Perhaps we had better worship our Noada instead of Pu," suggested Furp.

"You took the words out of my mouth," said Ope.

Thus, O-aa was sitting pretty in Tanga-tanga, as Hodon the Fleet One set sail from Amoz on his hopeless quest and David Innes drifted toward the end of the world in the Dinosaur II, as Perry christened his second balloon.

PART III

TIGER GIRL

I

"You say there is another shore," said Gamba to Dian; "perhaps there is, but we shall never reach it."

"We can try," replied the girl. "Had we remained in your land we should surely have been killed, either by the savages of which you told me, by the wild beasts, or by your own people. If we must die, it is better to die trying to reach safety than to have remained where there never could be safety for us."

"I sometimes wish," said Gamba, "that you had never come to Lolo-lolo."

"You don't wish it any more than I," replied the girl.

"We were getting along very well without a Noada," continued the man, "and then you had to come and upset everything."

"Things should have been upset," said Dian. "You and Hor were robbing the people. Pretty soon they would have risen and killed you both, which would have been a good thing for Lolo-lolo."

"I might not have gotten into all this trouble," said Gamba, "if I hadn't fallen in love with you. Hor knew it; and he made that an excuse to turn the people against me."

"You had no business falling in love with me. I already have a mate."

"He is a long way off," said Gamba, "and you will never see him again. If you had come to my house and been my wife before all this happened, you and I could have ruled Lolo-lolo as long as we lived. For a bright girl it seems to me that you are very stupid."

"You were stupid to fall in love with me," said Dian, "but in a moment it may not make any difference one way or another—look what is coming," and she pointed.

"Pu be merciful!" cried the man. "This is the end. I told you that we should not come out upon this water which stands on end and is filled with death."

A great head upon a slender neck rose ten feet above the surface of the sea. Cold, reptilian eyes glared at them, and jaws armed with countless teeth gaped to seize them. The creature moved slowly towards them as though knowing that they could not escape, the water rippling along its glossy sides.

"Your bow and arrow!" cried Dian. "Put an arrow into its body at the waterline, and bend your bow as you have never bent it before. When it comes closer we will use our swords."

Gamba stood up in the canoe and drew a three-foot arrow back to its very tip; and when he released it, it drove true to its mark; burying two-thirds of its length into the saurian's body at the waterline. Screaming with pain and hissing with rage, the creature seized the end of the shaft and jerked it from the wound; and with it came a stream of blood spurting out and crimsoning the surface of the water. Then, still hissing and screaming, it bore down upon the two relatively puny humans in the frail canoe. Dian was standing now, her bronze sword grasped tightly in one hand, her bronze knife in the other. Gamba drove another arrow into the reptile's breast; and then dropped his bow into the bottom of the canoe and seized his sword.

Now, as though by magic, hundreds of small fishes,

about a foot long, attracted by the blood of the saurian, were attacking the maddened creature, which had paused to wrench the second shaft from its breast. Ignoring the voracious, sharp-fanged fishes which were tearing it to pieces, it came on again to attack the authors of its first hurts. With arched neck it bore down upon them; and as it struck to seize Dian, she met it with her bronze sword; striking at the long neck and inflicting a terrible wound, which caused the creature to recoil. But it came on again, raising a flipper with which it could easily have overturned or swamped the frail craft.

Gamba, realizing the danger, struck a terrific blow at the flipper while it was still poised above the gunwale of the canoe; and so much strength did he put into it that he severed the member entirely; and simultaneously Dian struck again at the neck. The great head flopped sideways, and with a final convulsive struggle the saurian rolled over on its side.

"You see," said Dian, "that there is still hope that we may reach the other shore. There are few creatures in any sea more terrible than the one which we have killed."

"I wouldn't have given one piece of bronze for our chances," said Gamba.

"They didn't look very bright," admitted Dian, "but I have been in much worse dangers than that before; and I have always come through all right. You see, I did not live in a walled city as you have all your life; and my people were always open to the attacks of wild beasts, and the men of enemy tribes."

They had taken up their paddles again, but now they were out where the full strength of the current gripped them; and they were moving far more rapidly down the strait than they were across it. Because of the current it was hard to keep the bow of the canoe pointed in the right direction. It was a constant and exhausting struggle. They were still in sight of the shoreline they had left, though the distant shore was not yet visible.

"We're not making very much progress in the right direction," said Dian.

"I am very tired," said Gamba. "I do not believe that I can paddle much longer."

"I am about exhausted myself," said the girl. "Perhaps we had better let the current carry us along. There is only one place that it can take us and that is into the Korsar Az. There, there will be no strong current and we can come to shore. As a matter of fact, I believe that we can get much closer to Sari along that coast than we would have been if we had been able to paddle directly across the strait." So Dian the Beautiful and Gamba the Xexot drifted along the nameless strait toward the Korsar Az.

Borne along by a gentle wind, David Innes drifted down across the Land of Awful Shadow toward the end of the world and the nameless strait, in the balloon which Abner Perry had named the Dinosaur II. He knew that his was an almost hopeless venture, with the chances of his balloon coming down near the exact spot where Dian had landed almost nil; and even if it did, where was he to look for her?

Where would she be, in a strange land, entirely unknown to her, provided that she was still alive, which seemed beyond reason; for, supplied with warm coverings as he was, and provided with food and water, he had already suffered considerably from the cold; and he knew that Dian had been without food, or water, or covering of any kind, other than her scant loincloth, at the time that her balloon had broken away.

Yet somehow he thought that she was not dead. It did not seem possible to him that that beautiful creature, so full of life and vigor, could be lying somewhere cold and still, or that her body had been devoured by wild beasts. And so he clung to hope with an almost fanatic zeal.

At last he came to the nameless strait, across which he had never been. He saw the waters of it below him, and far to his right two figures in a canoe. He wondered idly who they might be and where they might be going upon those lonely, danger-ridden waters; and then he forgot them and strained his eyes ahead in search of the farther shore, where, if at all, he felt sure that he might find his mate.

His balloon was floating at an altitude of only about a thousand feet when he approached the opposite side of the strait. His attention was attracted by two things. On the beach below him lay the wreck of a dismasted ship, which he recognized immediately; for he and Perry had designed her and superintended her building. He recognized her, and he knew that she was the Sari.

The other thing that had attracted his attention was a walled city, not far from the shore of the nameless strait. He knew that O-aa had been aboard the Sari when she had been abandoned by her crew; and he realized that perhaps O-aa had been captured by the people who lived in that city.

The presence of a walled city in Pellucidar was sufficiently amazing to arouse many conjectures in his mind. In a walled city there might live a semi-civilized people who would have befriended O-aa; and if Dian had landed near it, she might be in the city, too; or the people might have heard something about her, for a balloon would certainly have aroused their interest and their curiosity.

Now he saw that his balloon had accomplished that very thing; for people were running from the city gates, staring up at him, and calling to him. They might be cursing and threatening him, for all he knew; but he decided to come down, for here were people, and where there were people there would be rumors; and even the faintest rumor might lead him upon the right track. So he pulled the ripcord, and the Dinosaur II settled slowly towards Tanga-tanga.

As the basket of the balloon touched the ground David Innes found himself surrounded by yellow-skinned warriors, wearing leather aprons painted with gay designs, that fell from their waists both before and behind. On their heads were leather helmets; and they carried swords and knives of bronze, as well as bows and arrows.

Some of the warriors shouted, "It is Pu. He has come to visit our Noada."

"It is not Pu," cried others. "He comes in the same thing that brought the false Noada of Lolo-lolo."

David Innes understood the words, but not the purport of them; only that the reference to the false Noada who had come in a balloon convinced him that Dian the Beautiful had been here. He did not know who Pu might be, but he saw that they were divided among themselves as to his identity; and he also saw that no weapon was drawn against him.

"I have come down out of the sky," he said, "to visit your chief. Take me to him."

To many of the men of Tanga-tanga this sounded as though Pu spoke; and many who had said that it was not Pu wavered in their convictions.

"Go to the house of Furp, the go-sha," said one who was evidently an officer to a warrior, "and tell him that we are bringing a stranger to the temple to visit him and our Noada. If he is indeed Pu, our Noada will recognize him."

The gas bag, partially deflated, still billowed limply above the basket; and when David Innes stepped out and relieved it of his weight the balloon rose slowly and majestically into the air and floated away inland across the city of Tanga-tanga.

When David stood among them, those who thought that he was Pu, the god, fell upon their knees and covered their eyes with their hands. David looked at them in astonishment for a moment and then he quite suddenly realized that they must believe him a deity coming down from heaven; and that the name of this deity was Pu; and he thought to himself, what would a god do under like circumstances? He hazarded a guess, and he guessed right.

"Arise," he said. "Now escort me to the temple," for he recalled that the officer had said that that was where they were taking him. The officer's reference to "our Noada" and to "Furp, the go-sha," meant little or nothing to him; but he decided to maintain a godly silence on the subject until he did know.

They led him through the city gate and along narrow, crooked streets flanked by mean little houses of clay. Here he saw women and children, the women wearing painted leather aprons like the men and having headdresses of feathers, while the children were naked. He noted with some measure of astonishment the bronze weapons and ornaments, and realized that these people had advanced into the age of bronze. Their walled city, their painted aprons, craftsmanship displayed in their weapons and ornaments, suggested that if the inner world were closely following the stages of human development upon the outer crust, these people might soon be entering the iron age.

To David Innes, if his mind had not been solely devoted to the finding of his mate, these people might have presented an interesting study in anthropology; but he thought of them now only as a means to an end.

They had seen Dian's balloon. Had they seen her? Did they know what had become of her?

II

IN THE CENTER of the city was an open plaza, on one side of which was a large, domed building, a replica of the temple where Dian the Beautiful had ruled for a short time in the city of Lolo-lolo. To this building David Innes was conducted.

Within it were many people. Some of them fell upon their knees and covered their eyes as he entered. These were the ones who were not taking any chances; but the majority stood and waited. Upon a dais at the far end of the room sat a girl in a long leather robe, gorgeously painted in many colors with strange designs. Upon her head was a massive feather headdress. Upon her arms were many bronze bracelets and armlets, and around her neck were strands of ivory beads.

As David Innes came toward the throne O-aa recognized him. They had brought her word that one who might be Pu had come to visit Furp the Go-sha; and now, nimble-witted as ever, she realized that she must perpetuate this erroneous belief as the most certain way in which to insure David's safety.

She rose and looked angrily upon those who had remained standing.

"Kneel!" she commanded imperiously. "Who dares stand in the presence of Pu."

David Innes was close enough now to recognize her; and as she saw recognition in his eyes, she forestalled anything he might be about to say: "The Noada welcomes you, Pu, to your temple in the city of Tanga-tanga"; and she held out her hands to him and indicated that he was to step to the dais beside her. When he had done so, she whispered, "Tell them to rise."

"Arise!" said David Innes in a commanding voice. It was a sudden transition from mortality to godhood, but David rose to the occasion, following the lead of little O-aa, daughter of Oose, king of Kali.

"What are your wishes, Pu?" asked O-aa. "Would you like to speak with your Noada alone?"

"I wish to speak with my Noada alone," said David Innes with great and godly dignity; "and then I will speak with Furp the Go-sha," he added.

O-aa turned to Ope the high priest. "Clear the Temple," she said, "but tell the people to be prepared to return later with offerings for Pu. Then they shall know why Pu has come and whether he is pleased with the people of Tanga-tanga, or angry at them. And, Ope, have the lesser priests fetch a lesser bench for me, as Pu will sit upon my throne while he is here."

After the temple was cleared and the bench was brought and they were alone O-aa looked into David's eyes and grinned.

"Tell me what you are doing here, and how you got here," she said.

"First tell me if you have heard anything of Dian the Beautiful," insisted David.

"No," replied O-aa, "what has happened to her? I supposed, of course, that she was in Sari."

"No," replied David, "she is not in Sari. Abner Perry built a balloon and it got away, carrying Dian the Beautiful with it."

"What is a balloon?" asked O-aa; and then she said, "Oh, is it a great, round ball with a basket fastened to it in which a person may ride through the air?"

"Yes," said David, "that is it."

"Then it was Dian who came before I did. They have told me about this thing that happened. The what-you-call-it, balloon, came down low over Tanga-tanga; and they thought that the woman in it was their Noada come from Karana; and they went out and fought with the men of Lolo-lolo for her. But the men of Lolo-lolo got her and she was Noada there until maybe thirty sleeps ago, maybe more. Then the people turned against her; and she disappeared with Gamba, the go-sha of Lolo-lolo, whom the people also wished to kill. What became of them no man knows; but the woman must have been Dian the Beautiful, for she came in that thing that floated through the air. But how did you get here, David Innes?"

"I also came in a balloon," replied David. "I had Abner Perry build one, thinking that it might float in the same direction as had that which bore Dian away; for at this time of year the direction of the wind seldom varies, and a balloon is borne along by the wind."

"They told me that this visitor, who some of them thought might be Pu, had come down from Karana. Now I understand what they meant."

"What is Karana?" asked David.

"It is where Pu lives," explained O-aa. "It is where I live when I am not on earth. It is where those who worship Pu go when they die. It is a mighty good thing for me that Pu came from Karana when he did," she added.

"Why?" asked David. "What do you mean?"

"Ope, the high priest, and Furp, the go-sha, don't like me," replied O-aa. "They liked me at first, but now they don't like me any more. They don't like me at all. The people bring offerings to me, and many of these offerings are little pieces of metal, like the metal in my bracelets."

"It is bronze," said David Innes.

"Whatever it is, Ope the high priest and Furp the go-sha are very anxious to get hold of as much of it as they can; but I throw much of it back to the people because it is a lot of fun watching them fight for it; and that is why Ope and Furp do not like me. But it has made me very popular with the people of Tanga-tanga; and so, not only do Ope and Furp dislike me, but they fear me, also. I cannot understand why Ope and Furp and the people are so anxious to have these silly little pieces of metal."

David Innes smiled. He was thinking of how typical it was of woman that even this little cave girl had no sense of the value of money, before she even knew what money was, or what it was for. "You had better let Ope and Furp have their silly little pieces of metal," he said. "I think you will live longer if you do; for these little pieces of metal men will commit murder."

"It is all very strange," said O-aa. "I do not understand it, but I do not dare ask questions because a Noada is supposed to know everything."

"And I suppose that Pu is supposed to know more than a Noada," remarked David, with a wry smile.

"Of course," said O-aa. "As I know everything that there is to be known, you must know everything that there is to be known, and a great deal that there isn't to be known."

"There is one thing that I don't know, but that I would like to know very much," he said; "and that is where Dian is, and whether she is still alive. After that I would like to know how we are going to get out of here and get back to Sari. You would like to get back, wouldn't you, O-aa?"

"It makes no difference to me now," she said, sadly. "Since Hodon the Fleet One was killed by Blug I do not care where I am."

"But Hodon was not killed by Blug," said David. "It was Blug who was killed."

"And I ran away thinking that Hodon was dead and that I would have to mate with Blug," exclaimed O-aa.

"Oh, why didn't I wait and see! Tell me, where is Hodon?"

"Before I left Sari he asked for a ship and some men that he might go out upon the Lural Az and search for you; for he received the message that you sent to him in the event that he was not dead."

"And he will never find me," said O-aa, "and he will be lost on that terrible ocean."

After a while the people came back and brought offerings for Pu. David Innes saw the little pieces of metal and he smiled—crude little coins, crudely minted. For these the high priest and the king would drag the goddess from her pedestal; and doubtless kill her into the bargain. Unquestionably, these men of the bronze age were advancing toward a higher civilization.

O-aa took a handful of the coins and threw them to the people, who scrambled, screaming, upon the floor of the temple, fighting for them. Ope the high priest and Furp the go-sha looked on with sullen scowls, but O-aa felt safer now because she had Pu right there at her side.

After the people had left the temple Ope and Furp remained; and Ope, suddenly emboldened by his anger at the loss of so many pieces of metal, said to David, "How is it that you are so much older than the Noada?"

O-aa was momentarily horrified, for she recalled that she had once told Ope and Furp that she was the mother of Pu. She had also told them that Pu did everything she told him to do. To be a successful liar one must be quick to cover up; so, before David could answer, O-aa answered for him.

"You should know, Ope, being my high priest, that a Noada may look any age she wishes. It pleases me not to look older than my son."

David Innes was astounded by the effrontery of the girl. Metaphorically, he took his hat off to her. These people, he thought, would look far before they could find a better goddess than O-aa.

Ope, the high priest, tried another tack. "Will Pu, who knows all, be kind enough to tell our Noada that she should not throw away the pieces of bronze that the people bring here as offerings?"

David thought that since he was supposed to know all, it would be best to pretend that he did.

"The Noada was quite right," said David. "She has done this to teach you not to exact so much from the people. I have known for a long time that your priests were demanding more from them than they could afford to give; and that is one reason why I came from Karana to talk with you; and with Furp, who also exacts more in taxes than he should."

Ope and Furp looked most unhappy; but Furp spoke up and said, "I must pay my warriors and keep the city in repair; and Ope must pay the priests and keep up the temple."

"You are telling Pu the things that he already knows," said David. "Hereafter you will exact less taxes and fewer offerings; demanding only what you require for the proper maintenance of the city and the temple."

Ope was a simple fellow, who believed against his will that this was indeed Pu the god; and he was afraid; but Furp was a skeptic, as well as something of an atheist; at least, he bordered on atheism. But, with Ope, he bowed to the will of Pu; at least temporarily, and with mental reservation.

"There are many things that trouble my mind," said Ope to David. "Perhaps you will explain them to me. We have always been taught that there was Pu; and that he had one daughter, who was our Noada. But now I am not only told that Pu is the son of our Noada, but that she had three fathers, eleven brothers, and four sisters, all of the latter being Noadas."

Even O-aa flushed at the recital of this bare-faced lie

which she had told Ope in order to impress him with her knowledge of conditions in Karana. For a moment she was lost, and could think of nothing to say. She only wondered what reply David Innes would make.

"It is all very simple," he said, "when you understand it. As my high priest, Ope, you must know that Pu is all-powerful."

Ope nodded. "Yes, of course, I know that," he said importantly.

"Then you will understand why it is that Pu can be either the son or the father of your Noada. We can change about as we wish; and the Noada can have as many brothers, or as many sisters, or as many fathers, as I wish her to have. Is that clear to you?"

"Perfectly clear," said Ope. But it was not clear to Furp; and when he left the temple he started to implant in the minds of many a suspicion that the man who had come down out of the skies was not Pu at all, nor was the woman a true Noada. Furp planted the seed and was willing to wait and let it germinate, as he knew it would.

III

It happened that when Hodon the Fleet One reached the coast of Amoz, to set sail upon the Lural Az in search of O-aa, that Raj, the Mezop who had commanded the Sari, was there; and Hodon asked Raj to come with him and take command of the little ship in which he and his warriors were about to embark.

The Mezops were a seafaring people, and Hodon was fortunate in obtaining the services of one to command his ship; and it was also additionally fortunate that it was Raj, because Raj knew exactly where the Sari had been abandoned; and he also knew the winds and the ocean currents. Knowing these, and where they would ordinarily have carried the Sari, Raj set his course for the mouth of the nameless strait. After many sleeps they reached it; but they had to stand off for several more sleeps because of a terrific storm, which because of the seamanship of Raj, they weathered.

When the storm abated the wind and the currents swept the little ship into the mouth of the nameless strait, swept it close past the coast of the Xexot country, and the spot where the wreck of the Sari had lain until the storm they had just weathered had broken her up and removed all vestiges of the clue of the whereabouts of O-aa that it had previously constituted, and which would have led them immediately to the city of Tanga-tanga.

David Innes and O-aa sat upon the dais in the temple of Pu, ignorant of the fact that their friends were passing so near them.

Dian the Beautfiul and Gamba, paddling through the nameless strait toward the Korsar Az, did not see the great balloon that passed in the air high behind them. Only a few thousand yards separated Dian the Beautiful and David at that moment; and it was a cruel fate that had prevented them from knowing how close they had been to a reunion; for David could have brought the balloon down on the shore, and Dian could have returned to it.

Dian had seen to it that the canoe was stocked with food and water before they embarked upon their perilous journey. They took turns sleeping as they let the current carry them along. Time and again they were attacked by fearful creatures of the deep, for this strange thing upon the surface of the water attracted many to them. Some were motivated only by curiosity, but voracious appetites actuated the majority of them; and it was a constant source of surprise to Gamba that they emerged from each encounter victorious.

"I didn't think that we would live to sleep once after we set out from shore," he said.

"I was not so sure myself," replied Dian, "but now I think that we shall get through to the Korsar Az, and then go up the coast to a point opposite Amoz. We can cut across country there; but I believe that greater dangers lie ahead of us on land than on the sea."

"Is it a savage country?" asked Gamba.

"For a long way back from the shores of the Korsar Az it is a very savage country," replied Dian. "I have never been there, but our men who have ventured into it to hunt say that it is infested with savage beasts, and even more savage men."

"I wish," said Gamba, "that I had never seen you. If you had not come to Lolo-lolo, I should still be go-sha and safe behind the walls of my city."

"I wish you would stop harping on that," said Dian, "but I may say that if you had been a better go-sha you would still have been there; and if you want to go back, we can paddle to shore, and I will let you out."

After many sleeps they reached the end of the nameless strait, which narrowed right at the entrance to the Korsar Az; so that the waters rushed through with terrific velocity, and the little canoe was almost swamped many times before it floated out on the comparatively smooth surface of the Korsar Az. Now they turned in a northeasterly direction hugging the coast; and it was then that the storm that had held Hodon off the mouth of the nameless strait in the Sojar Az, struck them and carried them far from shore.

Driving rain blinded them, and great seas constantly threatened to swamp them; so that while one paddled in an effort to keep the canoe from turning broadside into the trough of the seas, the other bailed with one of the gourds that Dian had thoughtfully brought along for that purpose.

They were both exhausted when a shoreline suddenly rose before them, dimly visible through the rain. Now Dian could see a wide, white beach up which enormous rollers raced, to break thunderously upon the shore; and toward this the storm was carrying them, nor could any puny efforts which they might put forth avert the inevitable end.

It did not seem possible to the girl that they could live that terrific surf; but she determined to try to ride it in, and so she told Gamba to paddle with all his strength; and she did likewise.

On and on the little canoe raced; and then, riding just below the crest of an enormous roller, it shot with terrific speed towards the shore; and, like a surfboard, it was carried far up on the beach.

Surprised that they still lived, they leaped out and held it as the water receded; then they dragged it farther up on the shore, out of reach of the breakers.

"I think," said Gamba, "that you must really be a Noada; for no mortal being could come through what we have come through, and live."

Dian smiled. "I have never said that I wasn't," she replied.

Gamba thought this over, but he made no comment. Instead, he said presently, "As soon as the storm is over we can start for Amoz. It is good to be on land again and to know that we shall not have to face the dangers of the sea any more."

"We have a lot more sea to cross," said Dian, "before we reach Amoz."

"What do you mean?" demanded Gamba. "Have we not been driven ashore; are we not on land?"

"Yes, we are on land," replied Dian, "but that storm blew us away from that land where Amoz lies; and as it certainly did not blow us all the way across the enormous Korsar Az, it must have blown us onto an island."

Gamba appeared stunned. "Now there is no hope for us," he said. "This is indeed the end. You are no true Noada, or you would not have permitted this to happen."

Dian laughed. "You give up too easily," she said. "You must have been a very poor go-sha indeed."

"I was a good go-sha until you came along," snapped Gamba; "but now, great Noada," he said sarcastically, "what do we do next?"

"As soon as the storm dies down," replied Dian, "we launch the canoe and set out for shore."

"I do not want to go on the water again," said Gamba.

"Very well, then," replied Dian, "you may remain here; but I am going."

Beyond the beach rose cliffs to the height of a hundred feet or more, topping them Dian could see green, jungle-like verdure; and not far away a waterfall leaped over the cliff into the sea, which lashed the face of the cliff itself at this point, throwing spray so high into the air that at these times the waterfall was hidden. In the other direction the sea again broke against the face of the cliff. They stood upon a narrow, crescent-shaped bit of land that the sea had never as yet claimed. To Gamba, as to you and me, the cliffs looked unscalable; but to Dian the cave girl they appeared merely difficult. However, as she had no intention of scaling them, it made no difference.

They were very uncomfortable for a long while, as they sat drenched by the heavy downpour. There was no cave into which they could crawl, and sleep was out of the question. They just sat and endured; Dian stoically, Gamba grumblingly.

At last, however, they saw the sun shining far out upon the sea, and they knew that the storm was passing over them and that it would soon be gone. Often it is a relief to have that eternal noonday sun hidden by a cloud; but now when the cloud passed they were glad of the sun's warmth again.

"Let us sleep," said Dian, "and if the sea has gone down when we awaken I shall set out again in search of the big land. I think you would be wise if you came with me, but do as you please. It makes no difference to me."

"You have a heart of stone," said the man. "How can you talk like that to a man who loves you?"

"I am going to sleep now," said Dian, "and you had better do likewise;" and she curled up in the wet grass with the hot sun beating down upon her beauitful body.

Dian dreamed that she was back in Sari, and that her people were gathered around her; and that David was there and she was very happy, happier than she had been for a long time.

Presently one of the people standing around her kicked her lightly in the ribs, and Dian awakened. She opened her eyes to see that there really were people surrounding her, but they were not the people of Sari. They were big men, who carried long, heavy spears and great bows; and their loincloths were made of the skins of tarags, and the heads of tarags had been cleverly fashioned to form helmets that covered their heads, with the great tusks pointing downward on either side of their heads at an angle of forty-five degrees, and the quivers which held their arrows at their backs were of the skin of the great carnivores—of the black and yellow hide of the tarag, the huge, sabre-tooth tiger that has been so long extinct upon the outer crust.

"Get up," said one of the men; and Dian and Gamba both came to their feet.

"What do you want of us?" demanded Dian. "We were leaving as soon as the sea went down."

"What were you doing here?" asked the man.

"The storm drove us onto this shore," replied Dian. "We were trying to reach the mainland."

"Who are you?"

"I am Dian, the mate of David Innes, the Emperor of Pellucidar."

"We never heard of you, or him, and I do not know what an emperor is."

"He is what you might call the chief of chiefs," explained Dian. "He has an army and a navy and many guns. He would be your friend if you would protect me and this man."

"What is a navy? What are guns?" demanded this man. "And why should we be kind to you? We are not afraid of this David Innes; we are not afraid of anyone in Pellucidar. We are the men of Tandar."

"What is Tandar?" demanded Dian.

"You mean to say you have never heard of Tandar?" exclaimed the warrior.

"Never," said Dian.

"Neither have I," said Gamba.

The warrior looked at them disgustedly. "This is the Island of Tandar that you are on," he said; "and I am Hamlar, the Chief."

"The sea is going down," said Dian, "and we shall soon be leaving."

Hamlar laughed; it was a nasty sort of a laugh. "You will never leave Tandar," he said; "no one who comes here ever does."

Dian shrugged. She knew her world, and she knew that the man meant what he said.

"Come," said Hamlar; and there was nothing to do but follow him.

Warriors surrounded them as Hamlar led the way toward the waterfall. Dian was barefooted, as she had left her sandals on the thwart of the canoe to dry. She would not ask Hamlar if she might get them, for she was too proud to ask favors of an enemy. She kept looking up at the face of the cliff to see where these men had come down, but she saw no sign of a place here that even she could scale; and then Hamlar reached the waterfall and disappeared beneath it, and a moment later Dian found herself on a narrow ledge that ran beneath the falls; and then she followed the warrior ahead of her into the mouth of a cavern that was as dark as pitch and damp with dripping water.

She climbed through the darkness, feeling her way, until presently she saw a little light ahead. The light came from above down a shaft that inclined slightly from the vertical, and leaning against its wall was a crude ladder. Dian had delayed those behind her in the darkness of the cavern, but now she clambered up the ladder like a monkey, soon overtaking those ahead of her. She could hear the warriors behind her growling at Gamba for climbing so slowly; and she could hear his grunts and cries as they prodded him with their spears.

From the top of the shaft a winding trail led through the jungle. Occasionally Dian caught glimpses of large animals slinking along other paths that paralleled or crossed the one they were on; and she saw the yellow and black of the tarag's hide.

A mile inland from the coast they came to a clearing at the foot of a towering cliff, in the sandstone face of which caves and ledges had been laboriously excavated and cut. She looked with amazement upon these cliff dwellings, which must have required many generations to construct. At the foot of the cliff, warriors lolled in the shade of the trees, while women worked and children played.

At least a score of great tarags slept, or wandered about among the people. She saw a child pull the tail of one, and the great carnivore turned upon it with an ugly snarl. The child jumped back, and the tarag continued its prowling. Aside from that one child, no one seemed to pay any attention to the brutes at all.

Attracted by the sight of Dian and Gamba, warriors, women and children clustered about; and it was evident from their remarks that they seldom saw strangers upon their island. The women wore loincloths and sandals of the skins of tarags. Like the men, the women were rather handsome, with well-shaped heads, and intelligent eyes.

Hamlar motioned to one of the women. "Manai," he said, "this one is yours," and he pointed to Dian. "Does anyone want the man?" he asked, looking around. "If not, we will kill him and feed him to the tarags."

Gamba looked around then, too, hopefully; but at first no one indicated any desire to possess him. Finally, however, a woman spoke up and said, "I will take him. He can fetch wood and water for me and beat the skins of the tarags to soften them"; and Gamba breathed a sigh of relief.

"Come," said Manai to Dian, and led the way up a series of ladders to a cave far up in the face of the cliff. "This," she said, stopping upon a ledge before an opening, "is the cave of Hamlar, the chief, who is my mate." Then she went in and came back with a bundle of twigs tied tightly together with strips of rawhide. "Clean out the cave of Hamlar and Manai," she said, "and see that none of the dirt falls over the edge of the cliff. You will find a big gourd in the cave. Put the dirt into it and carry it down to the foot of the cliff and dump it in the stream."

So Dian the Beautiful, Empress of Pellucidar, went to work as a slave for Manai, the mate of Hamlar, chief of Tandar; and she thought that she was fortunate not to have been killed. After she had cleaned the cave and carried the dirt down and dumped it in the stream, Manai, who had returned to the women at the foot of the cliff, called to her. "What is your name?" she asked.

"Dian," replied the girl.

"There is meat in the cave," said Manai. "Go and get it and bring it down here and make a fire and cook it for Hamlar and Manai, and for Bovar, their son."

While Dian was broiling the meat she saw Gamba pounding a tarag skin with two big sticks; and she smiled when she thought that not many sleeps ago he had been a king, with slaves to wait upon him.

Hamlar came and sat down beside Manai. "Does your slave work, or is she lazy?" he asked.

"She works," said Manai.

"She had better," said Hamlar, "for if she doesn't work, we will have to kill her and feed her to the tarags. We cannot afford to feed a lazy slave. Where is Bovar?"

"He is asleep in his cave," replied Manai. "He told me to awaken him when we ate."

"Send the slave for him," said Hamlar. "The meat is almost ready."

"Bovar's cave is next to ours, just to the right of it," Manai told Dian. "Go there and awaken him."

So again Dian the Beautiful clambered up the long series of ladders to the ledge far up on the face of the cliff; and she went to the opening next to that of Hamlar's cave and called Bovar by name. She called several times before a sleepy voice answered.

"What do you want?" it demanded.

"Manai, your mother, has sent me to tell you that the meat is ready and that they are about to eat."

A tall young warrior crawled out of the cave and stood erect. "Who are you?" he demanded.

"I am Manai's new slave," replied Dian.

"What is your name?" asked Bovar.

"Dian," replied the girl.

"That is a pretty name," he said; "and you are a pretty

girl. I think you are the prettiest girl I ever saw. Where do you come from?"

"I come from Amoz, which lies beside the Darel Az," replied Dian.

"I never heard of either one of them," said Bovar; "but no matter where you come from, you are certainly the prettiest girl I ever saw," repeated Bovar.

"Come down to your meat," said Dian as she turned to the ladder and started to descend.

Bovar followed her, and they joined Hamlar and Manai beside the leg of meat that was roasting over the fire on a pointed stick that Dian had driven through it, which was supported by forked sticks at either end.

"The meat is cooked," said Manai who had been turning it during Dian's absence. Dian took it from the fire then and laid it upon some leaves that were spread upon the ground, and Hamlar took his knife of stone and cut off a large piece and held it on a pointed stick to cool a little; and then Manai cut off a piece, and then Bovar.

"May I eat?" asked Dian.

"Eat," said Hamlar.

Dian drew her bronze knife from its sheath and cut off a piece of meat. The knife cut slickly and smoothly, not like the crude stone weapons of the Tandars.

"Let me see that," said Bovar; and Dian handed him the knife.

"No one ever saw anything like this," said Bovar; and handed it to his father. Both Hamlar and Manai examined it closely.

"What is it?" demanded Hamlar.

"It is a knife," said Dian.

"I don't mean that," said Hamlar. "I mean, what is it made of?"

"It is a metal which the Xexots call 'androde'," replied the girl.

Bovar held out his hand for the knife and Manai gave it to him.

"Who are the Xexots?" said Hamlar.

"They are people who live a long way from here at the other end of the nameless strait."

"Do these people all have knives made of this metal?" asked Hamlar.

"Knives and swords, too." She did not tell him that her sword and Gamba's were in the canoe; for she hoped some day to be able to run away and put to sea again.

Dian held her hand out towards Bovar for the knife. "I shall keep it," he said. "I like it."

"Give it back to her," said Manai. "It is hers. We are not thieves." So Bovar handed the knife back to Dian; but he made up his mind then and there to possess it, and he knew just how to go about it. All that he would have to do would be to push Dian off the ledge that ran in front of this cave; and he was sure that Manai would let him have the knife; provided, of course, that no one saw him push Dian.

IV

MANY SLEEPS had passed since Pu came to Tanga-tanga, but neither David Innes nor O-aa had been able to concoct any scheme whereby they might escape. The temple guard was composed entirely of warriors handpicked by Furp; and as far as David Innes and O-aa were concerned, these guardsmen were their jailers.

Furp was convinced that they were just ordinary mortals who had come to Tanga-tanga by accident; but he knew that most of the people believed in them, and so he did not dare to act against them too openly. He would gladly have had them killed; for now he was not receiving from Ope, the high priest, even a quarter as many pieces of bronze as he had before the advent of the Noada.

It was a little better since Pu had come, but the avaricious Furp wanted much more. Ope, the high priest, was secretly their enemy, and for the same reason that Furp was; but being a simple and superstitious fool, he had convinced himself that it was really a true god and goddess who sat upon the dais of the temple.

Though their enemies were powerful, those who believed in Pu and the Noada were many; and they were loved by these because the amount of their taxes and offerings had been greatly reduced, and now they had pieces of bronze with which to buy more food, and such other things as they required.

Both David and O-aa felt the undercurrent of intrigue against them, and they also felt that many of the common people were their friends; but these were never allowed to speak with them alone, as they were always surrounded by the priests of the temple, or the temple guards.

"I wish I might talk with some of these people alone," said David upon one of the few occasions where he had an opportunity to speak even to O-aa without being overheard by a priest or a warrior. "I think they are our friends, and if anyone were plotting against us, they would tell us if they had the opportunity."

"I am sure of it," said O-aa. "They have always liked me; and now they like you, too; for between us we have saved them a great many pieces of metal."

Suddenly David snapped his fingers. "I have it!" he exclaimed. "In the world from which I come there is a great and old religious faith whose communicants may come and confess theirs sins and be forgiven. They come alone and whisper to the priest, telling him what is troubling their hearts; and no one but the priest may hear them. Pu is going to ordain that the people of

Tanga-tanga have this privilege, with one great advantage over confessors in that other world, in that they may confess their sins directly to the ear of their god."

"Ope won't let you do it," said O-aa.

"There is a good, old American expression, which you would not understand, that explains succinctly just how I purpose winning Ope over."

"What are you going to do, then?" inquired O-aa.

"I am going to scare the pants off him," said David.

"What are pants?" asked O-aa.

"That is neither here nor there," replied David.

"Here comes Ope now," said O-aa. "I shall watch while you scare his pants off."

Ope, the high priest, came sinuously towards them; his gait reminding David of the silent approach of a snake.

David glared at the high priest sternly. "Ope," he said in a terrible voice, "I know what you have been thinking."

"I-I-I-I don't know what you mean," stammered the high priest.

"Oh, yes you do," said David, "Don't you know that you could be struck dead for thinking such thoughts?"

"No, most gracious Pu; honestly, I have not thought a bad thought about you. I have not thought of harming you—" and then he stopped suddenly; realizing, perhaps, that he had given himself away.

"I even know what you are thinking this instant," cried David; and Ope's knees smote together. "See that there is no more of it," continued David; "and be sure that you obey my slightest wish, or that of your Noada."

Ope dropped to his knees and covered his eyes with his palms. "Most glorious Pu," he said, "you shall never have reason to upbraid me again."

"And you'd better tell Furp to be careful what he thinks," said O-aa.

"I shall tell him," said Ope, "but Furp is a wicked man, and he may not believe me."

"In spite of the wickedness of Tanga-tanga, I am going to bring a great blessing to its people," said David. "Have built for me immediately against the wall beside the dais a room two paces square, with a door, and place two benches within it. The room should be two and a half paces high, and have no ceiling."

"It shall be done at once, most glorious Pu," said Ope, the high priest.

"See that it is," said David, "and when it is done summon the people to the temple; for I would speak to them and explain this wonderful blessing that I am bringing them."

Ope, the high priest, was dying to know what the blessing was, but he did not dare ask; and he was still worrying and cudgeling his brain as he went away to arrange to have artisans build a clay room such as David had demanded.

I am sure that he is really Pu, thought Ope, the high priest. *I am thinking good thoughts of him and of our Noada; and I always must. I must keep thinking good thoughts of them, good thoughts; and I must not let Furp put any bad thoughts into my head.* He thought this last thought in the hope that Pu was listening to it and would place all the blame upon Furp for the bad thoughts which Ope knew only too well he had been entertaining.

When the little room beside the dais was completed David directed that the people be summoned to the temple; and the lesser priests went out in their hideous masks and beat upon drums and summoned the people to come to the temple of Pu; and the temple was so crowded with people that no more could get in, and those who could not get into the temple filled the plaza.

It was O-aa who addressed them: "Pu has decided to

confer upon the people of Tanga-tanga a great blessing," she said. "Many of you have sinned; and if you have sinned much and have not been forgiven by Pu, it will be difficult for you to get into Karana after you die. Therefore, Pu has had constructed this little room here, where you may go, one at a time, and sit with Pu and confess your sins, that Pu may grant you forgiveness. You cannot all come at once, but between sleeps Pu will listen to the sins of twenty. Go forth into the plaza now and explain this to the others who are there; and then let twenty return to the temple to confess."

The people rushed out into the plaza then, and explained this marvelous thing to those who had not heard O-aa's words; and there was almost a riot before twenty had been selected to lay their sins before Pu prior to the next sleep.

David went into the little room, and the first of those who were to confess came and kneeled before him, covering his eyes with his hands. David told him to raise and sit on the other bench; and then he said, "You may now confess your sins, and be forgiven."

"Many sleeps ago," said the man, "before you and our Noada came, I stole pieces of metal from a neighbor who had money; because the priests and the go-sha had taken so many of mine from me that I did not have any to buy food for my family."

"When you are able to do so, you may return the pieces to the man from whom you took them," said David, "and you shall be forgiven. Did you know," continued David, "that if you have heard words spoken against Pu or the Noada, and have not come and told them, that that is a sin?"

"I did not know that," said the man, "but I have heard words spoken against you and the Noada. The warriors of Furp go among the people, telling them that you and the Noada are not from Karana; but that you are from Molop Az, and that some day soon you will destroy Tanga-tanga and take all its people to the Molop Az for the Little Men to devour. I did not believe that, and there are a good many others who do not believe it, but there are some who do; and these warriors are trying to incite them to murder you and the Noada."

"What is your name?" asked David; and when the man had told him David scratched the name with the point of his dagger in the clay of the wall of the little room. The man watched this process almost fearfully, for he knew nothing of the alphabets, or of writing. "This," said David, "is the sign of your forgiveness. It will stand as long as the temple stands, and Pu and the Noada remain here in safety. Now go on about your business, whatever it may be, and as you work learn the names of as many as possible who are loyal to Pu and the Noada; so that if we are ever in trouble you may summon them to the temple to defend us."

The man left the temple, and it did not occur to him that it was strange that god and a Noada who were all-powerful should require the help of mortals to defend them.

After many sleeps David had spoken with many of the citizens; and he had scratched upon the walls of the little room the names of those that he thought could be depended upon to be loyal to him and to O-aa. Nor was Furp idle during this time, for he had determined to rid himself of these two who were constantly increasing their hold upon the people; and depriving him of the pieces of bronze which he had been accustomed to collect from the temple and from the people.

Both Furp and Ope were quite concerned about this new confessional which permitted Pu to speak secretly with the people; but they would have been more concerned had they known that Pu, who now controlled the finances of the temple, was giving pieces of bronze to those who were loyal to him, in the privacy of the confessional, with which to purchase swords, and bows and arrows.

Ah-gilak, the little old man from Cape Cod, was much concerned over the fate of David Innes, whom he greatly admired, not only because of his ability and courage, but because David was from Hartford, Connecticut; and he felt that in this outlandish world at the center of the earth New Englanders were bound together by a common tie.

"Dod-burn it," he said to Abner Perry, shortly after David had departed, "how is this ding-busted idiot goin' to get back if that contraption carries him across the nameless strait that everyone says is at the end of the world?"

"I don't know" said Abner Perry sadly; "and to think that it is all my fault, all my fault. Because I am a careless absentminded old fool, I have sent the two I loved best to death."

"Well, settin' around cryin' over split milk ain't goin' to butter no parsnips, as the feller said," rejoined Ah-gilak. "What we ought to do is do sump'n about it."

"What can we do?" asked Abner Perry. "There is nothing that I would not do. I have been seriously considering building another balloon with which to follow them."

"Humph!" ejaculated Ah-gilak. "You sure are the dod-burndest old fool I've ever heard tell of. What good could you do if you did float over the nameless strait in one of them contraptions? We'd only have three of you to look for, instead of two. But I got a idea that I've been thinking about ever since David left."

"What is it?" asked Perry.

"Well, you see," explained the little old man, "afore the Dolly Dorcas was wrecked in the Arctic Ocean in

1845 I'd been a-plannin' that when I got back to Cape Cod I'd build me a clipper ship, the finest, fastest clipper ship that ever cut salt water. But then, of course the Dolly Dorcas she did get wrecked, and I drifted down here into this dod-burned hole in the ground; and I ain't never had no chance to build no clipper ship; but now, if I had the men and the tools, I could build one; and we could go down and cross this here nameless strait, and maybe we could find David and this here Dian the Beautiful."

Abner Perry brightened immediately at the suggestion. "Do you think you could do it, Ah-gilak?" he asked. "For if you can, I can furnish you the men and the tools. We haven't got a ship left seaworthy enough to navigate the nameless strait in safety; and if you can build one and sail it, I can furnish the men to build it, and the men to man it."

"Let's start, then," said Ah-gilak. "Procrastination is the mother of invention, as the feller said."

With this hope held out to him, Abner Perry was a new man. He sent for Ghak the Hairy One, who was king of Sari; and who theoretically ruled the loose federation of the Empire of Pellucidar while David was absent. Perry explained to Ghak what Ah-gilak had proposed, and Ghak was as enthusiastic as either of them. Thus it was that the entire tribe of Sarians, men, women and children, trekked to Amoz, which is on the Darel Az, a shallow sea that is really only a bay on the coast of the Lural Az.

They took with them arms and ammunition and tools —axes with hammers and chisels and mattocks, all the tools that Perry had taught them to make, after he himself had achieved steel following his discovery and smelting of iron ore, and the happy presence of carbon in the foothills near Sari.

Ghak sent runners to Thuria, Suvi, and Kali; and

eventually a thousand men were gathered at Amoz, felling trees and shaping the timbers; and hunters went forth and killed dinosaurs for the peritonea which was to form the sails.

Ah-gilak did not design the huge clipper ship he had planned to build at Cape Cod, but a smaller one that might be equally fast, and just as seaworthy.

Ja, the Mezop, came from the Anoroc Islands with a hundred men who were to help with the building of the ship and man it after it was launched; for the Mezops are the seafaring men of the Empire of Pellucidar.

The women fabricated the shrouds and the rigging from the fibers of an abacálike plant; and even the children worked, fetching and carrying.

No man may know how long it took to build that clipper ship, in a world where it is always noon and there are no moving celestial bodies to mark the passage of time; a fact which always annoyed Ah-gilak.

"Dod-burn that dod-blasted sun!" he exclaimed. "Why don't it rise and set like a sun oughta? How's a feller goin' to know when to quit work? Gad and Gabriel! It ain't decent."

But the Pellucidarians knew when to quit work. When they were hungry they stopped and ate; when they were sleepy they crawled into the darkest place they could find and went to sleep. Then the little old man from Cape Cod would dance around in a frenzy of rage and profanity, if their sleeping or their eating interfered with the building of the clipper. However, the work progressed, and eventually the clipper was ready to launch. The ways were greased, and every preparation had been made. A hundred men stood by the blocks, ready to pull them away.

"Dod-burn it!" exclaimed Ah-gilak. "We got to christen 'er, and we plumb forgot to find a name for her."

"You designed her and you built her," said Abner

Perry; "and so I think that you are the one who should have the privilege of naming her."

"That's fair enough," said Ah-gilak, "and I'm going to call her the John Tyler, because I voted for him for president at the last election; that is, I voted for him and William Henry Harrison; but when Harrison died Tyler became president."

"Why, that was a hundred and eighteen years ago, man!" exclaimed Abner Perry.

"I don't give a dod-blasted whoop if it was a thousand and eighteen years ago," said Ah-gilak. "I voted for Harrison and Tyler at the last election."

"Do you know what year it is now?" asked Abner Perry.

"David Innes tried to tell me that I was a hundred and fifty-three years old," said Ah-gilak; "but he has lived down here in this dod-burned hole in the ground so long he's crazy. They don't none of you know what year this is. They ain't no years here; they ain't no months! they ain't no weeks; they ain't no days; they ain't nothin' but noon. How you going to count time when it's always noon? Anyhow I'm going to name her the John Tyler."

"I think that's an excellent name," said Abner Perry.

"Now we ought to have a bottle of something to bust on her bow while I christen her," said Ah-gilak. "If a thing's worth doin' at all, don't put it off till tomorrow, as the feller said."

The best substitute for a bottle of champagne which they could find was a clay jug filled with water. Ah-gilak held it in his hand and stood by the bow of the clipper. Suddenly he turned to Abner Perry. "This ain't right," he said. "Who ever heard of a man christening a ship?"

"Stellara, the mate of Tanar, the son of Ghak is here," said Abner Perry. "Let her christen the John Tyler;"

and so Stellara came, and Ah-gilak told her what to do; and at his signal the men pulled the blocks away immediately after Stellara had broken the jug of water on the bow of the clipper and said, "I christen thee the John Tyler."

The ship slipped down the ways into the Darel Az; and the people of Thuria and Sari and Amoz and Suvi and Kali, screamed with delight.

The cannon had been put aboard her before they launched her; and now they set about rigging her, and this work Ah-gilak insisted must be done by the Mezops, who were to be the sailors that manned the ship; so that they would know every rope and spar. It was all a tremendous undertaking for people of the stone age, for they had so much to learn and when the ship was rigged the Mezops had to be drilled in making sail and taking it in quickly. Fortunately they were not only seafaring men, but semi-arboreal, as they lived in trees on their native islands. They ran up the shrouds like monkeys, and out upon the yardarms as though they had been born upon them.

"They may be red Injuns," said Ah-gilak to Perry, "but they're goin' to make fine sailormen."

Vast quantities of water in bamboo containers was stored aboard, as was the salt meat, vegetables, nuts, and quantities of the rough flour that Abner Perry had taught the Pellucidarians to make.

At last the Mezops were well drilled, and the John Tyler prepared to sail. Ah-gilak was skipper, Ja was the first mate and navigator. The second and third mates were Jav and Ko, while Ghak the Hairy One commanded two hundred picked warriors; for, being cavemen, they anticipated having to do battle after they had landed in the terra incognita beyond the nameless strait.

They had neither compass, nor sextant, nor any chronometer; but they had a man from Thuria aboard who could point the general direction; and Ja knew the great ocean currents that flowed directly along their course.

With all sails set to a fair wind, the John Tyler tossed the white water from her bow as she sailed gallantly out into the Lural Az in her quest for David Innes and Dian the Beautiful; and, for the first time since Dian had floated away toward the Land of Awful Shadow, Abner Perry felt hope budding in his breast; and for the first time in one hundred thirteen years the little old man from Cape Cod was really happy.

V

"I AM TIRED of being a slave," said Gamba to Dian, as they met beside the stream where Dian was filling a large gourd with water and Gamba was washing the lioncloths of his mistress. "That woman nearly works me to death."

"It is better than being killed and fed to the tarags," said Dian.

"I am afraid of the tarags," said Gamba. "I don't see why they let the terrible things hang around the way they do."

"They are tame," said Dian. "Manai told me that they catch them when they are cubs and tame them for hunting and for battle. There is a tribe on the other side of the island, two or three long marches away, with which Hamlar's tribe is always at war. The name of this tribe is Manat; and as the Tandars have tamed and trained tarags, so the Menats have tamed and trained tahos."

"What a terrible place," grumbled Gamba. "Why did we have to be cast ashore here?"

"You do not know when you are well off," said Dian. "If you had stayed in Lolo-lolo, you would have been killed; and if that woman had not taken you to be her slave, you would have been fed to the tarags. Are you never satisfied? Bovar said that you were very lucky to find a master at all, because nobody likes your yellow skin."

"And I do not like Bovar," snapped Gamba.

"Why?" asked Dian.

"Because he is in love with you."

"Nonsense!" said Dian.

"It is true," said Gamba. "He is always following you around with his eyes when he is not following you around with his feet."

"He does not want me," said Dian; "he wants my bronze knife"; she clled the metal androde.

"In the name of Pu!" exclaimed Gamba. "Look what's coming!"

Dian turned to see three great tarags slinking toward them. She and Gamba were some little distance from the cliff, and the tarags were between the cliff and them. Gamba was terrified, but Dian was not. The great beasts came and rubbed against the girl and nuzzled her hands, while Gamba sat frozen with terror.

"They will not hurt us," said Dian. "They are my friends. Every time that I can, I bring them pieces of meat."

One of the beasts came and smelled of Gamba; and then it bared its terrible fangs and growled, and the man shook as with palsy. Dian came and pushed against the beast's shoulder to turn it away, at the same time scratching it around one of its ears; then she walked away with her gourd of water, and the three beasts followed her.

For a long time Gamba sat there, wholly unnerved and unable to resume his work. But presently a woman came and spoke to him. "Get to work," she said, "you lazy ja-lok. What do you suppose I am feeding you for, to sit around and do nothing? Much more of this and you will be tarag meat."

"I am sick," said Gamba.

"Well, you had better get well," said the woman, "for I won't feed any sick slave." So Gamba, who had been a king, resumed his washing; and when it was done, he wrung the water out of the loincloths and took them and stretched them on a flat rock, where he rubbed them and rubbed them with a smooth stone to squeeze every remaining drop of water from them and to keep them soft as they dried in the hot sun. While he was doing this, his mistress came by again.

"You have not cleaned the cave since my last sleep," she said irritably.

"I have been doing the washing," said Gamba. "When that is done, I intended to clean the cave."

"You could have done both twice over if you hadn't been loafing," said the woman. "I don't know what to do. It is almost impossible to get a decent slave lately. I have had to feed the last three to the tarags, and it looks as though you would go the same way."

"I will try to do better," said Gamba. "I will work very hard."

"See that you do," said the woman, whose name was Shrud.

Dian shared a cave with some other slaves on the very lowest level. Such, of course, in a cave village, may be the least desirable, as the lower level is close to the ground and more easily accessible to wild beasts and enemies. She could go into it and sleep when her work was done; but it always seemed that she had no more than closed her eyes before Manai, or Hamlar, or Bovar, called her.

It was Bovar who called her most often, and usually

for no other reason than that he wished to talk with her. He had long since given up all thoughts of killing her in order to obtain her bronze dagger, for he had become infatuated with her; but according to the customs of his tribe, he could not take a slave as a mate. However, this fact did not wholly discourage Bovar, for he knew of a cave hidden deep in the jungle; and he toyed with the thought of stealing Dian and taking her there.

Once, after a fitful sleep, Bovar awoke cross and irritable. As he came out on the ledge before his cave he saw Dian walking toward the jungle. Two great tarags paced beside her. Dian was having ideas. She was going to run away, find the beach where her canoe lay, and paddle out upon the Korsar Az in an effort to reach the mainland. She had asked Gamba to go with her, but he had said that they would only be caught and fed to the tarags; so she had decided to go alone.

As Bovar reached the foot of the lowest ladder, one of the great tigers lay stretched in sleep across his path. He gave it a vicious kick in the ribs to make it get out of his way; and the beast sprang up with bared fangs, growling hideously. Bovar prodded it with his long, heavy spear; and it screamed and stepped back; then it slunk away, still growling. Paying no more attention to the tarag, Bovar looked around at the men and women of his trible, who were down at the foot of the cliff. No one was paying any attention to him. The men were lying around in the shade of trees, half asleep; and the women were working. Bovar walked nonchalantly towards the jungle into which Dian had disappeared. He did not look back; if he had, he would have seen a tarag slinking after him.

Gamba was scrubbing the floor of his mistress' cave. He had carried up a gourd of water and a smooth flat stone and a bundle of grasses. His knees were raw and bleeding from contact with the sandstone floor. As Shrud passed him on her way out of the cave, she kicked him in the side.

"Work fast, you lazy slave," she said.

This was more than Gamba could endure; it was the last straw, that he, a king, should be so abused and humiliated. He decided that death were better, but that he would have his revenge before he died, so he reached out and seized Shrud by an ankle, and as she fell forward he dragged her back into the cave. She clawed and struck at him, but he leaped upon her and drove his bronze dagger into her heart again and again.

When he realized what he had done, Gamba was terrified. Now he wished that he had gone with Dian, but perhaps she had not gone yet. He washed the blood from his dagger; and dragged Shrud's body to the very farthest end of the cave, where it was darkest; then he came out onto the ledge. Dian was nowhere in sight.

Gamba hastened down the ladders to the lowest level; and going to Dian's cave, he called her name; but there was no response. He started to cross the clearing toward the jungle in the direction that he thought Dian would take to reach the cove where their canoe lay; but he had gone only a short distance when Shrud's mate called to him.

"Where are you going, slave?" he demanded.

"Shrud has sent me into the jungle for fruit," replied Gamba.

"Well, hurry up about it," said the man. "I have work for you to do."

A moment later a runaway slave disappeared into the jungle.

It was noon in the city of Tanga-tanga and in all directions the world curved upward to be lost in the midst of the distance that merged with the blue vault of heaven to form a dome, in the center of which blazed the fiery sun that hung always at zenith.

In the temple a frightened man sat on a bench in the little room, facing his god.

"It will be soon, most gracious Pu," he said; "and if they find that I have been here, they will kill me; for there are those who know that I know."

"How will it come?" asked David.

"A great crowd will come to the temple with offerings. There will be warriors among them, and they will press close to the dais; and when one gives the word, they will fall upon you and our Noada and kill you. Furp will not be here, so that no blame may be attached to him by the people; but it is Furp who is directing it."

David read aloud to the man the names that he had scratched upon the wall of the little room, the names of those who were loyal to him and to O-aa. He read them twice, and then the third time. "Can you remember those names?" he asked.

"Yes," replied the man; "I know them all well."

"Go to them, then, and tell them that Pu says that the time has come. They will know what you mean."

"As I do," said the man; and he knelt, covering his eyes with his hands; and then he arose and left the temple.

David returned to the dais and sat upon his throne; and presently O-aa entered from her apartments, with the lesser priests in their hideous masks and the drums, according to the custom of the temple. She had come to the dais and seated herself beside David Innes.

"The time has come," he whispered to her.

"I have a sword and a dagger under my robe," she said.

Ope the high priest had never been able to persuade David to wear any robes of office, nor had David discarded his weapons. He had told Ope that Pu always dressed thus, and that it was only those who served Pu who wore the robes of office.

Time dragged heavily for these two, who might be waiting for death, but presently men commenced to struggle into the temple. David recognized some among these as those who were loyal to him. He held the first two fingers of his right hand across his breast. It was the sign that had been decided upon to recognize friend from foe; and all the men who had come in, even those whom he had not recognized, answered his sign.

They came and knelt before the dais and covered their eyes; and after they had been bidden to arise, they still stayed close to the dais; and so that it might seem reasonable that they should remain there, David preached to them as he imagined a god might preach to his people. He spoke to them of loyalty and the rewards of loyalty, and the terrible fate of those who were untrue to their faith. He spoke slowly, that he might consume time.

More and more men were entering the temple. There were no women, which was unusual; and as each entered, David made the sign; and some of them answered and some did not, but those who answered pressed close around the dais until they entirely sourrounded the three sides of it, the fourth side being against the wall of the temple.

David continued to talk to them in quiet tones that gave no indication that he anticipated anything unusual, but he watched them carefully; and he noticed that many of those who had not answered this sign were nervous, and now some of them tried to push through closer to the dais; but the loyal ones stood shoulder to shoulder and would not let them pass; and everyone in the temple waited for the signal.

At last it came. A warrior screamed. "Death!" Just the one word he spoke, but it turned the quiet temple into a bedlam of cursing, battling men.

Instantly the signal was given, the loyal ones had wheeled about with drawn swords to face the enemies of their gods; and David had arisen and drawn his sword, too.

The fighting men surged back and forth before the dais. One of Furp's men broke through and struck at O-aa; and David parried the blow and struck the man down; then he leaped to the floor of the temple and joined his supporters; and his presence beside them gave them courage and strength beyond anything that they had ever dreamed of possessing, and it put the fear of God into the hearts of the enemy.

Twenty of Furp's men lay bleeding on the floor and the others turned to flee the wrath of Pu, only to find that retreat was cut off; for, according to David's plan, a solid phalanx of his supporters, armed with bow and arrow, sword, and dagger, barred the way.

"Throw down your arms!" cried David. "Throw down your arms, or die!"

After they had divested themselves of swords and daggers, he told his people to let them go; but he warned them never again to raise their hands against Pu or their Noada.

"And now," he said, "go back to him who sent you; and tell him that Pu has known all his wicked thoughts and has been prepared for him; and because of what he has done he will be turned over to the people to do with as they see fit; and when you go, take your dead and wounded with you."

The vanquished warriors passed out of the temple with their dead and wounded, and David noted with a smile that they crossed directly to the house of the go-sha.

"It was easy to defeat the warriors of Furp when Pu was on our side," said one of David's supporters. "Now that will be the last of Furp, and Pu and his Noada will rule Tanga-tanga."

"Don't be too sure of that," said David. "Furp sent only a handful of men to the temple, for he did not anticipate any resistance. There will be more fighting before this is settled; and if you know of any more loyal men in the city, see that they are armed and ready to come at any moment. Let one hundred remain here constantly, for I am sure that Furp will attack. He will not give up his power so easily."

"Nor a chance to get all of our pieces of bronze as he once did," said one of the men bitterly.

The one hundred men remained and the others left and went through the city searching for new recruits.

David looked at O-aa and smiled and she smiled back. "I wish my eleven brothers had been here," she said.

VI

WHEN GAMBA entered the jungle, he commenced to run, hoping to overtake Dian; but the jungle was such a maze of trails that he soon realized that he was lost; and then he caught a glimpse of a large, yellow-striped creature slinking through the underbrush. Gamba was most unhappy. He wished that he had not killed Shrud, for then he would not have had to run away. He cursed the moment when Dian had come to Lolo-lolo; he cursed Dian; he cursed everybody but himself, who alone was responsible for his predicament; and, still cursing, he climbed a tree.

The tarag that had been stalking him came and stood under the tree and looked up and growled. "Go away," said Gamba, and picked a fruit that grew upon the tree and threw it at the tarag. The great beast snarled and then lay down under the tree.

As soon as Dian had entered the jungle she accelerated her pace; and the two great beasts which accompanied her strode upon either side, for here the trail was wide. Dian was glad of their presence, for they suggested protection, even though she did not know whether or not they would protect her in an emergency.

Presently she came to a natural clearing in the jungle; and when she was half-way across it she heard her name called. Surprised, she turn about to see Bovar.

"Where are you going?" he demanded.

"To the village," she said.

"You are going in the wrong direction, then. The village is back this way."

"These trails are confusing," said Dian. "I thought I was going in the right direction." She realized now that there was nothing to do but go back to the village and wait for another opportunity to escape. She was terribly disappointed, but not wholly disheartened; because, if it had been so easy to go into the jungle this time without arousing suspicion, there would be other times when it would be just as easy.

As Bovar came toward her she saw a tarag slink into the clearing behind him; and she recognized it immediately as the third member of the terrible trinity the affections of which she had won.

"You won't have to go back to the village now," said Bovar. "You can keep on going in the direction that you were."

"What do you mean?" demanded Dian.

"I mean that I think you were trying to escape, and I am going to help you. I know a cave deep in the jungle where no one will ever find us and where, when I am not with you, you will be safe from man and beast."

"I shall go back to the village," said Dian; "and if you

will promise not to annoy me, I will not tell Hamlar nor Manai what you would have done."

"You shall not go back to the village," said Bovar. "You are going with me. If you do not go willingly, I will drag you through the jungle by the hair."

Dian drew her bronze knife. "Come and try it," she said.

"Don't be a fool," said Bovar. "In the village you are a slave. You have to clean three caves and prepare the food for four people and wash loincloths and fetch carry all day. In the jungle you would have but one cave to clean and but two people to cook for; and if you behaved yourself I would never beat you."

"You will never beat me whether I behave myself or not," replied Dian.

"Throw down that knife," added Bovar. Dian laughed at him and that made Bovar furious. "Drop it and come with me, or I will kill you," he said. "You shall never go back to the village now to spread stories about me. Take your choice, slave. Come with me or die."

Two of the tarags stood close beside Dian, imparting to her a sense of security—whether false or not she did not know, but at least their presence encouraged her to hope. The third tarag lay on its belly a few yards behind Bovar, the tip of its tail constantly moving. Dian knew what that sign often portended, and she wondered.

Bovar did not know that the tarag had followed him, nor that it lay there behind him, watching his every move. What was in the great beast's mind, no one may know. Since cubhood it had been taught to fear these men-things and their long, sharp spears.

Bovar took a few steps toward Dian, his spear poised to thrust. Dian had not thought that he would carry out his threat; but now, looking into his eyes, she saw determination there. She saw the tarag behind Bovar rise with barred fangs and then she had an inspiration. This cave girl knew what an unfailing invitation to any dangerous animal to attack is flight; and so she turned suddenly and ran across the clearing, banking her safety on the affections of these savage beasts.

Bovar sprang after her, his spear poised for the cast; and then the great beast behind him charged and sprang, and the two which had stood beside Dian leaped upon him with thunderous roars.

Dian heard one piercing scream and turned to see Bovar go down with all those terrible fangs buried in his body. That one piercing scream marked the end of Bovar, son of Hamlar the chief; and Dian watched while the great beasts tore the chief's son to pieces and devoured him. Inured to savagery in a savage world, the scene that she witnessed did not horrify her. Her principle reactions to the event were induced by the knowledge that she had been relieved from an annoying enemy, that she now would not have to return to the village, and that she had acquired a long, heavy spear.

Dian went and sat down in the shade of a tree and waited for the three beasts to finish their grisly meal. She was glad to wait for them, for she wanted their company and protection as far as the entrance to the shaft which led down to the beach where her canoe lay; and while she was waiting she fell asleep.

Dian was awakened by something rubbing against her shoulder and opened her eyes to see one of the tarags nuzzling her. The other two had slumped down near her, but when she awoke they stood up; and then the three of them strode off into the jungle and Dian went with them. She knew that they were going for water and when they had drunk they would sleep; nor was she wrong, for when they had had their fill of water they threw themselves down in the shade near the stream; and Dian laid down with them and they all slept.

Gamba, in his tree a quarter of a mile away from the clearing where Bovar had died, had heard a human scream mingling with the horrid roars and snarls of attacking beasts, and he had thought that Dian had been attacked and was dead; and Gamba, who had been king of Lolo-lolo, felt very much alone in the world and extremely sorry for himself.

In Tanga-tanga, Ope the high priest was in a quandary and very unhappy. He and the lesser priests had all been absent from the temple throne room at the time that the followers of Furp had attacked Pu and the Noada; and now he was trying to explain his absence to his god. His quandary was occasioned by the fact that he did not know which side was going to win in the impending battle, of the imminence of which he was fully cognizant.

"It might have seemed a coincidence to some," David was saying, "that you and all of the lesser priests were absent at the time that Furp's men attacked us, but Pu knows that it was no coincidence. You absented yourselves when you knew that we were in danger so that the people might have no grounds upon which to reproach you, no matter what the outcome of the attempt might be. You must now determine once and for all whether you will support us or the go-sha."

The lesser priests were gathered around Ope at the foot of the dais and they looked to him for leadership. He could feel their eyes upon him. He knew the great numerical strength of the go-sha's retainers, but he did not know that Pu, also, had a great number, nor did he know that they were armed. He thought that Furp's warriors would be met, if at all, by an unarmed mob which they could easily mow down with arrow, spear, and sword.

"I am waiting for your answer," said David.

Ope decided to play safe; he could explain his reasons to Furp later. "We shall be loyal to Pu and our Noada in the future as in the past," he said.

"Very well, then," said David. "Send the lesser priests out into the city to spread the word among the people that they must arm themselves and be prepared to defend the temple."

Ope had not expected anything of this sort and he was chagrined, for at the bottom of his heart he hoped that Furp would succeed in destroying these two, that he might again enjoy to the fullest extent the prequisites and graft of his office; but he realized that he must at least appear to comply with Pu's instructions.

"It shall be done at once," he said. "I shall take the lesser priests into my private chambers and explain their duties to them."

"You will do nothing of the sort," said David. "The lesser priests have heard the instructions that Pu has given. They will go out into the city at once and with each one of them I will send one of these loyal citizens to see that my instructions are carried out honestly."

"But—" commenced Ope.

"But nothing!" snapped David, and he looked at the lesser priests. "You will leave at once, and you will each be accompanied by one of these men," and as he detailed those who were to accompany the lesser priests, he told them that they had his permission, the permission of their god, to destroy any priest who failed to exhort the people enthusiastically to defend the temple of Pu.

It was not long thereafter that men commenced to congregate in the plaza before the temple. Through the great temple doorway David could see the house of the go-sha; and soon he saw warriors emerging from it, and others coming into the plaza from other directions. They marched straight toward the temple, before which stood the temple guards and the loyal citizens who had armed themselves to protect Pu and their Noada.

Furp's men tried to shoulder their way through to the temple, but they were immediately set upon, and the battle began. Soon the plaza was filled with the clash of swords, the shouts and curses of battling men, and the screams and groans of the wounded and dying.

From every narrow, crooked street loyal citizens swarmed to the defense of the temple; so that not one of Furp's men ever reached the great doorway.

Who may know how long that battle lasted, for it was noon when it commenced and noon when it ended; but to David and O-aa it seemed like an eternity.

When the last of Furp's retainers who were not dead or wounded were driven from the plaza, the dead lay thick upon every hand; and David Innes was the master of Tanga-tanga.

Furp and a couple of hundred of his retainers had fled the city; and it was later discovered that they had gone to Lolo-lolo and enlisted in the service of the new go-sha there, who was glad to acquire so many trained fighting men.

David sent word to the people that as long as he remained he would rule Tanga-tanga; and that when he left he would appoint a new go-sha, one who would not rob them; and then he sent for Ope the high priest.

"Ope," he said, "in your heart you have always been disloyal to your Noada and to Pu; therefore, you are dismissed from the priesthood and banished from Tanga-tanga. You may go to Lolo-lolo and join Furp, and you may thank Pu that he has not destroyed you as you deserve."

Ope was aghast. He was not prepared for this, as he had felt that he had played safe.

"B-but, Pu," he cried. "The people—the people, what of them? They will not be pleased. They might even turn against you in their wrath. I have been their high priest for many thousand sleeps."

"If you prefer to leave the issue to the people," said David "I will summon them and tell them how disloyal you have been, and turn you over to them."

At that suggestion Ope trembled, for he knew that he was most unpopular among the people. "I shall abide by the will of Pu," he said, "and leave Tanga-tanga immediately; but it pains me to think that I must abandon my people and leave them without a high priest to whom they may bring their grievances."

"And their pieces of metal," said O-aa.

"The people shall not be without a high priest," said David; "for I now ordain Kanje as the high priest of the temple of Pu." Kanje was one of the lesser priests whom David knew to be loyal.

Ope was conducted to the gates of the city by members of the temple guard, who had orders to see that he spoke to no one; and so the last of David's active and powerful enemies was disposed of, and he could devote his time to plans for returning to Sari, after prosecuting a further search for Dian, who, in his heart of hearts, he believed to be lost to him forever.

He sent men out to fell a certain type of tree in a near-by forest, and to bring them into the city; and he sent hunters out to kill several boses, which on the outer crust were the prehistoric progenitors of our modern cattle. These hunters were instructed to bring the meat in and give it to the people; and to bring hides to the women to be cleaned and cured.

When the trees were brought in he had them cut into planks and strips, and in person he surpervised the building of a large canoe with mast and sails and watertight compartments forward and aft.

The people wondered at the purpose for which this strange thing was being built, for they were not a seafaring people; and in all their lives had seen only one craft that floated on the water—that in which their Noada had come to them.

When the canoe was completed, he summoned the people to the plaza and told them that he and the Noada were going to visit some of their other temples in a far land, and that while they were gone the people must remain loyal to Kanje and the new go-sha whom David appointed; and he warned Kanje and the new go-sha to be kind to the people and not to rob them.

"For, wherever I am, I shall be watching you," he said.

He had the people carry the canoe down to the nameless strait, and stock it with provisions and with water, and with many weapons—spears, and bows and arrows, and bronze swords; for he knew that the crossing would be perilous.

The entire population of Tanga-tanga, with the exception of the warriors at the gates, had come down to the shore to bid Pu and the Noada farewell; and to see this strange thing set out upon the terrible waters. O-aa had come down with the people, but David had remained at the temple to listen to a report from some of the warriors he had sent out in search of a clue to the whereabouts of Dian. These men reported that they had captured a Lolo-lolo hunter, who claimed to have seen Gamba and Dian as they set forth upon the waters of the nameless strait in their little canoe. So David knew that if Dian were not already dead, she might have returned to Sari.

As he started for the gate of the city he heard sounds of fighting; and when he reached the gate he saw that his people by the shore had been attacked by a horde of warriors from Lolo-lolo and were falling back toward the city.

O-aa had been in the canoe, waiting for David, when

the attack came; and in order to escape capture, she had paddled out upon the nameless strait, intending to hold the craft there until the attackers had been dispersed and David could come down to the shore; but the current seized the canoe and carried it out into the strait, and though she paddled valiantly she could do nothing to alter its course.

VII

THE SHIP in which Hodon sailed in search of the Sari and O-aa was named Lo-har, in honor of Laja who had come among the Sarians from the country called Lo-har. It was a little ship, but staunch; and Raj the Mezop brought it through that nameless strait, and out upon the broad bosom of the Korsar Az in safety; and there they were becalmed and the current carried them where it would. Their fresh water was almost exhausted and they looked in vain for rain; and then in the distance they sighted land, toward which the current was carrying them. When they were scarcely a mile off shore, the current changed and Hodon saw that they were going to be carried past the end of what he now saw to be an island; so he filled the canoe with empty water containers, and with twenty strong paddlers he set forth for the shore; and as he neared it he saw a waterfall tumbling into the sea over the edge of a cliff.

As the canoe was being drawn up on a narrow beach in a little cove at the far end of which was the waterfall, Hodon saw another canoe that had been dragged up on the shore; and while his men carried the containers to the waterfall to fill them, he investigated.

In the bottom of the canoe were strange weapons such as he had never seen before, for the swords he found there were of a metal he had never seen before, and the spears and arrows were tipped with it. Upon a thwart rested two tiny sandals. Hodon picked one of them up and examined it, and instantly he recognized it as the work of a Sarian woman; for the women of each tribe have a distinctive way of making their sandals, so that they are easily recognized, as are the imprints they make upon soft earth or sand.

What Sarian woman other than Dian the Beautiful could these tiny sandals belong to? She alone was missing from Sari. Hodon was excited, and he hastened to the waterfall to tell his warriors; and they were excited, too, when they heard that Dian might be on this island.

As the men filled the remaining bamboo containers Hodon discovered the little ledge behind the falls and, in investigating, found the opening into the cavern. He felt his way into it until he came at last to the bottom of the shaft where rested the crude ladder up which Dian's captors had taken her. Hodon returned to his men and they carried the fresh water back to the canoe; and as they looked out toward the Lo-har they saw that a breeze had sprung up and that the little ship was standing in toward shore.

After the tarag, tired of waiting beneath the tree, arose and slunk off into the jungle, Gamba came down onto the ground and continued his flight. He walked quite a distance this time before he was treed again by sounds which he could not clearly interpret, but which resembled the growls of beasts mingled with the conversation of men; and presently there passed beneath him a dozen warriors, each one of which was accompanied by a ta-ho on a leash. Gamba recognized them instantly as Manats from the other side of the island; for, although he had never seen one of them before, he had heard them and their fierce fighting beasts described many times by the Tandars.

Gamba remained very quiet in his tree, for these Manats looked like fierce and terrible men, almost as fierce and terrible as their grim beasts.

And while Gamba watched them pass beneath him and disappear along the winding trail beyond him, Dian and her three beasts slept beside the little stream where they had quenched their thirst.

Dian was awakened when one of her beasts sprang to its feet with a hideous roar. Approaching were the twelve warriors of Manat with their fighting tahos. The three tarags, roaring and growling, stood between Dian and the approaching Manats.

With cries of encouragement, the Manats turned their twelve beasts loose; and Dian, seeing how greatly her defenders were outnumbered, turned and fled and while the tarags were battling for their lives, a Manat warrior pursued her.

Dian ran like a deer, far outdistancing the Manat. She had no idea in what direction she was running. She followed jungle trails which turned and twisted, and which eventually brought her back to the very clearing in which Bovar had been killed, and there she saw the Manats and their fighting beasts, but there were only seven of the latter now. Before they had died, her tarags had destroyed five of them.

The warriors did not see Dian, and for that she breathed a sigh of relief as she turned and hurried back along the trail she had come—hurried straight into the arms of the warrior who had been following her. They met at a sharp turn in the trail and he seized her before she could escape. Dian reached for her dagger, but the man caught her wrist; and then he disarmed her.

"You came back to me," he said, in a gruff voice, "but for making me run so far I shall beat you when I get you back to the village of Manat."

Dian said nothing, for she knew that nothing she might say could avail her.

Gamba, sitting disconsolate and terrified in his tree, saw the twelve terrible men of Manat return. There were only seven tahos with them now, but this time there was a woman. Gamba recognized her immediately and his sorrow almost overcame him—sorrow for himself and not for Dian; for now he knew that she could never lead him to the cove where the canoe lay and that if he found it himself, he would have to embark on those terrible waters alone. It is wholly impossible that anyone could have been more unhappy than Gamba. He dared not return to the village; he did not know in which direction the cove lay; and he was alone in a jungle haunted by hungry man-eaters, he who had always lived in the safety of a walled city. From wishing that he had never seen Dian, he commenced to wish that he had never been born. Finally he decided to find a stream near which grew trees bearing edible fruits and nuts; and to live up in these trees all the rest of his life, coming down only for water.

While Gamba was bemoaning his fate, Dian, the leash of one of the dead tahos around her neck, was being led across the Island of Tandar toward the country of the Manats; but she was not bemoaning anything, nor being sorry for herself. She could not clutter her mind with useless thoughts while every moment it must be devoted to thoughts of escape. There was never any telling at what instant an emergency might arise which would offer her an opportunity; yet, deep in the bottom of her heart, her fate must have seemed utterly hopeless.

The warrior who had captured Dian was an ill-natured brute, and the fact that he had lost his ta-ho in the fight with the tarags had not tended to improve his disposition. He jerked at the rope around Dian's neck roughly and unnecessarily; and occasionally on no pretext at all, he cuffed her; and every time he did one of these things he was strengthening the girl's resolve to kill him. She would almost have abandoned an opportunity to escape for the pleasure of driving a dagger into his heart.

With all sails set, the John Tyler rode the water of the nameless strait. Ja and Abner Perry and Ah-gilak stood upon the quarterdeck.

"I think," said Abner Perry, "that we should disembark a searching party as soon as possible. We may have a long shoreline to search and a big country, which we must comb until we find some clew to the whereabouts of Dian"; and the others agreed with him.

As they approached the shore the lookout shouted, "Canoe dead ahead."

As they bore down upon the little craft the bow was filled with warriors and Mezops, watching the canoe and its single occupant. They saw a figure in a long cloak and an enormous feather headdress; and when they got closer they saw that it was a woman.

O-aa had never seen a ship built or rigged like this one, which had evidently discovered her and was headed for her; but as far as she knew, only the men of the Empire of Pellucidar built any sort of ships, and so she hoped against hope that these might be men of the federation.

As the ship came about and lay to near her, she paddled to its side. A rope was thrown to her and she was hauled to the deck.

"Dod-burn it!" exclaimed Ah-gilak. "Gad and Gabriel! If it isn't O-aa! What in the name of all that's dod-blasted are you doing in that get-up, girl; and out here alone in a canoe?"

"Don't talk so much, old man," retorted O-aa, who could never forget that Ah-gilak had once planned on killing and eating her that time that they were being besieged in the cave by the sabre-toothed men. "Instead of talking," she continued, "get to shore and rescue David Innes."

"David Innes!" exclaimed Abner Perry. "Is David Innes there?"

"He is in that city you can see," replied O-aa, "and if the warriors from Lolo-lolo get in there, they will kill him."

The ship was under way again and Ah-gilak brought it as close into shore as he dared, and dropped anchor. Then Ghak and his two hundred warriors, and all but about twenty-five of the Mezops, took to the boats and made for shore. Nearly three hundred veterans they were and they were armed with muskets; crude things, but effective against men of the stone age, or of the bronze age either; for, besides making a good deal of noise, they emitted volumes of black smoke; and those whom they didn't kill, they nearly frightened to death.

In a long thin line, as David had taught them, they approached the city where the warriors of Lolo-lolo were attempting to force the gates.

When they were discovered, the Lolo-loloans turned to repel them, looking with contempt upon that long, thin line of a few hundred men who had the temerity to threaten a thousand bowmen. But the thunder of the first ragged volley and the black smoke belching at them, as twenty or thirty of their comrades fell screaming to the ground, gave them pause; but they advanced bravely in the face of a second volley. However, with the third volley, those who had not been killed or wounded turned and fled, and Ghak the Hairy One led his troop to the walls of Tanga-tanga.

"Who are you?" demanded a warrior standing upon the top of the wall.

"We are friends, and we have come for Pu," replied

Ghak, who had been coached by O-aa.

Almost immediately the gates were thrown open and David Innes emerged. From the temple he had heard the firing and he was sure that could have come only from the muskets of the empire.

Tears were streaming down Abner Perry's cheeks as he welcomed David aboard the John Tyler.

David listened while they told him of their plans to search for Dian, but he shook his head and told them that it was useless; that Dian had set out upon the nameless strait in a canoe with a single companion and that if she were not already back in Sari, she must be dead.

O-aa had inquired about Hodon, and when she had been told that he had come this way in search of her, she begged David Innes to continue on through the nameless strait into the Korsar Az in search of him; as he must have gone there if he had not already been wrecked.

While Gamba was searching for a stream where there were trees bearing nuts and fruits he was suddenly confronted by a band of strange warriors bearing weapons such as he had never seen before. He tried to escape them, but they overtook and captured him.

"Who are you?" demanded Hodon.

"I am Gamba, the go-sha of Lolo-lolo," replied the frightened man.

"I think we should kill him," said a Mezop. "I do not like the color of his skin."

"Where is Lolo-lolo," asked Hodon.

"It is on the other side of the nameless strait," replied Gamba, "where the country of the Xexots lies."

"You came from the other side of the nameless strait?"

"Yes; I came in a thing called a 'canoe.'"

"Did you come alone?" asked Hodon.

"No; I came with a woman who said that she came

from a country called Sari, and that her name was Dian the Beautiful."

"Where is she?" demanded Hodon.

"She was captured by the Manats, who live on the other side of this island."

"Can you lead us there?"

"No," replied Gamba; "I am lost. I do not even know the way to the coast where our canoe lies. If I were you, I would not go to the country of the Manats. They are terrible men and they lead tahos, who can kill and devour you. There were twelve Manats who captured Dian, and they had seven tahos with them."

"Can you show us where she was captured?"

"I can show you where I last saw her," replied Gamba; and this he did. There the trail of men and beasts was plain and to these men of the stone age the following of that trail was simple. They marched rapidly and almost without rest; and though ordinarily it was three long marches to the village of the Manats, Hodon and his hundred warriors reached it shortly after the first sleep.

The men who had captured Dian had only just arrived and her captor had taken her to his cave.

"Now," he said, "I am going to give you the beating I promised you. It will teach you to behave." He seized her by the hair and, stooping, picked up a short stick; and as he stooped Dian snatched her bronze dagger that the man had taken from her from the sheath at his side, and as he raised the stick she plunged it into his heart. With a scream he clutched at his breast; and then Dian gave him a push that sent him out of the cave to topple over the ledge and fall to the ground below.

A moment later she heard shouts and war cries; and she thought that they were caused by the anger of the Manats because of the killing of one of their fellows; and she stood in the shadow of the cave's entrance with the dagger in her hand, determined to sell her life dearly and take a heavy toll of her enemies.

From below rose the shouts of the warriors and the roars and growls of the tahos; and then, like a thunderbolt out of a clear sky, came the roar of musketry.

Dian could not believe her ears. What other people in all Pellucidar, other than the men of the empire and the inhabitants of far Korsar, had firearms? It was too good to hope that these might be Sarians; and if they were from Korsar, she was as well off here among the Manats as to be captured by the Korsarians.

She stepped to the mouth of the cave and looked out. The fighting was going on almost directly beneath her. The tahos were doing the most damage among the attackers, but one by one they were being shot down; for the Manat warriors, confused by the noise and the smoke, made only an occasional sally, only to be driven back with heavy losses; and at last the remnants of them turned and fled, as the last of the tahos was killed.

Dian had long since seen that these men were no Korsars. She recognized the copper skins of the Mezops and knew that she had been saved.

She stood upon the ledge and called down to them, and the men looked up and cheered. Then she went down and greeted Hodon and the others; and the first question that she asked was of David. "Why is he not with you?" she asked. "Has anything happened to him?"

"He left Sari in a balloon such as carried you away," explained Hodon, "in the hope that it would take him to the same spot where yours landed. We do not know what became of him."

"Why are you here?" asked Dian.

"We were looking for O-aa, who, when last seen, was adrift on the Sari."

"How did you happen to come here and find me?" asked Dian.

"We landed on the island for water and I saw your sandals on the thwart of your canoe; then we came inland in search of you and we found a man who had seen you captured by these Manats. After that it was easy enough to follow their trail."

They started immediately on the long trek back to the other side of the island; and when they entered the jungle Gamba came down out of a tree where he had been hiding during the fighting.

"This man said that he came here in a canoe with you," said Hodon. "Did he offer to harm you in any way?"

"No," said Dian.

"Then we shall let him live," said Hodon.

PART IV

SAVAGE PELLUCIDAR

I

As THE JOHN TYLER sailed through the nameless strait toward the Korsar Az in what seemed to David a fruitless search for the ship Lo-har and Hodon the Fleet One, a forgotten incident flashed into David's mind. As he had drifted across the strait in the balloon that Abner Perry had built for him that he might prosecute his search for Dian the Beautiful, he had seen, far below, a canoe with two occupants moving with the current toward the Korsar Az. And now, recalling what one of the Xexots had told him of seeing Dian and Gamba, the former king of Lolo-lolo, escaping in a canoe, he was certain that it must have been Dian and Gamba whom he had seen. So now he was anxious as O-aa to sail on into the Korser Az.

Ah-gilak, the little old man from Cape Cod who could not recall his name but knew that it was not Dolly Dorcas, didn't care where he sailed the ship he had designed and now skippered. He was just content to sail it, a small version of the great clipper ship he had dreamed of building nearly a hundred years before as soon as he got back to Cape Cod.

Of course Abner Perry was more than anxious to prosecute the search for Dian, since it had been through his carelessness that the balloon had escaped and borne her away. Ja and Jav and Ko and the other Mezops of the crew, being borne to the sea, were happy in this, to them, wonderful ship. Ghak the Hairy One, king of Sari, who commanded the two hundred warriors aboard, would have gone to the fiery sea of Molop Az for either David or Dian. The two hundred warriors, while loyal and valiant, were mostly unhappy. They are hill people, the sea is not their element, and most of them were often sick.

On the Lo-har, Hodon and Dian decided to cruise about the Korsar Az for a while before giving up the search for O-aa, whom they had about given up for lost. Then they would return to Sari.

The Korsar Az is a great ocean extending, roughly, two thousand miles from north to south. It is an un-chartered wilderness of unknown waters, and all but a short distance of its enormous shoreline a *terra incognita* to the crews of the Lo-har and the John Tyler, most of whom thought that its waters extended to the ends of the world and were bordered by lands inhabited by fierce enemies and roved by terrifying beasts, in all but the first of which conceits they were eminently correct.

Leaving Tandar, the island upon which he had found Dian, Hodon cruised to the south, while the John Tyler, entering the great sea from the nameless strait, turned her prow toward the north. Thus, fate separated them farther and farther.

Usually within sight of land, the John Tyler cruised in a north-easterly direction along the great peninsula upon the opposite side of which lie most of the kingdoms of the Empire of Pellucidar. For thirteen or fourteen hundred miles the ship held this course, while Ghak's two hundred sturdy warriors, sick and hating the sea, became more and more unhappy and discontented until they were close upon the verge of mutiny.

They were at heart loyal to Ghak and David; but they

were men of the stone age, rugged individualists unaccustomed to discipline. Finally they came to Ghak in a body and demanded that the ship turn back and head for home.

Ghak and David listened to them, Ghak with deep sympathy, for he, too, was sick of the sea and longed to feel the solid earth beneath his feet once more. And David listened with understanding and a plan. He spread a crude map before them.

"We are here," he said, pointing, "opposite the narrowest part of the peninsula." He moved his finger in a southeasterly direction. "Here is Sari. Between us and Sari lie seven hundred miles of probably rugged country inhabited by savage tribes and overrun by fierce beasts. You would have to fight your way for all the seven hundred miles." He ran his finger back along the coast and through the nameless strait and then up along the opposite shore of the peninsula to Sari. "The John Tyler is a safe and seaworthy ship," he said. "If you remain aboard her, you may be sick and uncomfortable at times, but you will reach Sari in safety. If you wish, we will land you here; or you may remain aboard. If you stay with the ship, there must be no more grumbling, and you must obey orders. Which do you wish to do?"

"How far is it back to Sari by sea?" asked one of the warriors.

"This is, of course, a crude map," said David, "and we may only approximate correct distances; but I should say that by sea the distance to Sari is around five thousand miles."

"And only seven hundred miles by land," said the man.

"About that. It may be more, it may be less."

"If it were seven hundred miles by sea and five thousand by land," spoke up another warrior, "and I had to fight for every mile, I'd choose to go by land."

As one man, the two hundred cheered and that settled the matter.

"Well, dod-burn my hide!" grumbled Ah-gilak. "Of all the gol-durned idjits I almost nearly ever seen! 'Druther hoof it fer seven hundred miles than ride home in style an' comfort on the sweetest ship ever sailed these dod-blasted seas. Ain't got no more sense 'n a white pine dog with a poplar tail. Howsumever, good riddance says I. There'll be more victuals for the rest of us, an' plenty water."

"Then everybody's happy," said David, smiling.

At the point they chose to land the Sarian warriors, there was a narrow beach at the foot of cliffs which extended in both directions as far as they could see. The lead showed no bottom at sixteen fathoms four hundred yards off shore. Closer than that Ah-gilak would not take his ship.

"Too gol-durned close now," he said, "but what wind there is is right."

Standing on and off a light breeze and a calm sea, the boats were lowered and the first contingent was put ashore. David, Abner Perry, Ghak, and O-aa were standing together watching the warriors disembark.

"You will accompany them, Ghak?" asked David.

"I will do whatever you wish," replied the king of Sari.

"Your place is with them," said David; "and if you go with them, you'll be back in Sari much sooner than we shall by sea."

"Why don't we all go with them, then?" suggested Perry.

"I have been thinking the same thing," said David, "but for myself. Not you. It would be too tough a trek for you, Abner. Don't forget that you must be well over ninety by this time."

Perry bridled. "Stuff and nonsense!" he exclaimed. "I can keep up with the best of you. And don't you forget,

David, that if I am over ninety, you are over fifty. I'm going along, and that settles it. I must get back to Sari. I have important things to do."

"You will be much more comfortable aboard the John Tyler," coaxed David. "And what have you so important to do, that can't wait in a world where time stands eternally still?"

"I have in mind to invent a steam locomotive and build a railway," said Perry. "I also wish to invent a camera. There is much to be done, David."

"Why a camera?" asked David. "You can't kill anyone with a camera."

Perry looked hurt. The man who had brought gunpowder, muskets, cannon, and steel for swords and spears and knives to this stone age world was inherently the sweetest and kindest of men. But he just couldn't help "inventing."

"Be that as it may, David," he said with dignity, "I am going with Ghak," and David knew that that was that.

"How about you, O-aa?" asked David. "With two hundred warriors fully armed with Perry's appurtenances of civilization, I am sure that we can make the journey with safety; and you can be back in Kali with your own people far sooner than by making the long trip by sea."

"Hodon is somewhere on the Kosar Az searching for me, I am sure," replied O-aa; "so I shall stay with the John Tyler. I should much rather go with you than remain with the little old man whose name is not Dolly Dorcas and whom I do not like, but by so doing I might miss Hodon."

"Why do you call him the little man whose name is not Dolly Dorcas, and why do you dislike him?" asked Perry.

"He has forgotten his own name. He had none. So I called him Dolly Dorcas. I thought that was his name, but it was the name of the ship he was on that was wrecked. So he was always saying, 'my name is not Dolly Dorcas', until we gave him the name Ah-gilak. And I do not like him, because he eats people. He wanted to eat me. He ate the men who were shipwrecked with him. He was even going to start eating himself. He has told us these things. He is an evil old man. But I shall go with him, because I wish to find my Hodon."

"Gracious me!" exclaimed Perry. "I had no idea Ahgilak was such a terrible person."

"He is," said O-aa, "but he had better leave me alone, or my thirteen brothers will kill him."

II

As THE JOHN TYLER drew away from shore, little O-aa leaned on the rail and watched the last of the Sari warriors clamber up the cliff and disappear in the junglelike growth which surmounted it. A moment later she heard savage cries floating out over the water, and then the loud reports of muskets and the screams of wounded men.

"Men do not have to wait long for trouble on land," said Ko, the Mezop Third Mate, who leaned against the rail at her side. "It is well that you decided to return by sea, little one."

O-aa shot a quick glance at him. She did not like the tone of his voice when he called her little one. "My people can take care of themselves," she said. "If necessary they will kill all the men between here and Sari. And I can take care of myself, too," she added.

"You will not have to take care of yourself," said Ko. "I will take care of you."

"You will mind your own business," snapped O-aa.

Ko grinned. Like nearly all the red Mezops he was handsome, and like all handsome men he thought that he had a way with the women and was irresistable. "It is a long way to Sari," he said, "and we shall be much together; so let us be friends, little one."

"We shall not be much together, we shall not be friends, and don't call me little one. I do not like you, red man." Little O-aa's eyes snapped.

Ko continued to grin. "You will learn to like me—little one," he said. O-aa slapped him full in the face. Ko's grin vanished, to be replaced by an ugly snarl. "I'll teach you," he growled, reaching for her.

O-aa drew the long, slim steel dagger David had given her after she came aboard the John Tyler; and then a thin, cracked voice cried, "Avast there, you swabs! What goes on?" It was Ah-gilak the skipper.

"This she-tarag was going to knife me," said Ko.

"That's only part of it," said O-aa. "If he ever lays a hand on me I'll carve his heart out."

Ja, attracted by the controversy, crossed the deck to them in time to hear Ah-gilak say, "She is a bad one. She needs a lesson."

"You had better not try to give me a lesson, eater of men," snapped O-aa, "unless you want your old belly ripped open."

"What is this all about, O-aa?" asked Ja.

"This," said O-aa, pointing at Ko, "spoke to me as no one but Hodon may speak to me. And he called me little one—me, the daughter of Oose, King of Kali. And when I slapped him, he would have seized me—had I not had my knife."

Ja turned on Ko. "You will leave the girl alone," he said. Ko scowled but said nothing, for Ja is king of the Mezops of Anoroc Island, one whom it is well to obey. Ko turned and walked away.

"Dod-burn it!" exclaimed Ah-gilak. "They's always

trouble when you got a woman aboard. I never did like shippin' a woman. I got me a good mind to set her ashore."

"You'll do nothing of the sort," said Ja.

"I'm skipper of this here ship," retorted Ah-gilak. "I can put her ashore if I've a mind to."

"You talk too much, old man," said Ja, and walked away.

"You gol-durned red Indian," grumbled Ah-gilak. "That's insubordination. Tarnation! it's mutiny, by gum. I'll clap you in irons the fust thing you know," but he was careful to see that Ja was out of earshot before he voiced his anger and made his threats, for now, except for himself, all the officers and crew of the John Tyler were Mezops and Ja was their king.

The John Tyler beat back along the coast toward the nameless strait; and every waking moment O-aa scanned the surface of the great sea that curved upward, horizonless, to merge in the distant haze with the vault of the heavens. But no sign of another ship rewarded her ceaseless vigil. There was life, the terrible marine life of this young world; but no ship bearing Hodon.

O-aa was very lonely. The Mezops, with the exception of Ko, were not unfriendly; but they are a taciturn people. And, further, she had little in common with them that might have promoted conversation. And she hated the sea, and she was afraid of it. She might cope with enemies among men, but she could not cope with the sea. She had begun to regret that she had not gone overland to Sari with David Innes and his party.

Time dragged heavily. The ship seemed to stand still. There were adverse winds; and once, when she came on deck after sleeping, they were becalmed and a dense fog lay upon the water. O-aa could not see the length of the ship. She could see no ocean. There was only the lapping of little waves against the hull and the gentle movement of the ship to indicate that she was not floating off into space in this new element. It was a little frightening.

Every sail was set and flapping idly. A figure materialized out of the fog. O-aa saw that it was the little old man, and the little old man saw that the figure by the rail was O-aa. He glanced around. There was no one else in sight. He came closer.

"You are a hoo-doo," he said. "You brought bad winds. Now you have brought calm and fog. As long as you are aboard we'll have bad luck." He edged closer. O-aa guessed what was in his mind. She whipped out her dagger.

"Go away, eater of men," she said. "You are just one step from death."

Ah-gilak stopped. "Gol-durn it, girl," he protested, "I ain't goin' to hurt you."

"At least for once you have spoken the truth, evil old man," said O-aa. "You are not going to hurt me. Not while I have my knife. All that you intended to do was to throw me overboard."

"Of all the dod-gasted foolishness I ever heard, that there takes the cake, as the feller said."

"Of all the dod-gasted liars," O-aa mimicked, "you take the cake, as the feller said. Now go away and leave me alone." O-aa made a mental note to ask some one what the cake was. There is no cake in the stone age and no word for it.

Ah-gilak walked forward and was lost in the fog. O-aa stood now with her back against the rail, that no one might sneak up on her from behind. She knew that she had two enemies aboard—Ko and Ah-gilak. She must be always on the alert. The outlook was not pleasant. The voyage would be very long, and during it there would be many opportunities for one or the other of them to harm her.

Again she berated herself for not having accompanied David and his party. The sea was not her element. She longed for the feel of solid ground beneath her feet. Even the countless dangers of that savage world seemed less menacing than this vile old man who bragged of his cannibalism. She had seen men look at her with hunger in their eyes, but the hunger look in the watery old eyes of Ah-gilak was different. It connoted hunger for food; and it frightened her more even than would have the blazing eyes of some terrible carnivore, for it was unclean, repulsive.

A little breeze bellied the sails of the John Tyler. It sent the fog swirling about the deck. Now the ship moved again. Looking across the deck, O-aa saw something looming close alongside the John Tyler. It was a land—a great, green clad cliff half hid by the swirling fog. She heard Ah-gilak screaming orders. She heard the deep voice of Ja directing the work of the sailors—a calm, unruffled voice.

O-aa ran across the deck to the opposite rail. The great cliff towered high above, lost in the fog. It was scarcely a hundred feet away. At the waterline was a narrow beach that could scarcely be dignified by the name of beach. It was little more than a foothold at the base of this vertical escarpment.

Here was land—beloved land! Its call was irresistible. O-aa stepped to the top of the rail and dived into the sea. She struck out strongly for the little ledge. A kind Providence protected her. No voracious denizen of this swarming sea attacked her, and she reached her goal safely.

As she drew herself up onto the ledge the fog closed in again, and the John Tyler disappeared from view. But she could still hear the voices of Ah-gilak and Ja.

O-aa took stock of her situation. If the tide was out, then the ledge would be submerged at high tide. She examined the face of the cliff in her immediate vicinity; and concluded that the tide *was* out, for she could see the marks of high tides far above her head.

Because of the fog, she could not see far either to the right or to the left above her. To most, such a situation would have been appalling; but the people of Kali are cliff dwellers. And O-aa, being a Kalian, had spent all of her life scaling cliffs. She had found that there are few cliffs that offer no footholds. This is especially true of cliffs the faces of which support vegetation, and this cliff was clothed in green.

O-aa wished that the fog would go away before the tide came in. She would have liked to examine the cliff more carefully before starting the ascent. She could no longer hear voices aboard the John Tyler. O-aa was alone in a strange world that contained no other living thing. A tiny little world encompassed by fog.

A wave rolled in and lapped her ankles. O-aa looked down. The tide was coming in. Something else was coming in, also. A huge reptile with formidable jaws was swimming toward her, and it was eyeing her quite as hungrily as had Ah-gilak. It was a nameless thing to O-aa, this forty foot monster. I would have advantaged little O-aa nothing to have known that this creature that was intent on reaching up and dragging her down into the sea was Tylosaurus, one of the rulers of the Cretaceous seas of the outer crust, eons ago.

III

AH-GILAK HAD SEEN the green cliff loom close alongside the John Tyler at the same moment as had O-aa, but it connoted something very different to the ancient skipper than to O-aa. To the one it meant disaster, to the other escape. And each reacted in his own way. Ah-gilak screamed orders and O-aa dived overboard.

With the lightly freshening breeze, the ship hauled away from danger, at least from the imminent threat of that particular cliff. But who knew what lay just ahead in the fog?

Again the wind died, the sails hung limp, the fog closed in tighter than before. The tide and a strong current bore the helpless ship on. But where? Abner Perry's crude compass did 180s and 360s, as the current and the tide turned the John Tyler slowly this way and that.

"She ain't nuthin' but a dod-burned derelict," groaned Ah-gilak, "jest driftin' around. It all comes from shippin' a woman, dod-burn 'em. If we're driftin' to sea, we're all right. If we're driftin' t'other way, she'll go ashore. Gad an' Gabriel! I'd ruther pitch a whole slew o' women overboard than lose a sweet ship like the John Tyler."

"Shut up!" said Ja. "You talk too much. Listen!"

With a palm, Ah-gilak cupped an ear. "I don't hear nuthin'," he said.

"You're deaf, old man," said Ja.

"I can hear as good as the next feller, as the feller said," remonstrated Ah-gilak.

"Then you can hear the surf that I hear," said Ja.

"Surf?" screamed Ah-gilak. "Where? How far?"

"There," said Ja, pointing. "And close."

The Lo-har was fogbound. She had been cruising northeast after a futile search in the other direction. Hodon was loath to give up and admit that O-aa was hopelessly lost to him. Dian the Beautiful was apathetic. She knew that David might have been borne almost anywhere by the balloon that had carried him in search of her, and that she stood as good a chance of finding him while searching for O-aa as in any other way. But she was resigned to the fact that she would never see him again; so she encouraged Hodon to search for his O-aa.

Raj and the other Mezops were content just to sail. They loved the sea. Gamba, the Xexot, who had been a king, did not love the sea. It frightened him, but then Gamba was afraid of many things. He was not of the stuff of which kings are supposed to be made. And he was always whining and finding fault. Hodon would long since have pitched him overboard had not Dian interceded in his behalf.

"How many more sleeps before we reach your country?" he asked Dian.

"Many," she replied.

"I have already lost count of the number of times I have slept since I came aboard this thing you call a ship. We should be close to your country by now. The world is not so large that one can travel for so many sleeps without seeing it all."

"Pellucidar is very large," said Dian. "You might travel many thousands of sleeps and yet see but little of it. Furthermore, we have not been traveling toward Sari."

"What?" shrieked Gamba. "Not travelling toward your country?"

"Hodon has been searching for his mate."

"He did not find her," said Gamba, "so I suppose that we are not travelling toward Sari."

"No," said Dian. "We are getting farther and farther from Sari, at least by water."

"Make him turn around, and sail toward Sari," demanded Gamba. "I, Gamba the King do not like the ocean nor the ship."

Dian smiled. "King of what" she asked.

"I shall probably be king of Sari when we get there," said Gamba.

"Well, take my advice and don't tell Ghak the Hairy One," said Dian.

"Why not? Who is this Ghak the Hairy One?"

"He is king of Sari," explained Dian, "and he is a very large person and very fierce when he is crossed."

"I am not afraid of him," said Gamba.

Again Dian smiled.

O-aa did not scream as the great jaws of the reptile opened wide to seize her, nor did she faint. Had our foremothers of the stone age wasted time screaming and fainting, when danger threatened, the human race would have died a-borning. And perhaps the world would have been a better, kinder place to live for all the other animals who do not constantly make war upon one another as do men.

Like a human fly, O-aa scrambled up the face of the cliff a few feet; then she looked back and made a face at Tylosaurus, after which she considered carefully her new position. Because of the fog, she could see but a few yards in any direction. How high the cliff she could not know. The greenery which covered it consisted of lichen and stout liana-like vines which depended from above. As there was no earth on this vertical rock in which plant life might take root, it was obvious to O-aa that the lianas were rooted in earth at the top of the cliff. She examined them carefully. Not only were they, in themselves, tough and sturdy; but the aerial tendrils with which the vines clung to the face of the cliff added still greater strength and permanency. Making use of this natural ladder, O-aa ascended.

Some fifty feet above the surface of the sea she came to the mouth of a large cave from which emanated a foul stench—the stink of putrid carrion—and as she drew herself up and peered over the sill of the opening, three hissing, screaming little horrors rushed forward to attack her. O-aa recognized them as the young of the thipdar. Paleontologists would have classified them as pterodactyls of the Lias, but they would have been surprised at the enormous size to which these flying reptiles grow in the Inner World. A wing span of twenty feet is only average. They are one of the most dreaded of Pellucidar's many voracious carnivores.

The three that attacked O-aa were about the size of turkeys, and they came for her with distended jaws. Clinging to her support with one hand, O-aa whipped out her knife, and beheaded the leader of the attack. But the others came on, their little brains, reacting only to the urge of hunger, had no room for fear.

The girl would gladly have retreated, but the insensate little terrors gave her no respite. Sqawking and hissing, they hurled themselves upon her. She struck a terrific blow at one of them, and missed. The momentum of the blow carried her blade against the vine to which she clung, severing it just above her left hand; and O-aa toppled backward.

Fifty feet below her lay the ocean and, perhaps, Tylosaurus and Death. We, whose reactions have been slowed down by generations of civilization and soft, protected living, would doubtless have fallen to the ocean and, perhaps, Tylosaurus and Death. But not O-aa. Simultaneously, she transferred the knife to her mouth, dropped the severed vine and grabbed for new support with both hands. She found it and held. "Whe-e-ool" breathed O-aa.

It had been a close call. She started up again, but this time she detoured around the cave of the thipdars. She had much to be thankful for, including the fog. No adult thipdar had been in the cave, nor need she fear the return of one as long as the fog held.

A hundred feet above the sea she found the summit of the vertical cliff. From here, the mountain sloped upward at an angle of about forty-five degrees. Easy going for O-aa this. Practically level ground. There were trees. They kept looming up out of the fog as she advanced. Trees are beloved of Pellucidarians. Beneath their branches, sanctuary from the great earth bound carnivores.

Now that she had found trees, O-aa had no further need of fog. She wished that it would lift. She was getting as sick of the fog as she had been of the sea. But she knew that the fog was better than the sea. It would go away some time. The sea, never.

She climbed upward, alert, listening, sniffing the air. And presently she emerged from the fog into the bright sunlight of Pellucidar's eternal noon. The scene was beautiful. And if you think that primitive peoples do not appreciate beauty you are crazy. In any event, O-aa did. The mountain continued to rise gently toward its peak. Splendid trees dotted its slope. Green grass grew lush, starred with many flowers; and below her, shining bright in the sun, the fog rolled, a silent, silver sea.

By the time she reached the summit, the fog had disappeared as miraculously as it had come. O-aa looked in all directions, and her heart sank. In all directions she saw water. This single mountain rose from the depths of the ocean to form a small island. A mile away, she could see the mainland. But that mile of water seemed to the little cave girl of the mountains as effectual a barrier to escape as would a hundred miles of turbulent sea.

And then O-aa saw something else—something that sent her heart into a real nose dive. Sneaking toward her was a jalok, the fierce dog of Pellucidar. And there was no tree nearby.

IV

THE JOHN TYLER went ashore and the surf pounded her against the rocks. Ah-gilak burst into tears as he envisioned the breaking up of his beloved clipper ship. The he cursed fate and the fog and the calm, but especially he cursed O-aa. "Shut up, old man!" commanded Ja. He gave orders that the boats be lowered on the off-shore side of the ship. The powerful Mezops manned them and held them from the ship's side with their spears as the rollers came in.

Ja and Jav and Ko checked off the men to see that all were present. "Where is the girl" asked Ja. No one had seen her, and Ja sent men to search the ship for her. They returned to report that she was not on board, and Ja turned fierce eyes on Ah-gilak.

"What did you do with her, old man?" demanded Ja.

"I did nothing to her."

"You wanted to put her ashore. I think you threw her overboard."

"We do not need him any more," said Jav. "I think we should kill him."

"No! No!" screamed Ah-gilak. "I did not throw the girl overboard. I do not know what became of her. Do not kill me. I am just a poor old man who would not harm any one."

"We all know that you are a liar," said Ja, "so nothing you may say makes any difference. However, as no one saw you throw the girl overboard I shall give you the benefit of the doubt and not kill you. Instead, I shall leave you aboard the ship."

"But it will break up and I shall be drowned," pleaded Ah-gilak.

"That is your affair, not mine," said Ja. So the Mezops abandoned the wreck of the John Tyler, leaving Ah-gilak behind.

The Mezops reached the shore in safety and shortly after, the fog lifted. A strong wind sprang up, blowing from the land toward the sea. The Mezops saw the sails of the John Tyler fill.

"The old man is in bad way," said Jav.

"Look!" cried Ko. "The ship is moving out to sea."

"The tide came in and floated her," said Ja. "Maybe we should not have abandoned her so soon. I do not like the land."

"Perhaps we could overhaul her in the boats," suggested one.

So they manned the boats and paddled after the John Tyler. Ah-gilak saw them coming and guessed their intention. Impelled by the urges—fear of the Mezops and a desire for revenge—he took the wheel and steered a course that took full advantage of the wind; and the John Tyler picked up speed and showed a pretty pair of heels to the sweating Mezops, who soon gave up the chase and started back toward shore.

"The old son of a sithic!" exclaimed Jav. The sithic is a toadlike reptile.

The jalok is a big, shaggy hyaenodon, with a body as large as a leopard's but with longer legs. Jaloks usually hunt in packs, and not even the largest and fiercest of animals is safe from attack. They are without fear, and they are always hungry. O-aa knew all about jaloks, and she wished that she was up a tree—literally. She certainly was, figuratively. She was also behind the eight ball, but O-aa knew nothing of eight balls. To be behind the eight ball and up a tree at the same time is very bad business.

O-aa drew her knife and waited. The jalok lay down and cradled his powerful jaws on his oustretched front legs, and eyed O-aa. This surprised the girl. She had expected the beast to rush her. The animal looked like a big, shaggy dog; but O-aa was not deceived by appearances. She knew that sometimes jaloks were tamed, but they were never domesticated. This one was probably not hungry, and was waiting until he was.

I can't stay here forever, just waiting to be eaten, thought O-aa; so she started along slowly in the direction she had been going. The jalok got up and followed her.

Below her stretched a gentle declivity down to a narrow coastal plain. A little stream, starting from some place at her left, wound down the mountainside. It was joined by other little streams to form a little river that meandered across the plain down to the sea. It was all a scene of exquisite beauty—a little gem set in an azure sea. But for the moment it was all lost on O-aa as she glanced behind and saw the jalok following her.

If I climb a tree, thought O-aa, *the jalok will lie down beneath it until I come down or fall out.* O-aa knew her jaloks; so she kept on walking.

She had descended about a half mile when she heard a savage growl ahead and to her left. As she looked, a codon broke from the cover of some tall grass and charged her. O-aa knew that she was lost, but she held her knife in readiness and waited her end. Then something flashed by her. It was the jalok. He met the codon, a huge timber wolf, long extinct upon the outer crust, at the moment that it leaped for O-aa.

Then followed what bade fair to be a battle royal between these two savage, powerful beasts; and O-aa took advantage of their preoccupation to make good her escape. As she ran down the mountainside, the roars and growls of the battling beasts filled her ears. But not for long. Suddenly they stopped. O-aa glanced back, and again her heart sank. The jalok was coming toward her at a run. Behind him, she could see the still form of the codon lying where it had died.

O-aa stood still. The end was inevitable. She might as well face it now. The jalok stopped a few yards from her; then it moved toward her again *wagging its tail!* That has meant the same thing in the dog family from the

Cretaceous age to the present day, on the outer crust or in the Inner World at the earth's core.

O-aa sheathed her knife and waited. The jalok came close and looked up into her face, and O-aa placed a hand upon its head and scratched it behind an ear. The great beast licked her hand, and when O-aa started down toward the sea again, it walked at her side, brushing against her. Not since she had lost Hodon had O-aa felt so safe. She tangled her fingers in the shaggy collar that ringed the jalok's neck, as though she would never let him go again.

Until this moment she had not realized how friendless and alone she had been since she had said goodby to David and Abner Perry and Ghak. But now she had both a friend and a protector. O-aa was almost happy.

As they neared the beach, the jalok moved toward the right; and O-aa followed him. He led her to a little cove. Here she saw an outrigger canoe drawn up on the beach above high water. The jalok stopped beside it and looked up at her. In the canoe were the weapons and the loincloth of a man. And in these things, O-aa read a story. She could see by the general appearance of the articles in the canoe that they had lain untouched for some time. She knew that a man did not go naked and unarmed far from his weapons. And thus she reconstructed the story: A warrior had paddled from the mainland with his jalok to hunt, perhaps. He had gone into the sea to bathe, and had been seized and devoured by one of the innumerable voracious creatures which swarm in the waters of the Korsar Az. Or perhaps a thipdar had swooped down and seized him. At any rate, she was confident that he had gone never to return and she had fallen heir to his weapons, his canoe, and his jalok. But there remained a mile of terrifying water between herself and the mainland!

She looked across to the farther shore just in time to see the John Tyler put to sea. She could not know that the ship bore only Ah-gilak. The others, far down the coast, were too far away for her to see them. She looked at the canoe and out again across the water. The jalok lay at her feet. She ruffled his shaggy mane with a sandalled foot, and he looked up at her and bared his fangs in a canine grin—terrible fangs set in mighty jaws that could tear her to pieces in a moment.

O-aa sat down on the ground beside the jalok and tried to plan for the future. What she was really trying to do was raise her courage to a point that would permit her to launch the canoe and paddle across that fearsome mile. Every time it reached the sticking point she would look out and see a terrible head or a dorsal fin break the surface of the sea. Then her courage would do a nose dive. And when she realized that the wind was against her, she breathed a sigh of relief for so excellent an excuse to delay her departure.

She examined the contents of the canoe more closely. She saw a stone knife, a stone tipped spear, a tomahawk with a well shaped stone head and a wooden haft, a bow, a quiver of arrows, two paddles, a pole six or seven feet long, a woven fibre mat, and some cordage of braided grasses. These articles suggested something to O-aa that would never have entered her head before she began her adventures on that unfamiliar medium which rolled and tossed in illimitable vastness to form the Sojar Az and Korsar Az. O-aa had learned much that was no part of the education of a cave girl from Kali.

She examined further and found a hole in a thwart and beneath it a corresponding receptacle in the bottom of the canoe. Now she knew what the pole was for and the fibre mat and the cordage. All she had to do, she decided, was wait for a favorable wind. That would be much better than paddling; and as she intended to wait for a strong wind, it would result in a much shorter passage, which would cut down the odds that were always against the survival of any who put to sea in Pellucidar.

Her doom postponed until the wind changed, O-aa realized that she was hungry. She took the spear, the quiver of arrows, and the bow and set forth to hunt. The jalok accompanied her.

V

AH-GILAK LASHED the wheel and went below to ascertain the damage that had resulted from the ship's pounding on the rocks. He found her sound as a roach, for the Sarians had selected their lumber well and built well.

Returning to the wheel, he took stock of his situation. It did not appear too rosy. Twenty or thirty men were required to man the John Tyler. Obviously, one little old man could not. With the wind he had now, he could hold on as long as there was ocean ahead. He might even maneuver the ship a little, for Ah-gilak had spent a lifetime under sail. But a storm would be his undoing.

Without stars or moon, with a stationary sun, he could not navigate even had he had the necessary instruments and a dependable chart, none of which he had. Nor could he have navigated the nameless strait could he have found it. Ah-gilak was in a bad way, and he knew it; so he decided to beach John Tyler at the earliest opportunity and take his chances on land.

O-aa followed the little river. She moved warily, taking advantage of cover-trees, tall grasses, underbrush. She moved silently, as silently as the great beast at her side. Her left hand grasped her bow and several arrows, another arrow was fitted to the bow and drawn part way back, presenting an analogy to a loaded .45 with a full clip in the magazine and the safety off.

Suddenly three horses broke from nearby underbrush, and in quick succession two arrows brought two of them down. O-aa rushed in and finished them with her knife, while the jalok pursued and dragged down the third.

O-aa picked up the two horses she had shot and waited while the jalok devoured his kill; then they started back toward the canoe. The girl knew her prey as orthopi; but you would have recognized them as Hyracotherii of the Lower Eocene, the early ancestors of Seabiscuit and Whirlaway, little creatures about the size of foxes.

The girl gave one of the orthopi to the jalok; then she made fire and cooked much of the other for herself. Her hunger satisfied, she lay down beneath a tree and slept.

When she awoke, she looked around for the jalok; but he was nowhere to be seen. O-aa was swept by a wave of loneliness. She had been heartened by the promise of companionship and protection which the savage beast had offered. Suddenly the future looked very black. In her fit of despondency, the shore of the mainland seemed to have receded; and she peopled the world with terrifying menaces, which was wholly superfluous, as Nature had already attended to that.

She gave herself up to self-pity for only a short time; then she lifted her chin and braced her shoulders and was the self-sufficient cave girl of Kali once more. She looked out across the water, and realized that the wind had changed while she slept and was blowing strongly toward the mainland.

Going to the canoe, she stepped the mast and rigged the sail to the best of her ability, which was not mean; for O-aa was a highly intelligent young person, observant and with a retentive memory. She tugged on the canoe and found that she could move it, but before she dragged it into the sea she decided to look around once more for the jalok.

She was glad that she had, for she saw him coming

down toward her carrying something on his back. When he was closer, she saw that it was the carcass of small deer which he had thrown across his shoulders, still holding to it with his jaws—carrying it as the African lion has been known to carry its prey.

He came up to her, wagging his tail, and laid his kill at her feet. O-aa was so glad to see him that she dropped to her knees and put both arms around his shaggy collar and hugged him. Doubtless, this was something new in the jalok's life; but he seemed to understand and like it, for he bared his fangs in a grin and licked the girl's face.

Now O-aa was faced with a problem. If she waited to cook some of the deer and eat, the wind might change. On the other hand she couldn't bear to abandon so much good meat. The alternative was to take it with her, but would the jalok let her take the carcass away from him? She determined to experiment. Seizing the deer, she started to drag it down toward the water's edge. The jalok watched her; then, apparently getting the idea, he took hold of it and helped her. O-aa realized what she had become almost convinced of, that here was a well trained hunting animal that had worked with and for his dead master.

Having deposited the deer on the beach, O-aa dragged the canoe down to the water. It taxed her strength, but at last she was rewarded by seeing it afloat. Then she carried the deer to it.

She had no name for the jalok, and did not know how to call him to get into the canoe. She did not need to know. As she climbed over the gunwale, he leaped aboard and took his station in the bow.

The stern of the canoe was still resting on the sandy bottom, but the sail had filled and was tugging to free it. A few vigorous shoves with a paddle freed the little craft, and O-aa was on her way across the frightful water.

Steering with a paddle, O-aa kept the nose of her craft

pointed at a spot on the opposite shore and the wind always directly astern. As the wind freshened, the canoe fairly raced through the water. This was much better than paddling and much faster. O-aa could imagine that this would be a delightful way to travel were it not for the innumerable horrors that infested the ocean and the terrific storms which occasionally whipped it into fury.

Constantly searching the surface of the sea for signs of danger, the girl glanced back and saw the long neck and small head of a tandoraz, which, in Pellucidarian, means mammoth of the sea. The reptile was following the canoe and gaining on it slowly. O-aa well knew what was in that tiny brain. She also knew that the best she could do with any of her weapons was to infuriate it.

Had she known a god, she would have prayed to him for more wind; but, knowing no god, she had to depend entirely on her own resources. Suddenly her eyes fell upon the deer. If she couldn't destroy the tandoraz, perhaps she might escape it if she could but delay it.

The shore was not far away now, and the canoe was racing through the water almost as fast as the reptile was swimming; although O-aa was none too sure that the creature was exerting itself anywhere near to the limit of its powers. Nor was it.

With a steel knife that David had given her she ripped open the belly of the carcass and eviscerated it. Glancing back, she saw that the tandoraz was almost upon her. The cold, reptilian eyes glared down upon her. The snake-like jaws gaped wide.

Dragging the viscera to the stern of the canoe, she dropped it overboard directly in front of the hissing creature. The next couple of seconds were an eternity. Would the thing take the bait? Would the stupid mind in its tiny brain be thus easily diverted from the fixed idea that it had been following?

The odor of fresh animal matter and blood turned the

scale in O-aa's favor. The neck arched and the head struck viciously at the viscera. As the tandoraz stopped to tear at this luscious tid-bit, the canoe drew away. The distance widened. The shore was quite close now, but there was a heavy surf pounding on a sandy beach.

O-aa had resumed the paddle and was steering once more. Her heart was filled with rejoicing. Her escape from death had been all too close, and by comparison the menace of the heavy surf seemed trivial. She looked back at the tandoraz, and her heart missed a beat. Evidently sensing that its prey was escaping, it was coming through the water at terrific speed in pursuit.

O-aa glanced forward again. She was confident that the canoe would reach the surf before the tandoraz could overhaul it. But what then? She didn't believe that the canoe could live in what seemed to her the mountainous waves that broke upon the shore and rolled far up the beach. The reptile would be upon them as they were thrown into the water. It could not get them all. She could only hope that the thing would seize the carcass of the deer rather than upon her or the jalok which still sat in the bow of the canoe all unconscious of the tragedy of the past few minutes.

Again the "mammoth of the sea" loomed above her. The canoe was caught by a great roller and lifted high. O-aa felt a sudden surging rush as though the canoe, sentient of impending danger, sought to escape in a burst of speed.

Riding high now, just over the crest of the roller, the outrigger raced toward the beach like a frightened deer; and in a swirl of foamy water came to rest on the sand well out of reach of the tandoraz. O-aa leaped out and held it from being drawn out again by the receding waves, and with the next she dragged it well up to safety. Then she threw herself down on the sand, exhausted.

The jalok came and sat down beside her. She stroked

its shaggy coat. "We made it," she said. "I didn't think we should." The jalok said nothing. At least not in words. He put a great paw on her and licked her ear. "I shall have to give you a name," said O-aa. "Let me see. Ah, I have it! Rahna. That is a good name for you, Rahna." Rahna means killer.

VI

O-aa sat up and took stock of her situation. Beyond the sandy beach the ground rose slowly to a low ridge four or five hundred yards inland. Beyond the ridge were rolling hills, upcurving in this horizonless world to blend with distant mountains which, in turn, blended into the haze of distance.

The ground between O-aa and the ridge was carpeted with Bermuda grass and stunted shrubs, with here and there a windblown tree. The trees reminded O-aa that she was courting death to lie here thus in the open, an invitation to the first winged reptile that might discover her.

She arose and returned to the canoe, where she threw the carcass of the deer across one shoulder and gathered up her weapons. Then she looked down at the jalok and said, "Come, Rahna!" and walked to the nearest tree.

A man coming down out of the rolling hills paused at the edge of the low ridge which O-aa had seen a few hundred yards inland. At the man's side was a jalok. The man was naked but for a G-string. He carried a stone tipped spear, a stone knife, a bow and arrows. When he saw the girl, he dropped to the ground, where he was hidden by low bushes. He spoke to the jalok, and it lay down beside him.

The man noted the canoe pulled up on the beach. He noted the jalok which accompanied the girl. He saw the carcass of the deer. At first he had thought the girl a man, but closer inspection revealed that he had been mistaken. He was also mystified, for he knew that here there should be no girl with a jalok and a canoe. This was the man's country, and the men of the stone age knew all that went on in their own little neck-of-the-woods.

O-aa cut a generous hindquarter from the carcass and gave it to Rahna. She used the tomahawk and her steel knife. Then she gathered dry grasses and bits of dead wood, made fire, and cooked her own meal. O-aa, a slender little blonde, tore at the meat with firm, white teeth; and devoured enough for a couple of farm hands. Pellucidarians store up energy through food, for oftentimes they may have to go for long periods without food. Similarly, they store up rest by long sleeps.

Having stored up all the energy she could hold, O-aa lay down to store up rest. She was awakened by the growling of Rahna. He was standing beside her, his hair bristling along his spine.

O-aa saw a man approaching. A jalok paced at his side. The girl seized her bow and arrows and stood up. Both jaloks were growling now. O-aa fitted an arrow to her bow. "Go away!" she said.

"I am not going to hurt you," said the man, who had seen that O-aa was very lovely and very desirable.

"I could have told you that myself," replied the girl. "If you tried to, I could kill you. Rahna could kill you. My mate, my father, or my seven brothers could kill you." It had occurred to O-aa that possibly thirteen brothers were too many to sound plausible.

The man grinned and sat down. "Who are you?" he asked.

"I am O-aa, daughter of Oose, King of Kali. My mate is Hodon the Fleet One. My seven brothers are very large, fierce men. My three sisters are the most beautiful women in Pellucidar, and I am more beautiful than they."

The man continued to grin. "I never heard of Kali," he said. "Where is it?"

"There," said O-aa, pointing. "You must be a very ignorant person," she added, "for Kali is the largest country in the world. It requires the caves of a whole mountain range to house her warriors who are as many as the grasses that you can see as far as you can see."

"You are very beautiful," said the man, "but you are a great liar. If you were not so beautiful, I would beat you for lying so much. Maybe I shall anyway."

"Try it," challenged O-aa. "I have not killed anyone since I last slept."

"Ah," said the man, "so that is it? You killed my brother."

"I did not kill your brother. I never saw your brother."

"Then how did you get his canoe, his jalok, and his weapons? I recognize them all."

It was then that O-aa realized that she had lied a little too much for her own health; so she decided to tell the truth. "I will tell you," she said.

"And see that you tell the truth," said the man.

"You see that mountain that sticks up out of the sea?" she asked, pointing at the island. The man nodded. "I leaped into the sea," continued O-aa, "on the other side of that mountain from a big canoe to escape an old man whose name is not Dolly Dorcas. Then I crossed to this side of the mountain where I saw Rahna."

"His name is not Rahna," said the man.

"Maybe it wasn't, but it is now. And don't interrupt me any more. Rahna saved me from a codon, and we became friends. We came down to the edge of the water and found a canoe with these weapons and a man's loincloth in it. If it was your brother's canoe, I think he must have gone in the water and been eaten by a tandoraz, or possibly a thipdar flew down and got him. I did not kill your brother. How could I have killed a warrior when I was armed only with a knife? As you can see, all my other weapons are those I found in the canoe."

The man thought this over. "I believe that you are telling the truth at last," he said; "because had you killed my brother, his jalok would have killed you."

"Now will you go away and leave me alone?" demanded O-aa.

"Then what will you do?"

"I shall return to Kali."

"Do you know how far it is to Kali?"

"No. Kali is not far from the shore of the Lural Az. Do you know how far it is to the Lural Az?"

"I never heard of the Lural Az," said the man.

"You are a very ignorant person," said O-aa.

"Not as ignorant as you, if you think you can reach Kali by going in the direction you pointed. In that direction there is a range of mountains that you cannot cross."

"I can go around it," said O-aa.

"You are a very brave girl," said the man. "Let us be friends. Come with me to my village. Perhaps we can help you on your way to Kali. At least, warriors can go with you as far as the mountains, beyond which none of our people have ever gone."

"How do I know that you will not harm me?" asked O-aa.

The man threw down all his weapons and came toward her with his hands raised. Then she knew that he would not harm her. "We will be friends," she said. "What is your name?"

"I am Utan of the tribe of Zurts." He turned and spoke to his jalok, saying, "Padang." "Tell your jalok that we are friends," he said to O-aa.

"Padang, Rahna," said O-aa. Padang is Pellucidarian for friend or friends.

The two jaloks approached one another a little stiff-legged; but when they had sniffed about each other, they relaxed and wagged their tails, for they had been raised together in the village of Zurts. But there was no playful bouncing, as there might have been between domesti-cated dogs. These were savage wild beasts with all the majesty and dignity that is inherent in their kind. Adult wild beasts have far more dignity than man. When peo-ple say in disgust that a person acts like a beast, they really mean that he acts like a man.

"You can handle a paddle?" Utan asked O-aa.

"I have paddled all over the seas of Pellucidar," said O-aa.

"There you go again! Well, I suppose that I shall have to get used to it. Anyway, you can help me paddle my brother's canoe to a safe place."

"It is my canoe," said O-aa.

Utan grinned. "And I suppose that you are going to paddle it across the mountains to Kali?"

"I could if I wanted to," said O-aa.

"The better I know you," said Utan, "the less I doubt it. If there are other girls like you in Kali, I think I shall go with you and take one of them for my mate."

"They wouldn't have you," said O-aa. "You are too short. You can't be much more than six feet tall. All our men are seven feet—except those who are eight feet."

"Come on, little liar," said Utan, "and we will get the canoe."

Together they dragged the outrigger into the water. O-aa climbed into the bow, the two jaloks leaped in, and just at the right moment Utan gave the craft a shove and jumped in himself.

"Paddle now!" he said. "And paddle hard."

The canoe rose to the crest of a roller and slid down the other side. The two paddled furiously until they were beyond the heavy rollers; then they paralleled the shore until they came to the mouth of a small river, up which Utan turned.

It was a pretty little river overhung by trees and full of crocodiles. They paddled up it for about a mile until they came to rapids. Here, Utan turned in to the bank on their right; and together, they dragged the canoe up among the lush verdure, where it was well hidden.

"Your canoe will be quite safe here," said Utan, "until you are ready to paddle it over the mountains to Kali. Now we will go to my village."

VII

HODON, RAJ, DIAN, AND GAMBA were standing on the quarterdeck of the Lo-har; and, as always, Hodon was searching the surface of the sea for the little speck that, in his heart of hearts, he knew he would never see—the little speck that would be the Sari in which O-aa had been carried away by winds and currents on the Sojar Az and, doubtless, through the nameless strait into the Korsar Az. The little lateen rigged Lo-har had been beset by fog and calm, but now the weather had cleared and a fair wind filled the single sail.

Hodon shook his head sadly. "I am afraid it is hopeless, Dian," he said. Dian the Beautiful nodded in acquiescence.

"My men are becoming restless," said Raj. "They have been away from home for many, many sleeps. They want to get back to their women."

"All right," said Hodon. "Turn back for Sari."

As the little ship came about, Gamba pointed. "What is that?" he asked.

They all looked. In the haze of the distance there was a white speck on the surface of the sea. "It is a sail," said Raj.

"O-aa!" exclaimed Hodon.

The wind was blowing directly from the direction in which the sail lay; so the Lo-har had to tack first one way and then another. But it was soon apparent that the strange ship was sailing before the wind directly toward them, and so the distance between was constantly growing shorter.

"That is not the Sari," said Raj. "That is a big ship with more sail than I have ever seen before."

"It must be a Korsar," said Dian. "If it is, we are lost."

"We have cannon," said Hodon, "and men to fight them."

"Turn around," said Gamba, "and go the other way. Maybe they have not seen us."

"You always want to run away," said Dian, contemptuously. "We shall hold our course and fight them."

"Turn around!" screamed Gamba. "It is a command! I am king!"

"Shut up!" said Raj. "Mezops do not run away."

"Nor Sarians," said Dian.

The village of the Zurts, to which Utan led O-aa, lay in a lovely valley through which a little river wandered. It was not a village of caves such as O-aa was accustomed to in Kali. The houses here were of bamboo thatched with grass, and they stood on posts some ten feet above the ground. Crude ladders led up to their doorways.

There were many of these houses; and in the doorways, or on the ground below them, were many warriors and women and children and almost as many jaloks as there were people.

As Utan and O-aa approached, the jaloks of the village froze into immobility, the hair along their backbones erect. Utan shouted, "Padang!" And when they recognized him, some of the warriors shouted, "Padang!" Then the jaloks relaxed, and Utan and O-aa entered the village in safety; but there had to be much sniffing and smelling on the part of the jaloks before an *entente cordiale* was established.

Warriors and women gathered around Utan and O-aa, asking many questions. O-aa was a curiosity here, for she was very blonde, while the Zurts had hair of raven black. They had never seen a blonde before.

Utan told them all that he knew about O-aa, and asked Jalu the chief if she might remain in the village. "She is from a country called Kali which lies the other side of the Terrible Mountains. She is going to try to cross them, and from what I have seen of her she will cross them if any one can."

"No one can," said Jalu, "and she may remain—for thirty sleeps," he added. "If one of our warriors has taken her for a mate in the meantime, she may remain always."

"None of your warriors will take me for a mate," said O-aa, "and I will leave long before I have slept thirty times."

"What makes you think none of my warriors will take you for a mate?" demanded Jalu.

"Because I wouldn't have one of them."

Jalu laughed. "If a warrior wanted you he would not ask you. He would take you."

It was O-aa's turn to laugh. "He would get a knife in his belly," she said. "I have killed many men. Furthermore, I have a mate. If I am harmed, he would come and my eleven brothers and my father, the king; and they would kill you all. They are very fierce men. They are nine feet tall. My mate is Hodon the Fleet One. He is a Sarian. The Sarians are very fierce people. But if you are kind to me, no harm will befall you. While I am here, Rahna and I will hunt for you. I am a wonderful hunter. I am probably the best hunter in all Pellucidar."

"I think you are probably the best liar," said Jalu. "Who is Rahna?"

"My jalok," said O-aa, laying her hand on the head of the beast standing beside her.

"Women do not hunt, nor do they have jaloks," said Jalu.

"I do," said O-aa.

A half smile curved the lip of Jalu. He found himself admiring this yellow haired stranger girl. She had courage, and that was a quality that Jalu the chief understood and admired. He had never seen so much of it in a woman before.

A warrior stepped forward. "I will take her as my mate," he said, "and teach her a woman's place. What she needs is a beating."

O-aa's lip curved in scorn. "Try it, bowlegs," she said.

The warrior flushed, for he was very bowlegged and was sensitive about it. He took another step toward O-aa, threateningly.

"Stop, Zurk!" commanded Jalu. "The girl may remain here for thirty sleeps without mating. If she stays longer, you may take her—if you can. But I think she will kill you."

Zurk stood glaring at O-aa. "When you are mine," he snarled, "the first thing I will do is beat you to death."

Jalu turned to one of the women. "Hala," he directed, "show this woman a house in which she may sleep."

"Come," said Hala to O-aa.

She took her to a house at the far end of the village. "No one lives here now," she said. "The man and the woman who lived here were killed by a tarag not long ago."

O-aa looked at the ladder and up at the doorway. "How can my jalok get up there?" she asked.

Hala looked at her in surprise. "Jaloks do not come into the houses," she explained. "They lie at the foot of the ladders to warn their owners of danger and to protect them. Did you not know this?"

"We do not have tame jaloks in my country," said O-aa.

"You are lucky that you have one here, now that you have made an enemy of Zurk. He is a bad man; not at all like Jalu, his father."

So, thought O-aa, *I have made an enemy of the chief's son.* She shrugged her square little shoulders.

Ah-gilak had bowled along in a southwesterly direction for some time before a good wind. Then the wind died. Ah-gilak cursed. He cursed many things, but principally he cursed O-aa, who had brought all his misfortunes upon him, according to his superstition.

When the wind sprang up again, it blew in the opposite direction from that in which it had been blowing before the calm. Ah-gilak danced up and down in rage. But he could do nothing about it. He could sail in only one way, and that was with the wind. So he sailed back in a north-easterly direction. He lashed the wheel and went below to eat and sleep.

VIII

As THE LO-HAR and John Tyler approached one another, the former made no effort to avoid the larger ship. Her guns were loaded and manned, and she was prepared to fight.

It was Raj who first noticed something peculiar about the strange ship. "There is no one on deck," he said. "There is no one at the wheel. She is a fine ship," he added half to himself. Then an idea popped into his head. "Let's capture her," he said.

"No! No!" cried Gamba. "They haven't seen us. Sail

away as fast as you can."

"Can you bring the Lo-har alongside her?" asked Dian.

"Yes," said Jav. He summoned his men from below and gave them their orders.

The Lo-har came about ahead of the John Tyler which was making far better headway than the smaller vessel. As the John Tyler overhauled her, Jav drew in closer to the other ship. As their sides touched, the agile Mezops swarmed aboard the John Tyler with lines and made the Lo-har fast to her.

The impact of the two ships as they came together awoke Ah-gilak. "Dod-burn it! what now?" he cried, as he scrambled up the ladder to the main deck. "Tarnation!" he exclaimed as he saw the score of Mezops facing him. "I've gone plumb looney after all." He shut his eyes and turned his head away. Then he peeked from a corner of one eye. The copper colored men were still there.

"It's the little Ah-gilak," said one of the Mezops. "He eats people."

Now Ah-gilak saw more people coming over the side of his ship, and saw the sail of the little Lo-har. He saw Raj and Hodon, and a beautiful girl whom he had never seen before. With them was a yellow man. But now Ah-gilak realized what had happened and the great good luck that had overtaken him at the very moment when there seemed not a ray of hope in all the future.

"Gad and Gabriel!" he exclaimed. "It never rains but they's a silver lining, as the feller said. Now I got a crew. Now we can get the hell out o' this here Korsar Az an' back to Sari."

"Who else is aboard?" asked Hodon.

"Not a livin' soul but me." He thought quickly and decided that perhaps he had better not tell all the truth. "You see we had a little bad luck—run ashore in a storm. When the crew abandoned ship, I guess they plumb forgot me; and before I could get ashore, the wind changed and the tide came in an', by all tarnation, the first thing I knew I was a-sailin' off all by myself."

"Who else was aboard?" insisted Hodon.

"Well, they was Ja, and Jav, and Ko, an' a bunch of other Mezops. They was the ones that abandoned ship. But before that O-aa got a yen to go ashore—"

"O-aa?" cried Hodon. "She was aboard this ship? Where is she?"

"I was just a'tellin you. She got a yen to go ashore, and jumped overboard."

"Jumped overboard?" Hodon's voice rang with incredulity. "I think you are lying, old man," he said.

"Cross my heart, hope to die," said Ah-gilak.

"How did she get aboard this ship?" continued Hodon.

"Why, we picked her up out of a canoe in the nameless strait; and she told us where David was, an' we went back an' rescued him."

"David?" exclaimed Dian. "Where is he?"

"Well, before the John Tyler went ashore, David an' Abner Perry an' Ghak an' all his Sarian warriors decided they could get back to Sari quicker across country than they could by sailin' back. Course they was plumb looney, but—"

"Where did they go ashore?" asked Dian.

"Gad an' Gabriel! How'd I know? They ain't no charts, they ain't no moon, they ain't no stars, and the dang sun don't never move; so they ain't no time. They might o' went ashore twenty years ago, for all a body can tell."

"Would you recognize the coast where they landed?" persisted Dian.

"I might an' I might not. Reckon as how I could though."

"Could you recognize the spot where O-aa jumped overboard?" asked Hodon.

"Reckon not. Never seed it. She jumped over in a fog."

"Haven't you any idea?"

"Well, now maybe." Ah-gilak being certain that O-aa had drowned or been eaten by one of the reptiles that swarm the Korsar Az, felt that it would be safe to give what information he could. "As a matter of fact," he continued, "'t warn't far from where the John Tyler went ashore."

"And you would recognize that spot?"

"I might an' I might not. If I recalls correctly they was an island 'bout a mile off shore near where the John Tyler hit."

"Well, let's get going," said Hodon.

"Where?" demanded Ah-gilak.

"Back along the coast to where O-aa 'jumped overboard' and to where David Innes went ashore."

"Now wait, young feller," remonstrated Ah-gilak. "Don't you go forgettin' that I'm skipper o' this ship. It's me as'll give orders aboard this hooker."

Hodon turned to Raj. "Have your men bring all the water, provisions, ammunition, and personal belongings from the Lo-har; then set her adrift."

Ah-gilak pointed a finger at Hodon. "Hold on young feller—"

"Shut up!" snapped Hodon, and then to Raj: "You will captain the John Tyler, Raj."

"Gad and Gabriel!" screamed Ah-gilak. "I designed her, I named her, an' I been skipper of her ever since she was launched. You can't do this to me."

"I can, I have, and I'll do more if you give me any trouble," said Hodon. "I'll throw you overboard, you old scoundrel."

Ah-gilak subsided and went away and sulked. He knew that Hodon's was no idle threat. These men of the Stone Age held life lightly. He set his mind to the task of evolving a plan by which he could be revenged without incriminating himself. Ah-gilak had a shrewd Yankee mind unfettered by any moral principles or conscience.

He leaned against the rail and glared at Hodon. Then his eyes wandered to Dian, and he glared at her. Another woman! Bad luck! And with this thought the beginnings of a plan commenced to take shape. It was not a wholly satisfactory and devastating plan, but it was better than nothing. And presently he was aided by a contingency which Hodon had not considered.

With the useful cargo of the Lo-har transferred to the John Tyler and the former set adrift, Raj came to Hodon, a worried expression on his fine face.

"This," he said, with a wave of a hand which embraced the John Tyler, "is such a ship as I and my men have never seen before. She is a mass of sails and ropes and spars, all unfamiliar to us. We cannot sail her."

For a moment Hodon was stunned. Being a landsman, such a possibility had never occurred to him. He looked astern at the little Lo-har, from which the larger ship was rapidly drawing away. Hodon realized that he had been a trifle precipitate. While there was yet time, perhaps it would be well to lower the boats and return to the Lo-har. The idea was mortifying.

Then Raj made a suggestion. "The old man could teach us," he said. "If he will," he added with a note of doubt in his voice.

"He will," snapped Hodon, and strode over to Ah-gilak. Raj accompanied him.

"Ah-gilak," he said to the old man, "you will sail the ship, but Raj will still be captain. You will teach him and his men all that is necessary."

"So you are not going to throw me overboard?" said Ah-gilak with a sneer.

"Not yet," said Hodon, "but if you do not do as I have said and do it well, I will."

"You got your nerve, young feller, askin' me, a Yankee

skipper to serve as sailin' master under this here gol-durned red Indian."

Neither Hodon nor Raj had the slightest idea what a red Indian was, but from Ah-gilak's tone of voice they were both sure that the copper colored Mezop had been insulted.

"I'll sail her fer ye," continued Ah-gilak, "but as skipper."

"Come!" said Hodon to Raj. "We will throw him overboard."

As the two men seized him, Ah-gilak commenced to scream. "Don't do it," he cried. "I'll navigate her under Raj. I was only foolin'. Can't you take a joke?"

So the work of training Raj and his Mezops commenced at once. They were quick to learn, and Ah-gilak did a good job of training them; because his vanity made it a pleasure to show off his superior knowledge. But he still nursed his plan for revenge. His idea was to cause dissension, turning the copper colored Mezops against the white Hodon and Dian. Of course Ah-gilak had never heard of Communists, but he was nonetheless familiar with one of their techniques. As he worked with the Mezops, he sought to work on what he considered their ignorance and superstition to implant the idea that a woman on shipboard would be certain to bring bad luck and that Dian was only there because of Hodon. He also suggested to them that the latter felt superior to the Mezops because of his color, that he looked down on them as inferior, and that it was not right that he should give orders to Raj. He nursed the idea that it would be well for them all should Dian and Hodon accidently fall overboard.

The Mezops were neither ignorant nor superstitious, nor had they ever heard of race consciousness or racial discrimination. They listened, but they were not impressed. They were only bored. Finally, one of them said to Ah-gilak, "Old man, you talk too much about matters which have nothing to do with sailing this ship. We will not throw Hodon the Fleet One overboard, neither will we throw Dian the Beautiful overboard. If we throw anyone overboard it will be you."

Ah-gilak subsided.

IX

After O-aa had slept, she came to the doorway of her house and looked around. The village seemed very quiet. There were only a few people in sight and they were at the far end of the village. She descended the ladder. Rahna, who had been lying at the foot of it, stood up and wagged his tail. O-aa scratched him between his ears.

"I am hungry," she said; "so you must be, too. We will hunt."

She had brought her weapons. Those of the Stone Age who would survive have their weapons always at hand.

"Come, Rahna!" she said, and started up the valley away from the village.

A man, standing in the doorway of a hut farther down the village street, saw them leave. It was Zurk, the son of Jalu the chief. When a turn in the little valley hid them from his sight, he started after them with his jalok. He was a heavy barreled man, short on his bowed legs; and he lurched from side to side a little as though one leg were shorter than the other. His face was coarse and brutal, with beetling brows overhanging close-set eyes.

O-aa and Rahna moved silently up the valley, searching for game. There was a high wind blowing from the direction of the sea, and presently the sun was obscured by black clouds. There was a flash of lightning followed by the deep roar of thunder. The wind rose to violence and rain commenced to fall. But none of these things appeased O-aa's hunger; so she continued to hunt.

The valley turned suddenly to the right, paralleling the coast; and it became narrower. Its walls were neither high nor steep at this point; so O-aa ascended the right hand wall and came out upon a tree dotted mesa. Here there were tall grasses in which the smaller game might hide.

And Zurk followed with his jalok. O-aa's spoor in the light mud of the new fallen rain was easy to follow. When Zurk came out upon the mesa, O-aa, who had been advancing slowly, was not far ahead. So intent was she on her search for game that Zurk closed rapidly on her without attracting her attention or that of Rahna. The wind and the rain and the rumbling thunder were all on the side of Zurk.

Zurk's plan was made. He would shoot the girl's jalok; then she would be at his mercy. He closed up the distance between them to make sure that he would not miss. He fitted an arrow to his bow. He made no sound, but something made O-aa look behind her at that very moment.

Her own bow was ready for the kill, for any game that she or Rahna might flush. Recognizing Zurk, seeing his bow drawn, she wheeled and loosed an arrow. Zurk's bow string twanged simultaneously with hers, but the arrow was aimed at O-aa and not at Rahna.

Zurk missed, but O-aa's arrow drove through the man's shoulder. Then O-aa turned and fled. Zurk knew that on his short bowed legs he could not overtake her. He spoke sharply to his jalok and pointed at the fleeing girl. "Rah!" he snapped. Rah means kill.

The powerful, savage brute bounded in pursuit.

The seas fled before the wind, mounting as the wind mounted. The John Tyler carried but a rag of sail. She handled well, she was seaworthy. Ah-gilak was proud of her. Even when the storm reached almost tornado proportions he did not fear for her.

Gamba the king, cowering below, was terrified, reduced almost to gibbering idiocy by fear. Dian watched him with disgust. And this thing had dared to speak to her of love! Hodon was nervous below deck. Like all mountain men, he wanted to be out in the open. He wanted to face the storm and the danger where he could see them. Below, he was like a caged beast. The ship was pitching wildly, but Hodon managed to fight his way to a ladder and then to the deck above.

Both the wind and the current had combined with malevolent fury in an attempt to hurl the John Tyler on the all too near shore. Dead ahead loomed the green island upon which O-aa had been cast when she leaped overboard in the fog. Ah-gilak realized that he could make no offing there, that he would have to pass between the island and the shore, only a bare mile away. And through unchartered waters, below the tumbling surface of which might lie reefs and rocks. Ah-gilak was not happy.

Hodon saw the mountainous waves and wondered that any ship could live in such a sea. Being a landsman, he saw the high seas as the only menace. Ah-gilak feared for the things he could not see—the reefs and the rocks —and the current that he and the ship fought. It was a titanic battle.

Hodon, clinging to a stanchion to keep from falling, was quite unconscious of a real danger that confronted him on the deck of the John Tyler. The ship rose to meet the great seas and then drove deep into the troughs, but so far she had shipped but little green water.

Ah-gilak saw the man, and his toothless mouth grimaced. The wind and the blinding rain beat about him. The tornado whipped his long white beard. *There won't be no call to throw the dod-burned idjit overboard,* he thought. Raj saw Hodon and called a warning to him, but the wind drove his voice down his throat.

Just before the ship reached the shelter of the island's lee, a monstrous sea loomed above her. It broke, tons of it, over her, submerging her. The John Tyler staggered to the terrific impact, then slowly she rose, shaking the water from her.

Ah-gilak looked and grinned. Hodon was no longer by the stanchion. In the shelter of the island, Ah-gilak hove to and dropped anchor. The John Tyler had weathered the storm and was safe.

Raj's eyes searched the tumbling waters, but they were rewarded by no sight of Hodon. The Mezop shook his head sadly. He had liked the Sarian. Later, when Dian came on deck, he told her; and she, too, was sad. But death comes quickly and often in the Stone Age.

"Perhaps it is just as well," said Dian. "They are both gone now, and neither is left to grieve." She was thinking of how often she had wished for death when she had thought David was dead.

Ah-gilak shed crocodile tears, but he did not fool the Mezops. Had they not known that it would have been impossible, they would have thought that he had been instrumental in throwing Hodon overboard; and Ah-gilak would have gone over, too.

A great comber threw Hodon far up the beach, and left him exhausted and half dead. The enormous sea had buffetted him. His head had been beneath the surface more often than it had been above. But the tide and the wind and the current had been with him. As had a kindly Providence, for no terrible creature of the deep had seized him. Perhaps the very turbulence of the water had saved him, keeping the great reptiles down in the relative quiet far below the surface.

Hodon lay for a long time where the sea had spewed

him. Occasionally a wave would roll up and surge around him, but none had the depth or volume to drag him back into the sea.

At last he got slowly to his feet. He looked back and saw the John Tyler riding at anchor behind the island. Because of the torrential rain he could but barely discern her; so he knew that those on board could not see him at all. He thought of building a fire in the hope that its smoke might carry a message to them, but there was nothing with which to make fire.

Before the storm struck them, Ah-gilak had said that he thought the ship was approaching the spot at which the Mezops had abandoned her. If that were the case, then the island was close to the place at which O-aa was supposed to have leaped overboard. If she had survived, which he doubted, she would be making her way right now toward Kali, hundreds of miles away. Perhaps, somewhere in this unknown land of terrors, she was even now pursuing her hopeless journey.

That he might ever find her in all this vast expanse of plain and hill and mountain he knew to be wholly unlikely, even were she there. But there was the chance. And there was his great love for her. Without a backward glance, Hodon the Fleet One turned his face and his steps northeast toward Kali.

X

O-AA RAN LIKE the wind. She did not know that Zurk had set his jalok on her. She thought only of escaping the man, and she knew that on his bowed legs he could never overtake her.

Zurk pulled upon the arrow embedded in his shoulder. It had just missed his heart. The rough stone tip tore at the tender wound. Blood ran down the man's body. His features were contorted with pain. He swore. He was very careful as he withdrew the shaft lest the point should be deflected and touch his heart. The girl and the jalok were out of sight, having passed through bushes into a slight depression.

Rahna had followed his mistress, loping easily along a few yards behind her. Suddenly another jalok flashed past him, straight for the fleeing girl.

Hodon the Fleet One turned his face and his steps northeast toward Kali. Hodon knew nothing about the points of the compass, but his homing instinct told him the direction to Sari; and, knowing where Kali lay in relation to Sari, his homeland, he knew the direction he must take.

He had been walking for some time, when, emerging from a clump of bushes, he came upon a man sitting with his back against the bole of a tree. Hodon was armed only with a knife, which was not well in a world where the usual greeting between strangers is, "I kill."

He was very close to the man before he saw him, and in the instant that he saw him, he saw this his body was smeared with blood and a little stream of blood ran down his chest from a wound in his breast close to his left shoulder.

Now the Sarians, because of the influence of David Innes and Abner Perry, are less savage and brutal than the majority of Pellucidarians. Although Perry had taught them how to slaughter their fellow men scientifically with muskets, cannon, and gunpowder, he had also preached to them the doctrine of the brotherhood of man; so that their policy now was based on the admonition of a man they had never heard of who had lived in a world they would never see, to "speak softly and carry a big stick," for Abner Perry had been a worshipper of Teddy Roosevelt.

The man's head was bowed, his chin lay upon his breast. He was barely breathing. But when he realized that some one had approached him he looked up and snarled. He expected to be killed, but he could do nothing about it.

Hodon turned back to the bushes through which he had just passed and gathered some leaves. He made a little ball of the most tender of them and came back to the man. He knelt beside him and plugged the hole in his chest with a little ball of leaves, stopping the flow of blood.

There was questioning in Zurk's dull eyes as he looked into those of the stranger. "Aren't you going to kill me?" he whispered.

Hodon ignored the question. "Where is your village?" he asked. "Is it far?"

"Not far," said Zurk.

"I will help you back to it," said Hodon, "if you promise me that the warriors will not kill me."

"They will not kill you," said Zurk. "I am the chief's son. But why do you do this for a stranger?"

"Because I am a Sarian," said Hodon proudly.

Hodon helped Zurk to his feet, but the man could scarcely stand. Hodon realized that he could not walk; so he carried him pickaback, Zurk directing him toward the village.

The wind blew and rain fell, but the storm was abating as Hodon carried the chief's son into the village. Warriors came from their houses with ready weapons, for Hodon was a stranger to be killed on sight. Then they saw Zurk, who was unconscious now, and hesitated.

Hodon faced them. "Instead of standing there scowling at me," he said, "come and take your chief's son and carry him to his house where the women can care for him."

When they had lifted Zurk from his back, Hodon saw

that the man was unconscious and that he might be killed after all. "Where is the chief?" he asked.

Jalu was coming toward them from his house. "I am the chief," he said. "You are either a very brave man or a fool to have wounded my son and then brought him to me."

"I did not wound him," said Hodon. "I found him wounded and brought him here, else he would have died. He told me that if I did this the warriors would not kill me."

"If you have spoken the truth the warriors will not kill you," said Jalu.

"If the man dies before he regains consciousness, how will you know that I have spoken the truth?" asked Hodon.

"We will not know," said Jalu. He turned to one of his warriors. "Have him treated well, but see that he does not escape."

"The brotherhood of man is all right," said Hodon, "if the other fellow knows about it." They did not know what he was talking about. "I was a fool not to let him die," he added.

"I think you were," agreed Jalu.

Hodon was taken to a house and a woman was sent to take him food. Two warriors stood guard at the foot of the ladder. The woman came with food. It was Hala. She looked at the handsome prisoner with questioning eyes. He did not look stupid, but then one could not always tell just by looks.

"Why did you bring Zurk back when you know that you might be killed? What was he to you?" she asked.

"He was a fellow man, and I am a Sarian," was Hodon's simple explanation.

"You, a Sarian?" demanded Hala.

"Yes. Why?"

"There is a Sarian with us, or there was. She went

away, I think to hunt; and she has not returned."

Hodon paled. "What was her name?" he asked.

"Oh, I was wrong," said Hala. "She is not a Sarian. It is her mate that is a Sarian. She comes from another country where the men are nine feet tall. She has eleven brothers and her father is a king."

"And her name is O-aa," said Hodon.

"How do you know?" demanded Hala.

"There is only one O-aa," said Hodon, enigmatically. "Which way did she go?"

"Up the valley," said Hala. "Zurk followed her. Zurk is a bad man. It must have been O-aa who wounded him."

"And I have saved him!" exclaimed Hodon. "Hereafter I shall leave the brotherhood of man to others."

"What do you mean by that?"

"It is meaningless," said Hodon. "I must get out of here and follow her."

"You cannot get out," said Hala. Suddenly her eyes went wide in understanding. "You are Hodon the Fleet One," she said.

"How did you know that?"

"That is the name of O-aa's mate. She said so, and that he is a Sarian."

"I must get out," said Hodon.

"I would help you if I could," said Hala. "I liked O-aa and I like you, but you will only get out of this village alive if Zurk regains consciousness and says that he promised that you would not be killed."

"Will you go then and find out if he has regained consciousness?" he asked her.

O-aa heard a savage growl close behind her. She turned to see a strange jalok reared on its hind feet to seize her and drag her down. As she leaped, quick as a chamois, to one side, she saw something else. She saw

Rahna spring upon the strange jalok and hurl it to the ground. The fight that ensued was bloody and terrifying. The two savage beasts fought almost in silence. There were only snarls of rage. As they tore at one another, O-aa circled them, spear in hand, seeking an opportunity to impale Rahna's antagonist. But they moved so quickly that she dared not thrust for fear of wounding Rahna instead of the other.

Rahna needed no help. At last he got the hold for which he had been fighting—a full hold of the other jalok's throat. The mighty jaws closed, and Rahna shook the other as a terrier shakes a rat. It was soon over. Rahna dropped the carcass and looked up into O-aa's eyes. He wagged his tail, and O-aa went down on her knees and hugged him, all bloody as he was.

She found the leaves she needed, and a little stream, and there she washed Rahna's wounds and rubbed the juices of the leaves into them. After that, she flushed a couple of hares and some strange birds that have not been on earth for a million years. She fed Rahna, and she ate her own meat raw, for there was nothing dry with which to make fire.

She did not dare go back to the village, both because she feared that she might have killed Zurk and feared that she hadn't. In one event, Jalu would kill her if her deed were discovered; in the other, Zurk would kill her. She would go on toward Kali, but first she would sleep. Beneath a great tree she lay down, and the fierce hyaenodon lay down beside her.

XI

THE GREAT STORM passed on. Again the sun shone. The seas subsided. Saddened, Dian suggested that they turn back toward Sari. "What is the use of going on?" she demanded. "They are all dead."

"Perhaps not," said Raj. "Perhaps not all. David, Abner, Ghak, and over two hundred warriors can make their way anywhere in Pellucidar. They may be waiting for us in Sari when we return."

"Then let's return as soon as possible," said Dian.

"And even for O-aa and Hodon there may be hope."

Dian shook her head. "Had they been together, possibly; but alone, no. And then, even if Hodon reached shore, he was armed with only a knife."

So they weighed anchor, put about, and laid a course for the nameless strait.

At the same time, David, Perry, and Ghak, were holding a council of war, so to speak. There was no war except with the terrain. With the two hundred fierce Sarians, armed with muskets and well supplied with ammunition, the party had moved through the savage world with not a single casualty.

They lived off a country rich in game, fruits, vegetables berries, nuts. But the terrain had almost beaten them. The backbone of the great peninsula they were attempting to cross is a mountain range as formidable as the Himalayas and practically insurmountable for men clothed only in G-strings. Its upper reaches ice-locked and snowbound presented an insurmountable barrier to these almost naked men of the Stone Age.

When they reached the mountains, they had moved in a northerly direction searching for a pass. Many sleeps had passed, but still the unbroken facade of the Terrible Mountains barred the way to Sari. Time and again they had followed deep canyons, hoping that here at last was a gap through which they could pass. And time and again they had had to retrace their steps. Now, as far as the eye could reach until vision was lost in the haze, the Terrible Mountains stretched on seemingly into infinity.

"There is no use going on in this direction," said David Innes.

"Well, where in the world shall we go?" demanded Abner Perry.

"Back," said David. "There are no mountains on the Lidi Plains nor in the Land of Awful Shadow. We can cross there to the east coast and follow it up to Sari."

So they turned back toward the southwest, and started anew the long, long trek for home.

Later, many sleeps later, the three man point, which David always kept well ahead of his main body, sighted warriors approaching. One of the warriors of the point ran back to notify David, and presently the Sarians advanced in a long thin skirmish line. Their orders were not to fire until fired upon, and then to fire one volley over the heads of the enemy. David had found that this was usually enough. At the roar and the smoke, the enemy ordinarily fled.

To David's astonishment, the strange warriors also formed a line of skirmishers. This was a tactful innovation brought to Pellucidar by David. He had thought that only warriors trained under the system of the Army of the Empire used it. The two lines moved slowly toward another.

"They look like Mezops," said David to Ghak. "They are copper colored."

"How could there be Mezops here?" demanded Ghak.

David shrugged. "I do not know."

Suddenly the advancing line of copper colored warriors halted. All but one. He advanced, making the sign of peace. And presently David recognized him.

"First I saw the muskets," said Ja, "and then I recognized you."

Ja told of the loss of O-aa and the abandonment of the

John Tyler and how it had sailed out to sea with only Ah-gilak.

"So they are both lost," said David sadly.

"Ah-gilak is no loss," said Ja; "but the girl—yes."

And so Ja and Kay and Ko and the other Mezops joined the Sarians, and the march was resumed toward the Lidi Plains and the Land of the Awful Shadow.

A warrior came to the foot of the ladder leading to the house where Hodon was confined. He spoke to the guards, and one of them called to Hodon. "Sarian, come down. Jalu has sent for you."

Jalu sat on a stool in front of the house where Zurk lay. He was scowling, and Hodon thought that Zurk had died. "Zurk has spoken," said Jalu. "He said that you had told the truth. He said more. It was O-aa who loosed the arrow that wounded him. Zurk said that she was right to do it. He had followed her to kill her. Now he is sorry. I will send warriors with you to search for her. If you find her, or if you do not, the warriors will either bring you back here or accompany you to the foot of the Terrible Mountains, which is where O-aa wished to go. I do this because of what you did for Zurk when you might have killed him. Zurk has asked me to do this. When do you wish to start?"

"Now," said Hodon.

With twenty warriors and their jaloks, he set out in search of O-aa.

O-aa slept for a long time or for but a second. Who may know in the timeless world of Pellucidar? But it must have been for some considerable outer crust time; because things happened while she slept that could not have happened in a second.

She was awakened by Rahna's growls. She awoke quickly and completely, in full possession of all her faculties. When one is thus awakened in a Stone Age world, one does not lie with closed eyes and stretch luxuriously and then cuddle down for an extra cat nap. One snaps out of sleep and lays hold of one's weapons.

Thus, did O-aa; and looked quickly around. Rahna was standing with his back toward her, all the hairs along his spine standing on end. Beyond him, creeping toward them, was a tarag, the huge tiger of the Inner World. A jalok is no match for a tarag; but Rahna stood his ground, ready to die in protection of his mistress.

O-aa took in the scene instantly and all its implications. There was but one course to pursue were she to save both Rahna and herself. She pursued it. She swarmed up the tree beneath which she had been sleeping, taking her bow and arrows with her.

"Rahna!" she called, and the jalok looked up and saw her. Then the tarag charged. Freed from the necessity of sacrificing his life to save the girl's, Rahna bounded out of harm's way. The tarag pursued him, but Rahna was too quick for him.

Thus thwarted, the savage beast screamed in rage; then he leaped upward and tried to scramble into the tree after O-aa; but the limb he seized was too small to support his great weight, and he fell to the ground upon his back. Rahna rushed in and bit him, and then leaped away. Once more the great cat sprang after the jalok, but Rahna could run much faster. O-aa laughed and described the tarag and its ancestors with such scurrilous vituperation as she could command and in a loud tone of voice.

The tarag is probably not noted for its patience; but this tarag was very hungry, and when one is hungry one will exercise a little patience to obtain food. The tarag came and lay down under the tree. It glared up at O-aa. It should have been watching Rahna. The jalok crept stealthily behind it; then rushed in and bit it savagely in the rear, bounding away again instantly. Again the futile pursuit.

And again it came and lay down beneath the tree, but this time it kept its eyes on Rahna. O-aa fitted an arrow to her bow and drove it into the tarag's back. With a scream of pain and rage, the cat leaped into the air. But it would take more than one puny arrow to do more than infuriate it.

Another arrow. This time the tarag saw from whence it came, and very slowly and methodically it began to climb the bole of the tree. O-aa retreated into the higher branches. Rahna ran in and tore at the tarag's rump, but the beast continued its upward climb.

O-aa no longer felt like laughing. She guessed what the end would be. The mighty cat would climb after her until their combined weight snapped the tapering stem and carried them both to the ground.

It was upon this scene that Hodon and Utan and the other warriors broke. Utan recognized Rahna and knew that O-aa must be in the tree. Rahna turned on this new menace, and Utan shouted to O-aa to call him off. He did not want to have to kill the courageous animal.

With relief, O-aa heard the voices of men. Any man would have been welcome at that moment, and she shouted the single word, "Padang" to Rahna. Jalu had armed Hodon, and now twenty-one bow strings twanged and twenty-one arrows pierced the body of the tarag. But even these did not kill him. They did bring him down out of the tree and set him upon these enemies.

The men scattered, but they kept pouring arrows into the beast, and each time he charged one of them, jaloks leaped in and tore at him. But at last he died. An arrow reached his savage heart.

O-aa came down from the tree. She just stood and looked at Hodon in wide eyed silence. Then two tears ran down her cheeks, and in front of all the warriors Hodon the Fleet One took her in his arms.

XII

JALU'S TWENTY warriors accompanied O-aa and Hodon to the Terrible Mountains. "You can never cross them," said Utan. "You had better come back and join our tribe. Jalu said that he would accept you."

Hodon shook his head. "We belong in Sari, my mate and I. We may never reach Sari, but we must try."

"We will reach Sari," said O-aa. "You and I and Rahna can go anywhere. There is nothing we Sarians cannot do."

"I thought that you were from Kali where the men are nine feet tall," said Utan.

"I am from where my mate is from," said O-aa. "I am a Sarian."

"If I thought that there was another girl like you in Kali, I would go there," said Utan.

"There is no other girl like O-aa in all Pellucidar," said Hodon the Fleet One.

"I believe you," said Utan.

Jalu's warriors ate and slept, and then they started back for their village; and Hodon and O-aa took the long trail—in the wrong direction. They moved toward the northeast. But after all it proved to be the right direction, for before they had slept again they met David and his party. For all of them it was like meeting old friends who had returned from death.

Who may say how long it took them to make the incredible march of nearly two thousand five hundred miles down to the Lidi Plains and the Land of Awful Shadow and across to the east coast and back up to Sari? But at last they came to the village, the village that most of them had never expected to see again; and among the first to welcome them was Dian the Beautiful. The John Tyler had made the long trip in safety.

Every one was happy except Ah-gilak and Gamba. Ah-gilak had been happy until he saw O-aa. Gamba was never happy. Abner Perry was so happy that he cried, for those whom he thought his carelessness had condemned to death were safe and at home again. Already, mentally, he was inventing a submarine.

EDGAR RICE BURROUGHS

VENUS SERIES

.... 056523 Beyond the Farthest Star — 75¢
.... 092023 Carson of Venus — 75¢
.... 187708 Edgar Rice Burroughs: Master of Adventure — 95¢
.... 215624 Escape on Venus — 75¢
.... 495028 Lost on Venus — 75¢
.... 537027 The Moon Maid — 75¢
.... 537522 The Moon Men — 75¢
.... 645101 The Outlaw of Torn — 75¢
.... 665026 The Pirates of Venus — 75¢

PELLUCIDAR SERIES

.... 033255 At Earth's Core — 75¢
.... 046334 Back to the Stone Age — 95¢
.... 469973 Land of Terror — 75¢
.... 658526 Pellucidar — 75¢
.... 751321 Savage Pellucidar — 75¢
.... 797928 Tanar of Pellucidar — 75¢
.... 798520 Tarzan of the Earth's Core — 75¢